Three Shots
to the Wind

Sherry Harris

Kensington Publishing Corp.
www.kensingtonbooks.com

KENSINGTON BOOKS are published by

Kensington Publishing Corp.
119 West 40th Street
New York, NY 10018

All Kensington titles, imprints, and distributed lines are available at special quantity discounts for bulk purchases for sales promotion, premiums, fund-raising, educational, or institutional use.

Special book excerpts or customized printings can also be created to fit specific needs. For details, write or phone the office of the Kensington Sales Manager: Attn.: Sales Department. Kensington Publishing Corp., 119 West 40th Street, New York, NY 10018. Phone: 1-800-221-2647.

The K and Teapot logo is a trademark of Kensington Publishing Corp.

First Printing: April 2022
ISBN: 978-1-4967-3436-5

ISBN: 978-1-4967-3437-2 (ebook)

10 9 8 7 6 5 4 3 2 1

Printed in the United States of America

To Bob
The man who puts up with my deadline craziness—my rock, my love

And to Clare
The Angel on my Shoulder, I miss you

Heritage Businesses

Sea Glass—owner, Vivi Jo Slidell
Briny Pirate—owner, Wade Thomas
Redneck Rollercoaster—owner, Ralph Harrison
Russo's Grocery Store—owner, Fred Russo
Hickle Glass Bottom Boat—owners, Edith Hickle, Leah Hickle, Oscar Hickle
Emerald Cove Fishing Charters—owner, Jed Farwell

CHAPTER 1

The whine of a plane's engine had become part of the music of my life working at the Sea Glass Saloon. They flew over day after day, pulling banners advertising happy hours, restaurant specials, and amusements such as water parks and minigolf.

"Chloe, you've got to get out here," Joaquín Diaz yelled. He stood out on the deck of the Sea Glass, gesturing wildly for me.

It was ten thirty and we'd just opened. I grabbed the three beers I'd poured, dropped them to patrons sitting on tall stools at a high-top table, and ran to Joaquín's side.

"What?" I asked, looking across the expanse of white sand to the Gulf of Mexico. Snowbirds, the flock of people who abandoned their cold, wintery states and provinces for the warmer climes of the Florida Panhandle, walked and sunbathed on the beach. No local would sunbathe in January. I scanned for something more interesting. Something that would make Joaquín sound so urgent. Last October a sailboat had run aground not far from here, but I saw no such boat now.

Joaquín pointed up. I shaded my eyes with my hand and squinted into the bright January sun. A small plane was flying over the beach with a banner. It read: "I love you Chloe Jackson." What the haymaker? My eyes went wide as I tried to sort through why such a sign would be flying over the beaches of Emerald Cove, Florida.

"Oh, Chloe," Joaquín said, "somebody loves you, girl." His eyes were the same aquamarine color as the Gulf on its showiest days. Dark hair tumbled over his forehead. "Do you think it's Rip?"

He gave me a hip nudge and did a little dance with his hands clasped over his heart. Joaquín was a former professional backup dancer for the likes of Beyoncé, Ricky Martin, and Jennifer Lopez. Now he was a fisherman in the early morning and a bartender the rest of the day, but, boy, he still had moves.

I'd been dating Rip Barnett on and off for the past few months. His real name was Rhett, but he'd gotten a nickname in the fall and it stuck. We were solidly in the like zone, with a touch of lust thrown in. But we definitely weren't in the love zone, and Rip didn't seem like the kind of man who went for wild public gestures like this. No man I could think of would do this. Although the proof otherwise was flying right over my head.

"It's not from Rip," I said, my voice sounding crosser than Joaquín deserved.

Joaquín whipped out his phone and started snapping pictures.

"Stop that, Joaquín," I said, making a grab for his phone.

He held it out of my reach, which wasn't hard because he was a lot taller than I was at my five four.

"You're going to want to remember this, Chloe."

I had a terrible feeling he was wrong, and that I wouldn't forget this no matter how much I wanted to.

"What's going on?" Vivi Slidell asked. She came out and stood beside us. "We have a business to run and thirsty customers."

Vivi Slidell was my boss, even though I owned a quarter of the Sea Glass. She was tall, slender, worked out regularly, and had a sleek silver bob. As far as I was concerned, she was the poster child or woman, as the case may be, for how to live your best seventy-year-old life.

Joaquín pointed up. Vivi went through the same routine I had of squinting, looking up, and eyes widening.

"Is this from Rip?" Vivi asked. Exasperation poured through her voice like beer through a broken tap.

Vivi and Rip's grandmother had a long-running feud that had started with a boy when they were in high school and had continued on from there. It had made dating Rip awkward and sometimes secretive. I often wondered if the rebellious part of me enjoyed the sneaking-around aspect of our relationship. Although you'd think at twenty-eight I would have matured beyond such actions. And I guess the sneaking was unnecessary if Vivi was asking if the banner was from Rip. Our jig was up.

"No. It couldn't be." I almost shuddered at the thought. "He knows I'd hate something like that. Something that would make everyone gawk at me. Maybe it's my brothers." They loved to tease me, and this stunt seemed right up their alley except for the fact they wouldn't want to spend the money to prank me. Plus, it would take a lot of work to do this and they had busy lives, wives, kids, and plumbing jobs back in Chicago, where I'd grown up. They'd taken over my father's plumbing business when my parents packed up, bought an RV, and hit the road.

My phone buzzed in the back pocket of my leggings. Normally, I didn't pull it out at work, but right now I needed answers. I had five texts. The first four were from heritage business owners—local people whose families, like Vivi's, had opened their businesses when Emerald Cove was barely on the map, hence the heritage designation. The heritage businesses had been in Emerald Cove since the nineteen fifties or longer. The Sea Glass was one of the heritage businesses, and often a gathering place for the other owners, which included the Hickle Glass Bottom Boat, the Redneck Rollercoaster, which was a trolley, Russo's Grocery Store, the Briny Pirate restaurant, and the Emerald Cove Fishing Charters. They all wanted to know who loved me. The fifth one was from Rip. Great.

Is there something you need to tell me?

I clapped my hand to my forehead and then shoved my phone back into my pocket. As Vivi said, there were thirsty customers inside. I would deal with the rest of this later.

An hour later, during a lull, Joaquín, Vivi, and I stood behind the bar speculating who could be behind the "I love you Chloe Jackson" banner. The Sea Glass was more tiki hut than saloon, with its wooden walls decorated with lots of historic pictures and its concrete floors, which made it easy to clean up the sand our customers dragged in.

"What about that guy, Smoke?" Joaquín asked. "He's been in here a lot lately."

Smoke was one of the few full-time employees of the Emerald Cove Fire Department. He was a good-looking man and a transplant like me. He'd moved down here from Minneapolis a couple of years ago.

"Ewww, no. We're just friends." We'd gone water-skiing a couple of times before the weather got too cold, and he'd been over to my house to watch football with some of the other volunteer firefighters. But that was it. There'd been the occasional friendly hug. It didn't mean we weren't just friends.

"I don't know," Vivi said, "you know what they say. Where there's smoke, there's fire." Her eyes sparkled as she said it. She'd be happy if I had a boyfriend as long as it wasn't Rip.

A woman came staggering in from the deck, which wasn't entirely unusual. Only this woman wasn't drunk, she was carrying an enormous bouquet of flowers in a ceramic pot almost as big as she was. Purple lilacs. My favorite flower. I had the same sinking feeling I had when I saw the banner.

"Is there a Chloe Jackson here?" she asked.

I wanted to run out the back door. "That's me." The lilacs' perfumey scent was already competing with the smell of salt air, beer, and the lemon cleaner we used. I hustled over to help her. Together we managed to get the arrangement on the bar top.

"Ooohhh, Chloe, your favorite flowers," Joaquín said.

"They are beautiful," the florist said. "And hard to come by this time of year."

"Thank you," I said. I gave her a tip.

She started to turn, but then snapped back around. "Are you the Chloe Jackson that the 'I love you' banner was referencing?"

Hey! Maybe there was another Chloe Jackson in town. "I'm sure it must be some other Chloe Jackson."

The woman started shaking her head. "I've lived here all my life and our family floral business opened in the seventies. I don't recall anyone else named Chloe Jackson."

"Have you ever had amnesia or a concussion?" I asked hopefully. Not that I wished her harm, just a temporary memory lapse so maybe she'd forgotten all the other Chloe Jacksons who lived in Emerald Cove.

"Sorry, honey. I'm known for my recall."

She left. I stared at the lilacs for a moment, but I couldn't resist their charm, so I put my face near one, breathing in their delicious scent. I fingered one of the soft flowers, while I stared at the card, trying to work up the courage to open it.

"Want me to look?" Joaquín asked.

"No. I'll do it."

Joaquín plucked the card from its clear, plastic holder that looked like a cheap, mini version of Triton's trident. "Here you go."

I opened the envelope, pulled it out, and stared down. *I love you, Chloe Jackson*. No signature. I handed it over to Joaquín, who handed it to Vivi. They both laughed. I'm glad someone found this situation was funny.

"Wait," I said. "The florist must know who bought these."

"Go," Vivi said.

I raced out the back door, ran along the harbor to the parking lot, and caught the woman as she started her van.

"Who bought these?" I asked. "The card wasn't signed."

She frowned. "He paid cash."

Of course he did. "What did he look like?"

"He asked me not to say. Said he wanted to surprise you."

"Trust me, I'm surprised. Please, tell me?" There was a little whine to my voice that I didn't usually have.

"Honey, the florist-client relationship is sacred. If I started giving away all the secrets I know, it would ruin my business."

Oh, good grief. It wasn't like she was a psychiatrist or a lawyer. There were no oaths. "Please?"

She shook her head and drove off.

Thank heavens we were having a busy day, so 90 percent of the time I could keep my mind off the banner and the flowers. Although the flowers were hard to avoid. Even though we moved them to the other end of the bar, they scented the air. Also, my phone kept buzzing away and I kept ignoring it.

At one forty-five there was a knock on the back door. I went to answer it, but no one was there. I started to step out, looked down, and froze.

CHAPTER 2

I'd almost tripped over a magnum bottle of wine. I backed away from it like it was going to explode. It had a big white bow around the neck and a small card attached. My name was written on the card, but I didn't recognize the handwriting. A cold wind coming from the north had whipped up and cooled my face, which was heating up in frustration. Vivi came up behind me.

"Why are you backing away? What's out there? Please tell me it's not a dead body," she said.

There'd been a dead body behind the bar last June, so it wasn't outside the realm of possibility. I pointed down. Vivi stepped around me, spotted the bottle of wine, and let out a relieved laugh. Vivi picked up the wine.

"It looks like you have another gift," Vivi said as she handed me the bottle. "Your favorite sparkling blanc de blanc, and a magnum no less."

"Normally, I love being showered with gifts," I said as

I carried the bottle into the bar. Although, really, had anyone ever showered me with gifts before? The answer was a resounding no. Until today, I'd always thought of myself as someone who would love an extravagant gesture, but this was creepy.

Joaquín hustled over when he saw us. "What is it now?"

"Wine," Vivi said.

"Getting all these gifts is weird." I opened the card and, as with the others, it just read, "I love you Chloe Jackson." I showed it to Vivi and Joaquín.

"This is so exciting and romantic," Joaquín said. "One time, before we were married, I sent Michael a gift every hour for twelve hours. The last gift was dinner at our favorite restaurant."

"Somehow this doesn't feel exciting or romantic to me," I said.

"Who knows you well enough to do this?" Joaquín asked.

"Good point," Vivi said. They both looked at me expectantly.

"Anyone," I said. "Well, almost anyone. Joaquín knows my favorite flower. Vivi, you know my favorite sparkling wine. All anyone would have to do is look through my social media. It wouldn't be hard to figure out."

"Have you said anything to your family lately that would make them think you're lonely?" Vivi asked.

"No." I hadn't. Had I? "Do you think these are pity gifts?" I always told my family I missed them, and I did, but I couldn't think of any comment that would elicit this kind of response. "They would call or send a card. They wouldn't do anything this extravagant."

"I'll bet it's Rip," Joaquín said. He fanned himself dramatically. "It's so romantic." Then he did a side glance at Vivi, who bristled at the mere mention of his name and mouthed *sorry* to me.

I took my phone back out and scrolled through the messages. No one had taken responsibility for the gifts.

"Let's look at the security camera recordings to see if we can figure out who dropped off the wine. Maybe it's the mystery person," I suggested.

We quickly checked to make sure all our customers were happy and then crowded into Vivi's office, around her computer. A man wearing a T-shirt with a logo for the local wine shop walked up, set down the bottle, knocked, and left.

"I might as well call the wine shop to see if they know anything," I said, although I didn't hold out a lot of hope after the experience with the florist.

"Want me to call?" Vivi asked. "I've known the owner's mother my entire life. I used to babysit her."

"Yes, please." Vivi could be scary at times. If it took scaring someone to find out who was behind all this, I was all for it. A local talking to a local had a better chance of getting information anyway. I'd only lived here for seven months. Folks had accepted me for the most part, but in some ways I was still the new kid on the block—or the beach, as the case may be.

Joaquín and I went back out to the bar, leaving Vivi to make the call. I took orders and studied all the customers. Could one of them being doing this? But no one paid any extra attention to me. They just wanted their drinks. Vivi came out of her office a few minutes later. After I delivered the drinks Vivi, Joaquín, and I gathered together again.

"A woman placed the order. Someone around your age, Chloe. She paid cash and gave them the delivery instructions."

"A woman?" I said.

"Oh, and the plot thickens." Joaquín rubbed his hands together like he was an evil overlord.

He was enjoying this way too much.

"Yes. But she got into a car with someone parked out front. So she may have placed the order for someone else."

I looked from Vivi to Joaquín. Thought about how they knew my favorite things. Thought about how much Joaquín was enjoying this. "It's you two, right?"

Eyebrows rose. Faces looked shocked.

"I do love you, Chloe," Joaquín said.

Vivi nodded. I wasn't quite sure what that meant. Was she agreeing that Joaquín loved me or indicating she loved me too?

"But I love you in a why-don't-you-come-over-for-dinner or let-me-make-you-a-happy-drink way. Not an I'm-spending-all-my-hard-earned-money-on-you way. Not even for a great prank."

Vivi patted my cheek. Hmmm, she didn't say she didn't do it. On the other hand, I couldn't imagine her doing all this, certainly not as a joke. Had I said anything to her that would make her think I needed this kind of lavish gesture? I couldn't think of anything that would make them think I was emotionally needy. I'd flown home a few weeks ago to spend Christmas with my family. If I recalled, I'd told Vivi and Joaquín how happy I was to be back. That Emerald Cove was really starting to feel like home.

Something else was going on here, but I had no idea what.

"Chloe, you look really pale," Vivi said. "This is upsetting you more than I realized. Take the rest of the day off. Joaquín and I can easily handle this lot." She gestured to the bar seating area. The crowd had thinned out. "You run on home."

She meant that literally, as I'd taken to running back and forth to work lots of days now that the weather was cooler. For once I wasn't even going to argue with her. I was drained. "Thank you. I'm just going to take a break and then I'll come back." A run was just what I needed.

I grabbed the small purse I brought with me and slung it crosswise over my chest. I waved at Joaquín, went out on the deck, and onto the beach. There were still a lot of people out even though a strong, northern wind was blowing. I ran farther up on the beach than I normally did. Usually, I liked to be near the shore, but today I didn't want to dodge around the tourists. Gulls soared and dipped riding the updrafts. The Gulf was gray-colored with white caps on the waves. I thought of that saying, "A bad day at the beach is still better than a good day anywhere else."

The wind tugged at my short, brown hair. My house was about a twenty-minute run to the east. I passed the state beach and preserve that had once been land owned by Vivi's family. They'd donated it to the state so it would never be developed. It was a sanctuary for pelicans and other birds to roost in. The beach was pristine.

As I ran toward the coastal dune lake that was between the preserve and my house, I spotted Deputy Biffle walking toward a man who was gesturing wildly at the coastal lake. Coastal dune lakes were unique because of their close proximity to the Gulf, their shallow depth, and because there weren't many places in the world that had them. This area had seventeen. I heard sirens wailing. This couldn't be good.

"What's going on?" I asked when I got close enough to the men.

They both spun around, startled by my voice.

Deputy Biffle put up his hand for me to stop, but I stepped up beside him. As always, his uniform was pressed and his boots were polished, although bits of sand clung to them like barnacles on the underside of a boat. His hair, military short, was under his wide-brimmed, khaki-colored hat. He was thick and muscled in a way that shouted self-discipline. I knew his first name was Dan because someone had called him that last fall. I only thought of him as Deputy Biffle, though.

"Chloe—" Deputy Biffle started. His grim expression softened a little behind his ever-present mirrored aviator sunglasses.

Several beach patrol vehicles pulled up. I looked at the lake. Spotted a body floating in the rushes near the edge. I looked away.

"Chloe," Deputy Biffle said, "he has a picture of you."

CHAPTER 3

"Me?" My voice was shrill. It hurt my ears to hear it. If fingernails on a chalkboard were an emotion instead of a sound, that's how I felt.

"Yes, Chloe."

"Do you know who it is?"

"No."

That meant it probably wasn't someone local. It made me all the more anxious. I took a step closer. Mingled with dread was a shot of curiosity about why someone, a dead someone, had a picture of me. An ambulance trundled up the beach and another sheriff's deputy arrived. I took a couple of deep breaths, which was stupid because there was an odd scent that wasn't pine needles or sea air. I put a hand on my stomach as it twisted.

I took a closer look. I started shaking my head and

stepping back. My hands were out in front of me, as if I could push the sight away.

"Chloe, do you know him?" Deputy Biffle asked.

I tried to change the shaking of my head to a nod, but my body didn't seem to be on board. I continued to back away as little pin dots of black swirled on the outer edges of my vision like clouds before a waterspout. I put my hands on my knees and dropped my head, trying to stop the encroaching blackness.

"Medic." I heard Deputy Biffle shout it as he put a hand under my elbow. His voice sounded like he was across the lake from me.

I opened my eyes, saw a ceiling, and looked around. An ambulance. We weren't moving. I lifted my head and could see the coastal lake out the open back doors. An EMT stood out there looking in. "What happened?" I asked, sitting up.

Deputy Biffle leaned against some equipment across from me. He looked at the EMT. "Give us a minute." When the EMT walked off he turned back to me. "You fainted. It's understandable. Seeing someone who's been shot is difficult."

I sat up. "I don't faint." Then the reality of what had happened, of what I'd seen, returned. I lay back down and closed my eyes, wishing I could unsee the body by the lake. A tear trickled from the corner of my eye.

"Chloe?" Deputy Biffle's voice was gentle.

I pushed myself up and swung my legs off the stretcher, so I was sitting up again. For once Biffle didn't have his aviator sunglasses on. His brown eyes were crinkled with concern.

"Do you know him?" He leaned forward for a moment as he asked.

"Yes." My voice was barely a whisper.

"Who is he?" Deputy Biffle asked.

"My ex-fiancé, Perry Franklin."

CHAPTER 4

That set off a flurry of questions from Deputy Biffle. He put his sunglasses back on. Maybe it was part of his interrogation technique. It was effective in making me squirm.

"Did you know he was in town?"

I could barely form words to answer. "No."

"When was the last time you contacted him?"

"When I broke off our engagement. It was over a year and a half ago."

"You haven't texted him or contacted him through social media?"

"No."

"Has he reached out to you?"

I thought for a minute. "A couple of times right after we broke up, but nothing significant." I was bewildered. How did Perry end up dead in the coastal lake near my house? Shot dead. What was he even doing down here? "I hurt him badly."

I'd never quite been able to shake the terrible feeling from the day I'd given him that two-carat solitaire diamond ring back. His face had crumpled. He'd cried. Each of those tears had been like one hundred tiny daggers stabbing my heart. He'd even begged, but I knew relenting would only lead to another scene like that one farther down the road. We weren't meant for each other. Hurting a good man for the right reasons had left a void in my heart.

Deputy Biffle alerted when I said the words "hurt him." It was a subtle straightening of his already upright posture that tipped me off. "What do you mean, you hurt him? Today? Are you confessing?"

"No." I shook my head violently, which led to the reappearance of the stupid black dots. I needed to get a grip. "Never. I'm talking about when I ended our engagement. Not that I hurt him physically." I could tell that's what Biffle was thinking. "I'm the one who broke off our engagement. He tried to convince me otherwise. Can we get out of this ambulance and get some air?"

Deputy Biffle dipped his head briefly in what I assumed was agreement and we climbed out. I turned my back to the lake and faced the Gulf. The cold north wind felt good as it hit my back.

"You haven't reached out to him. Or him to you, recently and yet here he is dead in a lake near your place."

"Exactly. Unless . . ." I said.

"Unless what?"

"I've had an odd day. First an airplane flew over the Sea Glass pulling a banner that said 'I Love You Chloe Jackson.' Then a bouquet of my favorite flowers arrived, and a bottle of my favorite sparkling wine. I couldn't figure out who would possibly do that. But maybe it was Perry." He would know those things about me. But why would he do it now, after all this time?

Deputy Biffle studied me for a couple of minutes. At least I think he did. His mirrored aviators were pointed in my direction, but he could have been looking over my head for all I knew. I resisted an urge to turn around and see if something or someone was behind me. I also resisted the urge to start babbling anything to fill the silence that felt like a canyon between us. I read enough crime fiction to know that's exactly what he wanted me to do.

"I saw the banner," Deputy Biffle finally said. "Do you know anyone who would think Perry was a threat to a relationship with you?"

"*No.*" Deputy Biffle certainly wouldn't know about my relationship with Rip. Rip would never kill someone he saw as a competitor. It was ridiculous and not worth bringing up.

"Where have you been all day?" he asked.

"Why would you ask that?" Then I got it. "You think I did this?"

"Will you please just answer the question?"

"I took a run around six this morning."

"Where did you run?"

"From my house to the harbor and back."

"You ran right by here?"

"I did." I shivered at the thought. "Do you think Perry was there then?" I couldn't bear it if he was.

"I don't know. Did you notice anything or anyone?"

"A few fishermen. A woman who runs most mornings. Nothing unusual." Had I even glanced over this way?

"And then?"

"I went home, showered, read for a bit, and made breakfast. I got to the Sea Glass at ten and have been there all day."

"You didn't have a lunch break?"

"I just sat at the bar and ate."

"And someone can confirm your whereabouts?"

"Not overnight or until I got to the bar."

"If you think of anything else, please let me know."

"I will." I'd ask him to do the same, but it was unlikely that a by-the-book man like Deputy Biffle would reciprocate. At least not until everything was tied up neatly and resolved in his eyes. "Who found Perry?"

"Him." Deputy Biffle pointed to an older man twenty yards to the left. "He was out for a run. Please don't tell anyone who the victim is until we can notify his next of kin."

That caused the waterworks to turn on—thinking of someone telling the soft-spoken Franklin family their youngest son was dead. Perry was one of five kids. All of them were much alike, except for his middle sister. A tatted-up, multi-pierced singer with a punk rock revival band. I gave Deputy Biffle their contact information, which was still on my phone.

"I'll let you know when we've made the notification." He turned to go, but paused. "I'm sorry you had to go through this. Do you want someone to walk you home?"

I shook my head. "No. I'll be fine." I really hoped I would be.

I trudged to my house, which I'd inherited last summer from my best friend Boone. He was Vivi's grandson and had died last spring while serving in Afghanistan. The two-bedroom, two-bath, cement-block house sat on top of a sand dune and had stunning views of the Gulf. It was surrounded on either side by loblolly pines, magnolia trees, and scrub oaks. At first the quiet here had freaked out this born-and-bred city woman. The only noise was that of the Gulf, the trees, and the birds. So unlike the honking, the traffic, and the crowds in Chicago. Both had their advantages, but I had come to love this place and my solitude.

Last fall Boone's absentee father had shown up claiming Boone had left everything to him. Fortunately, he'd been lying and was now serving time for impersonating a military officer among other charges. I plopped down on the steps at the back of the house that led to my screened-in porch. The beach curved just enough that I couldn't see Perry being loaded up in a body bag. For once the sight and sound of the Gulf didn't soothe me. Good, honest Perry. Our lives were just too different. I was always on the go, water sports, running, trivia nights with the librarians I had worked with. I'd always invited him along, but he liked to stay in, read biographies, do crossword puzzles. Not that I was opposed to any of those things. They were great Sunday morning activities in my book. However, only having Sunday mornings in common didn't make for a great relationship.

Who would kill Perry, though? It didn't fit with the man I knew. And why here of all places? Everything in my world had shifted today. Like I was the grains of sand that danced across highway 98 on Okaloosa Island on windy days. Unease. That was the only solid emotion except sadness I could latch on to right now. Surely Deputy Biffle didn't really think I'd have been involved with Perry's death, but he'd asked all those questions.

I sent a quick text to Joaquín and Vivi, telling them, in general terms, what had happened on my run home— there'd been a body in the coastal lake and it appeared to be a homicide. I added for the time being it was all I could say.

I immediately got two texts back, telling me there was no need for me to come back to work and asking if I needed anything. That was a relief. I'd fill them in when I got the okay from Detective Biffle. What loomed before me wouldn't be fun. I'd have to tell my parents and my brothers. I'd have to reach out to Perry's family. But I guess, in the grand scheme of life, it wasn't nearly as awful as what Perry's family would be dealing with.

I let myself into my house. It had an open floor plan with a living room, dining room, kitchen combo that all looked out on the screened-in porch that ran the length of the back. Not grand, like Perry's family's home or even the apartment he had in a high-rise condominium building. On each side of the house there was a bedroom/bathroom combo. The only difference between the two was that the bedroom I used had sliding glass doors that opened to the screened porch. Perry would have liked that.

The décor was mostly done in beiges and browns. Perry would have approved, although he'd added violent splashes of red as an accent color in his condo. Because I'd inherited the house from my friend Boone, I also had his masculine, oversize sectional. It wasn't my style, but I had to admit it was incredibly comfortable. I'd painted my bedroom the lightest shade of aqua, which Perry would have hated. *Walls should be neutral.* It was almost as if he was standing next to me saying it. I'd added aqua accents with pillows and artwork in bright colors to perk things up.

Many nights I left the slider partially open so I could

hear the Gulf better as I drifted off to sleep—a rod wedged in it so it couldn't be opened more than a few inches. The noise combined with the scent of pine and salt made for good sleeping. But now I was too restless for napping, and I was worried that people were going to start showing up here, including a reporter I'd met last fall. I didn't want to hide out and ignore people, but I also didn't want to talk to anyone. Even though both Joaquín and Vivi had said not to come in, either or both of them could show up at any time. I wasn't ready to see Rip either. As a volunteer fireman, he probably already knew there was a body in the lake near my house. That alone would be enough to send him over here sooner rather than later. I sent him a quick text saying I was fine and I'd talk to him later.

I threw on an oversized sweater. Then I grabbed a heavy coat and headed to my car. Fifteen minutes later, at three fifteen, I parked across the harbor from the Sea Glass and snuck over to the boat I'd inherited from Boone. It was a fifteen-foot, center-console boat perfect for going out on Choctawhatchee Bay or, on calm days, the Gulf. A few minutes later I'd unsnapped the tarp and was headed out of the harbor and down a bayou that led to the bay. Sunset was at five this time of year, so I couldn't stay out here long.

The water on the bay was choppy, stirred up by a north wind that blew not only cold air down here but snowbirds who were probably still out on the beach. Was that why Perry was here? Had he wanted to get away from the Chicago winter? It was so unlike him. He loved Chicago as much as I did, and it was one of the few things we'd had in common. A desire to always live there. Perry must have been shocked when he'd heard I'd moved to

Florida. Like my friend Ralph Harrison always said, "Life has a way at laughing at our plans."

I didn't mind the chop on the bay and accelerated into it. It tossed me around more than the thoughts in my head bounced from question to question. There were hardly any other boats out here. The jouncing and cold air had me slowing down before I wanted to. But I realized quickly that I wasn't going to outrace my thoughts no matter how fast I went.

I slowed to a stop, turned off the engine, and drifted, sitting on the bench seat at the front of the boat. I wrapped my coat tighter around me, glad I'd brought it with me when I moved my things from Chicago last fall. The waves slapped against the side, rocking me like I was a baby inside a cradle. A gull cried and something splashed in the water. The sound of another engine startled me.

I shaded my eyes to see where it was. Due west, heading in my direction. I recognized the boat and tried to decide if I was happy or not that I was going to have company.

CHAPTER 5

A few minutes later, Rip Barnett pulled up next to me in his big, shiny cabin cruiser. The boat he lived on. It dwarfed my boat.

"Permission to come aboard?" he asked. Rip had dark hair, green eyes, and a body honed with hard work and time in a gym. His smile dazzled, although it was masked with concern right now. His gaze caused shivers that had nothing to do with the cold.

"Why don't I come to you? I'm freezing."

He nodded, so I tossed him ropes from my boat so it wouldn't drift away. Rip held out his hand, so warm, and helped me onto his deck once he tied my boat to his.

"Chloe, your hand feels like a block of ice. Let's get inside." He held the door open for me.

"I forgot my gloves," I said as I walked past him. The warm air hit like a balmy tropical breeze.

"Hot chocolate?" he asked.

Who wouldn't like a man who kept hot chocolate in his galley because he knew I liked it?

"Yes, please." I watched as he got out the dark chocolate mix I liked, along with milk and marshmallows. Still cold, I kept my coat snuggled around me. "How did you find me?"

"I saw you go by in the harbor. But by the time I could get out onto the water, you were gone. I just made an educated guess and here I am." He stirred the mix and milk in a pan. When it was ready he poured it in a mug, topped it with marshmallows, and handed it to me.

"Thank you." I took it and sat on the couch, warming my hands. I didn't know how much he knew about what had happened this morning. Rip could be called to scenes like the one at the lake. But if he'd been there, he would have sought me out. Even if he wasn't there, he might have heard about what happened.

I took a sip of the hot chocolate and felt some marshmallow stick to my upper lip. Rip came over and sat next to me and gently wiped off the marshmallow with his thumb. Suddenly, I wasn't so cold. I set the hot chocolate down and took off my coat, wishing I'd dressed better.

"I heard you had a rough day," he said.

I picked up the hot chocolate and drank some more before I answered, wondering exactly what he'd heard. If he knew the body was that of my ex-fiancé. "I did." It started with that stupid banner being flown over the Sea Glass. That seemed like a month ago. "What do you know?"

"I know about the banner and the body."

"Nothing else?"

"What else is there?"

"The flowers and the wine."

He looked surprised. "There was more than the banner?"

"I got a giant bouquet of lilacs. They might as well have sent a whole shrub, there were so many flowers." Not that lilacs grew down here. It was too hot. "And a bottle of my favorite sparkling wine. Both had cards that said 'I love you Chloe Jackson' on them. No other signature."

Rip ran a finger down my neck. Now I was breaking out in goose bumps.

"I have to say, I was jealous when I saw that banner."

I couldn't be unhappy about that. "I'm sorry I didn't text you back earlier." I shook my head. "I didn't know what to make of all the gifts."

"It's okay. I heard you identified the body at the coastal lake near your house."

I took in a shaky breath. "I did."

"I'm sorry you had to go through that."

"Did you hear who it was?"

"No."

I liked that he didn't press me for an answer.

"Do you think the banner, flowers, and wine are connected to the body?"

Tears spilled over again. I hated crying. I wasn't usually weepy. Growing up, my brothers' endless teasing made me tough. "Show no pain" was one of my personal mottoes. Emotional pain was best hidden too, in my opinion.

"It was my ex-fiancé." Rip knew I'd been engaged. I'd told him months ago. But I'd never gone into details, only saying I'd broken it off.

He took the cup of hot chocolate from my hands and set it on the table before gathering me to him. I rested my head on his shoulder and closed my eyes. His heart thrummed a steady, comforting beat. We sat like that for a few minutes. He didn't pester me with questions that he must surely have, like what was Perry even doing down here. Questions I had no answers to. I finally pulled away, although I really didn't want to.

"I should get back," I said. "I need to stop at the Sea Glass and call my family. Probably Perry's as well."

"If you want to talk, I'll be around."

I drank the rest of my hot chocolate. "Thank you."

"Want me to tow your boat back? You can stay in here that way."

That was heart melting. "No." Going back on my own would almost be as good as a cold shower, which I really needed about now.

The back door to the Sea Glass was unlocked. I shouldn't have been surprised, but I shook my head as I went through. After the murder behind the Sea Glass last summer, where the murderer had stolen a knife from us and cast suspicion on Vivi, I'd thought I'd convinced Vivi and Joaquín to keep the door locked. Unfortunately, it didn't last long. Regulars and the heritage business owners all waltzed through the back entrance instead of going around to the front.

There were only a few customers scattered at tables around the bar. Vivi and Joaquín rushed over to me.

"Are you okay?" Joaquín asked. He wrapped me in his very toned arms. Between fishing and bartending, he didn't even need to go to the gym.

"I've had better days," I said.

That was when I noticed a huge bunch of balloons

with "I love you Chloe Jackson" written on some of them. There was also one of those fruit arrangements with a card on it. I could make out my name written on the card but knew that wasn't Perry's handwriting. He had very concise cursive with tiny, neat letters. I walked over to the arrangement and pulled out the card. This one had the usual *I love you Chloe Jackson*, but it also had a request for me to meet for dinner. Seven p.m. at the Breeze, a fancy restaurant in Sandestin, about fifteen minutes from here toward Destin.

I slumped onto a barstool and handed the card to Vivi. She read it and handed it to Joaquín.

"Oooohhhh," Joaquín said, "dinner with a mystery person." Joaquín paused. "I'm sorry. That was inappropriate, considering what you've been through today."

"It's not likely anyone will show up," I said. I closed my eyes for a moment, thinking of Perry.

"Because of the person in the lake?" Vivi asked. Her voice was gentle. Her brows knitted together with concern. "Can you tell us who it was?"

"I'm surprised you haven't already heard," I said. News traveled faster than the Sea Blaster thrill ride boat that took tourists out on the Gulf. I took out my phone to see if I'd heard from Deputy Biffle. I hadn't. Since I wanted to keep my word to him, I wouldn't say anything yet. Although I'd already broken that promise by telling Rip.

"Chloe, maybe you should go to the Breeze tonight. Just in case whoever is sending all of this doesn't have anything to do with who was in the lake," Joaquín said.

Maybe Joaquín was right, but the idea of getting dressed up to go somewhere after what had happened to Perry was exhausting. "Maybe you could go? Take

Michael." Michael was Joaquín's lovely husband, a former Navy intelligence officer. "I'll buy your dinner."

"Why don't I go with you?" Joaquín suggested. "If whoever is doing this doesn't see you, they might not reveal themselves."

"I'm pretty sure whoever is doing this is dead." My voice caught before I could get out the word "dead." "But okay, I'll go." Just in case. At least that would mean one mystery was solved. If this was a Nancy Drew book, it would be called *The Mystery of the Secret Gift Giver*. It would involve hidden staircases, roadsters, and broken lockets. I already knew that real-life mysteries were much more complex. That led me back to wondering who would have killed nice, dull Perry.

By the time I drove home at five thirty, Deputy Biffle had sent me a text saying the Franklins had been notified of their son's death. I went out to the screened porch and sat on the love seat that was part of a set of wicker furniture. I stared at my phone for a few minutes. I had to call the Franklins, but I really didn't want to. However, putting off the call wouldn't make it any easier.

I punched in the number. Mr. Franklin answered. His voice was somber as he said, "Franklin residence."

I was surprised he answered. A small part of me was hoping the call would go to voice mail. That's a lie. All of me was hoping the call would go to voice mail. "Mr. Franklin," we'd never gone beyond the formal during the time I dated and was engaged to Perry, "this is Chloe Jackson."

"Chloe." His voice choked on my name. "You've heard we lost our Perry."

"Yes, sir. I'm so sorry." There was a scuffling noise.

"You have your nerve calling here," Mrs. Franklin said.

She must have yanked the phone away from Mr. Franklin. I'd never called her by her first name, Irma. Her voice ripped my heart to shreds with its grief.

"It's your fault Perry was down there. And your fault he's dead."

"Mrs. Franklin . . ." I realized the call had been ended. What had she meant by that?

I dialed my friend Rachel. We'd known each other since ninth grade. We'd been roommates in Chicago until I'd come down here to help Vivi after Boone's death. While I was here last summer she'd gotten engaged, and her fiancé moved in with her. It had made my decision to stay here easier because my room had become a man cave. After she answered I told her that Perry was dead, leaving out the details.

"How did he die?" Rachel asked after she got over the shock of the news.

"I can't say, but he was murdered."

"Perry? Murdered?" The phone disconnected.

CHAPTER 6

I stared at my phone. First Mrs. Franklin hung up on me and now Rachel. It rang as I looked at it. Rachel.

"I'm sorry about that. I was so shocked I dropped my phone and ended the call by accident. He was murdered?"

"Yes. I can't believe it either, or that he was down here and didn't let me know." I filled her in on the gifts I'd received today. And the banner. "It's just so unlike him." Then I told her what his mother had said to me.

"Oh, Chloe." Rachel blew out a big breath of air. "I'm so sorry she said that to you." Rachel hesitated. "There are some things I haven't told you."

"What?" Rachel usually didn't dillydally around with her statements. She was a medical student at Northwestern. Practical, smart, fun. Rachel had been a wonderful roommate.

"Perry changed after you broke up with him."

"How so?" I knew he was sad, but our lives hadn't intersected after we'd broken up. I'd gone to great lengths to avoid him before I moved down here.

"I think he knew you thought he was boring. We'd see him around occasionally."

Ouch. I'd been very careful not ever to say that to him. But maybe my actions had spoken louder than I thought they did.

"Why do you think that?"

"First, he started working out."

"Perry went to a gym?" I was astounded. It wasn't that Perry wasn't in good shape. It's just that he wasn't an avid exerciser like I was.

"But then he decided that wasn't exciting enough. So he tried his hand at Roller Derby."

"*Roller Derby*?" Perry was so gentle. I couldn't imagine him bashing people out of the way.

"Yes. Until he sprained an ankle."

Perry had always been a bit clumsy. I'd found it adorable early in our relationship.

"But once Perry recovered, he went to trapeze school. There's a well-known one here."

"No way." I couldn't picture Perry flying through the air with any ease. Perry was afraid of heights.

"It's true. Until he broke his wrist."

"That must have put a stop to trying to be exciting."

"He took poker lessons and was threatening to quit his job to become a professional poker player."

"Poker? What, until he got carpal tunnel and couldn't hold the cards?"

Rachel laughed. "No. He was still playing. According to Perry, it was exciting."

"No wonder his mom blames me." Perry would be a

terrible poker player. Most of the time he had a very expressive face. One like a happy puppy that showed every emotion. "Why didn't you ever tell me any of this?"

"Because Perry could climb Mount Kilimanjaro blindfolded and he still wouldn't be right for you. So why mention it?"

That was practical Rachel.

"I told him as much more than once," Rachel said.

"Do you know why he was down here?" I asked.

"Some accountants' convention. He said he could combine work and winning you back."

I shook my head, like I could shake off everything I'd just heard. It didn't work. "Had he been dating anyone since I broke things off with him?"

"A lot of women. Nothing serious."

That was another big change. Before me, Perry had dated his high school sweetheart all through college. He always said he hated playing the field. "Did you meet any of them?" I asked.

"A couple when we were at the bar down the block."

"How'd Perry meet them?"

"One woman he met through his accounting networking group and a few through online dates."

It was so hard picturing Perry meeting women online. "Do you remember their names?"

"Why do you want to know?"

That was an excellent question. Maybe one had followed Perry down here and killed him. Or someone they knew did. I could, at the very least, give the names to Deputy Biffle for him to check out. I could check them out online too. "Curiosity," I finally answered. "Maybe it will help the sheriff's department figure out what happened to Perry."

"I remember a few first names, but it never went beyond that. I'll text them to you."

"Let me know if you think of anything else," I said. "Tell Asher hi for me." Asher was Rachel's fiancé. He wasn't my favorite person because he had an ego higher than the Willis Tower—the tallest building in Chicago which I still called the Sears Tower. But if Rachel loved him, I'd give him my best shot. We hung up after talking a little longer.

Rachel sent the text with a list of five women. It was more than I'd expected. I didn't recognize any of the names but felt obligated to forward the list to Deputy Biffle. However, without last names I wondered how helpful they would be. Still, any of them could be possible suspects. And if they had Perry's phone maybe the names would match his contacts. That made me feel a little bit better. Taking action eased some of my pain.

After I'd talked to Rachel I'd sent a text to Vivi and Joaquín, explaining who the body in the lake was. My phone rang two seconds later. Joaquín.

"Chloe!!!! We just heard the news about your connection to the murder victim. Vivi's right here beside me. What can we do?"

"There's nothing that can be done," I said. "It's strange. I don't know how to feel. Sad, of course. Shocked too." Horrified, appalled. The list could go on, but I still couldn't settle on one emotion.

"Do you want to cancel our dinner?"

"No. I think we should proceed as planned."

"Okay." Joaquín sounded skeptical, drawing out the word "okay."

"Just in case it wasn't Perry who sent the gifts. More

important, just in case it had something to do with his . . .
death."

"I can come pick you up," Joaquín said.

"It's okay. I'll meet you there."

I showered and dressed in a simple black dress for my
dinner with Joaquín. As I drove over, and thought about
Perry, I remembered something Boone had said to me
once. I'd been whining about my dating life. Frankly, I
had a type—hot, jock. And more than one had stomped
all over my silly, little heart. I'd told Boone I was going
to find a man who was different from the usual.

He'd said, "Why don't you look closer to home?"

"You're brilliant," I'd replied. I remembered how
happy he'd looked. "I'll see if Rachel wants to go to the
bar down the street." It wasn't our usual haunt, and I'd
thought maybe this bar would attract a different type of
guy. Boone had had a bemused expression, which I'd
misinterpreted for approval. I didn't realize then, and didn't
learn until after his death, that when he said, "Closer to
home," he'd meant him. What an idiot I'd been.

I valet parked and spotted Joaquín waiting for me near
the entrance. He looked handsome in tan slacks and an
open-collared teal shirt instead of his usual Hawaiian
shirt. "You clean up nice," I said.

"So do you." He hugged me to him for a long moment
and kissed the top of my head before letting me go. "Are
you sure you want to do this?"

What choice did I have?

CHAPTER 7

"Yes," I said.

Joaquín held the door open for me. I stood there for a moment.

"It's not the lion's den, Chloe, and I'm here with you."

"Okay, then." I took a deep breath and we went to the hostess stand. "I'm Chloe Jackson. I'm not sure—"

"Right this way," the hostess said, smiling.

I scanned the room as we followed the waitress. There was no table with a man sitting by himself. No one paid much attention to me, but women were perking up at the sight of Joaquín. They always did. We were seated at a table by a window that overlooked the grounds of Sandestin. Palm fronds bent to the will of the north wind, which hadn't let up all day.

As soon as we sat down, a waiter arrived with an ice bucket holding my favorite champagne in it. Another waiter came over with a bouquet of long-stemmed white roses. I took them and then looked around for a place to put them, noticing that the vase wasn't your ordinary, run-of-the-mill florist vase. It was a heavy, cut crystal vase.

"Do you think a trio is next to serenade you?" Joaquín asked.

"If Perry was doing all this, he'd know how much I'd hate that." I sat so I could watch the restaurant entrance, my head jerking up anytime I noticed motion. I probably looked like a bobblehead doll.

A waiter brought out two bowls of lobster bisque and placed them in front of us.

"There must be some mistake," I said. "We haven't ordered yet."

The waiter winked at Joaquín. "The gentleman ordered in advance. And paid. Thank you for the generous tip." He stood at the table until we'd both taken a sip and murmured our approval. Even the waiter didn't want to leave Joaquín's side.

"Does lobster bisque have some kind of meaning for you and Perry?" Joaquín asked.

"We had it on our first date." In my gut I'd known that Perry would have been my mystery date for tonight, but this clinched it. Although Perry had never been a generous tipper. He figured out 18 percent to the penny and never rounded up. Maybe that was another thing that had changed about him.

My stomach and my heart warred over whether I should eat or not. While my stomach shouted, *Eat, this is delicious* and *When was the last time you ate?* my heart said, *"How can you eat when Perry is dead?* I took a couple more bites. What would the next dish bring?

"Surf and turf," Joaquín said as the waiter whisked

away our bowls and put fresh plates in front of us. He raised one of his manicured eyebrows at me.

"Our six-month anniversary meal," I answered.

"I hate to speak ill of the dead—" Joaquín started.

"But you're going to." I managed a smile at him. "No worries. I get it. I've said some things today about Perry that weren't exactly flattering."

Joaquín gestured toward the food. "Seems kind of predictable. You deserved better."

I flashed back to Perry floating in the lake. "Perry did too."

Joaquín reached over and squeezed my hand. "It's not on you that he's dead. You had nothing to do with it."

"Not according to his mom." I filled Joaquín in on my phone conversation with her.

"She's hurting right now. And she's wrong, Chloe."

As Joaquín ate and I nibbled, I told him about my conversation with Rachel.

"That is borderline nuts," Joaquín said. He leaned forward. "You might have thought you broke up with him because he was boring, but maybe you sensed something was off with him."

I let that idea roll around in my head for a few minutes. "I don't know."

"What was he like when you met him?"

"The exact opposite of my usual boyfriend. So, not built like a Greek god. Perry was cute in a boyish way instead of romance-book-cover handsome. Kind of shy instead of aggressive. I went up to him instead of waiting for him to come to me. That's one of the many reasons I felt bad about breaking off our engagement." I pushed some food around on my plate. "He was nice."

"You didn't date nice guys?" Joaquín looked at my plate. "If you aren't going to eat that lobster, pass it over. It would be a shame to let it go to waste."

I passed my lobster over to Joaquín. "I call my dating life 'the Chloe effect.' The guys I dated started out seeming nice enough, but after a couple of months they turned into raging jerks. Selfish or domineering or cheaters. One guy was all three."

"Chloe, it's not you. They let their true selves show. Did your family like Perry?" Joaquín asked.

"I'm not sure. Usually no one said much because they learned when I was in high school that if they said they didn't like someone, I liked them even more. I'm a dating wreck."

"You and Rip seem to be doing okay."

"That's because if you look in the dictionary for the definition of the word 'slow,' you'd see our picture next to it. Normally, I plunge into a relationship, but not with Rip." Was that because there was some underlying issue with him? Or me? Now that Joaquín presented his theory of Perry and me—that I saw something off about him—I'd always be second-guessing myself.

"Slow can be good. I held Michael at arm's length for a while. I didn't see the need to rush things. We became best friends first."

"My parents are best friends. I thought maybe Perry and I could be too." But that had never happened. "He tried to put me up on a pedestal and tried to cherish me. But I'm not the cherishing kind."

"I cherish you. I don't get what you mean by 'tried to cherish you.'"

"He wanted me to be like his mom. She's this seemingly fragile, catered-to woman. If having the vapors was still a thing, she'd have them. I'm more of a bulldog in the proverbial china shop." I remembered the tight smile Mrs. Franklin always had when I was around. I took attention away from her and she didn't like it one bit.

"That's not cherishing. That's smothering."

"If you get any more on point, I'm going to have to find a couch to lie down on and we'll start therapy. I never found the right word for my relationship with Perry. But smothering is perfect. I couldn't be who he wanted me to be."

The waiter came by and whisked away our plates.

"Shall we go?" I asked.

"I think our dessert is coming." Joaquín pointed behind me.

I turned in my chair and a flaming Baked Alaska was being brought to our table. I turned back to Joaquín. "Baked Alaska. The dessert his parents had when his father proposed to his mother. The dessert we had the night Perry proposed."

The waiter placed it on a tray by the table, cut two slices, plated them, and set them in front of us. "Bon appétit."

I took my fork and started shredding the piece.

"What are you doing?"

"Last time we had this I almost ate my engagement ring."

Joaquín chuckled. "How did you even end up engaged considering the way you felt?"

"We were in a restaurant. He got down on one knee. I looked up and both of our families were standing there. They all looked anxious. I didn't know what to do but say yes." I continued to dig through my dessert. "I was twenty-four but should have been smarter."

I jerked my head up and did another scan of the restaurant. Whew, our families weren't here, but there was a large round table in the middle of the restaurant with a bunch of people staring over at Joaquín and me. Most of the people at the table looked around my age, with the exception of one gray-haired man and a woman who looked a bit younger than me. What was going on?

"Don't be so hard on your twenty-four-year-old self," Joaquín said.

"Joaquín, dig through your dessert to check for a ring." I hoped he didn't find one, that I was wrong.

He did and seconds later lifted a ring out with his fork. "I think this was meant for you."

CHAPTER 8

It wasn't the ring that Perry had proposed with the first time. It was even bigger, gaudier. Not my style at all, but it made a statement. I heard a commotion and looked up to see a woman at the round table shoving back her chair and throwing down her napkin. Soon she worked her way through the other diners to our table. Her hair was blue/black and board straight. Her dark eyes flashed and her round face was flushed. She was so petite, I felt big.

"Where's Perry?" She pointed dramatically at Joaquín. "And who's this?" She did a double take when she took a closer look at Joaquín. "Oh, hi." She batted her eyelashes.

I never trusted eyelash batters. Even worse, I didn't want to tell her that Perry was in the local morgue. My face grew warm as I battled back tears. Joaquín glanced at me and lowered his fork so the ring rested on his plate. He batted his dark eyelashes right back at her, took her hand, and went into full charm mode, saving me from having to speak.

"I'm Joaquín Diaz. And you are?" He threw in another bat of his eyelashes.

Okay, so I guess there was an exception to my eyelash-batting rule as long as it wasn't something that was done routinely.

"I'm Suni Weatherly."

"Charming name," Joaquín murmured.

Suni blushed.

"How did you know Perry would be here?" Joaquín asked.

I was grateful he'd managed to speak, because I was still coming up with ways to break the news about Perry's whereabouts.

She waved a hand toward the large round table where she'd been seated. "Perry invited us. We're his coworkers and are all down here for an accounting conference."

That confirmed what Rachel had said. I'd have to let Deputy Biffle know, although he'd probably already found that out.

"Tonight was the end of a months' long campaign to win her," she flicked a glance at me, "back. It culminated with the banner flyover, the bouquet of lilacs, her favorite sparkling wine, balloons, fruit, and her favorite meal, then he was going to get down on one knee and propose." She flicked another look my way. "To her."

Months' long campaign? If only he'd let me in on it, I could have nipped this all in the bud. Or if Rachel had let me know. Suni didn't sound too thrilled with Perry's plan. And her glances at me screamed she thought I was the dirt beneath the rock, beneath the pond scum at the bottom of a lake. I sounded like I was channeling my inner Julia Roberts in *My Best Friend's Wedding*. Lake. Perry. Telling Suni.

Joaquín stood, maneuvered around Suni, pulled out my chair, and had me up and moving toward the entrance of the restaurant. He'd paused long enough to pick up the ring, which I would return to Perry's family. Suni followed us. When we were out of sight of the other diners, Joaquín turned toward Suni.

"Perry was unavoidably detained. I filled in for him."

I know Joaquín didn't like lying, so I appreciated his willingness to do so for me. He held the door open and we hustled out.

Outside, we gave the valet the tickets for our cars.

"Thank you for handling all that so smoothly." I was exhausted. The idea of another public engagement only with friends here this time instead of family made me sick. I imagined it in my head. I would have said no even if the Queen of England had been invited to watch.

"That's what friends are for. And now I know what your favorite meal is."

"That's Perry's favorite meal, not mine."

"It sounds like he was selfish, Chloe."

Memories of our relationship flashed through my head. "I'd never looked at it that way. I spent most of our engagement feeling guilty because I didn't want to give up my friends or the activities I enjoyed to sit home with Perry."

"You shouldn't have to. True love means allowing space for those things."

I envied Joaquín and Michael's relationship.

"We left your flowers," Joaquín said. "Do you want me to go back in to get them?"

"No. I don't need any more reminders of this day. But thank you."

The door opened behind us.

"Wait," Suni said. She hurried over to Joaquín and shoved a piece of paper at him.

Suni went back inside after he took it.

"What's that?" I asked.

Joaquín unfolded the paper and shook his head. "She's staying at the Sandpiper Hotel in Destin. Room 224."

I laughed. I couldn't help it. "Now who has someone who's smitten with them?"

"I guess she didn't notice my wedding ring."

"Or she didn't care."

Joaquín shrugged. "Here's your engagement ring. I don't want the responsibility."

Joaquín pressed it into my palm. It was still sticky from the Baked Alaska. I dropped it in my purse.

"That was a lot," I said. "And I think Suni has a thing for Perry."

"I thought the same thing."

"Could she be so angry she killed him? And then went to dinner with the group because otherwise they'd know something was up?"

"She'd have to be colder-blooded than the fish I catch to pull that off."

I stared off at a palm tree for a moment. A light shone on its base and the leaves rustled in the wind. "Or she can't care too much about Perry if she's handing out her phone number."

The valets brought our cars. "Thanks for coming tonight and for being so wonderful all day." I got up on my tippy-toes and kissed Joaquín's cheek.

"You're welcome. Are you all right to be alone?" Joaquín asked.

"I think maybe I need to be. Thanks." I climbed into my Beetle, not sure if I should be alone or not.

There was a car in my driveway and two people sitting on my small front porch when I pulled up to my house at eight thirty. Delores and Ralph Harrison rushed over to me as soon as I was out of the car and enveloped me in a hug. I'd met them last summer and we'd grown closer ever since. Delores was a 911 dispatcher and owned The Diner, one of my favorite restaurants on the town circle in Emerald Cove. Ralph owned the Redneck Rollercoaster. The business was born from a time when Black people weren't allowed to go to white amusement parks in this area, and Ralph's ancestors came up with a fun alternative. He was also a volunteer fireman.

"You didn't have to come over," I said, although I was glad to see them. I'd thought I'd wanted to be alone, but I didn't.

"We brought you some food," Delores said. "All your favorites." Delores had brassy red hair and a curvaceous figure. She always had on bright red lipstick and tonight was no exception.

"You don't know how happy I am to see you." My stomach rumbled, so much for not having any appetite. "Excuse me. How long have you two been sitting here?"

"Not long," Ralph said. "The food's still hot." Ralph's short Afro was graying. Now in their late sixties, the two of them had been high school sweethearts, but because of the times, their families didn't approve of their interracial relationship. They'd both married other people but eventually found their way back to each other and married.

"But we would have waited all night if we had to," Delores said.

"Let's go inside," I suggested.

We all picked up the bags of food they'd left on the porch, went in, and settled at my small dining room table. Delores had brought gumbo, shrimp po' boy sandwiches, French fries, and coleslaw. There were also pieces of Delores's famous Mile High Pecan Pie.

My appetite came roaring back and we all dug in.

"No talking about today until we eat," Delores said.

As I finished my last bite of pie, Delores and Ralph studied me. I filled them in on my day, pausing before I told them about seeing Perry. My appetite was gone, mostly because I was full, but partly from the vision of Perry in the lake. His arms had been folded over his chest and he'd clutched the photo of me in his hand. That was odd. I was glad Delores had said no talking until after we finished.

"Did you know him?" Delores asked.

"I'm surprised you haven't heard," I said. I pushed some crumbs from the pie crust around my plate.

"I was out fishing all day and Delores was at The Diner," Ralph said. "All we know is that there was a body at the coastal lake and you identified the man."

"Let me start at the beginning. I'm sorry I didn't answer your texts after the airplane flew over with the 'I Love You Chloe Jackson' banner."

"Honey, you don't worry about that," Delores said, patting my arm.

I filled them in about all that had gone on. There was a

lot of gasping, "oh, honeys," and more arm patting while I talked. When I got to the part about the ring I remembered it was still in my purse.

"Hang on," I said. I'd dropped my purse on the kitchen counter when we got into the house. I searched it, found the ring, and took it back to the table. "Look at this. He was going to propose."

"That's big," Ralph said.

"He didn't know you at all, did he?" Delores asked. "That doesn't look like something you'd wear."

How could Delores understand me more in seven months than Perry had in the two and a half years we were together?

"Have either of you heard any news about Perry's death? Do they have his phone? Did he fly down here or drive?" Something that might give Deputy Biffle a lead would be good.

"I haven't heard anything," Ralph said. "But like I said, I was fishing and I haven't been to the station."

"I don't know anything either. There was some speculation going on at The Diner during the dinner rush, but that's all it was. If you know what kind of car he has, that might help Deputy Biffle."

"He drove a classic Pontiac Trans Am." He had loved that car. It was the only thing about Perry that was flashy. "I didn't think to tell him earlier because I assumed Perry flew down here. Plus, it's been a year and a half. I'm not sure if he still had it. But I'll call him just in case."

Delores stood. "Come on, Ralph, let's get you home and get some salve on you before that arm of yours seizes up from fishing all day."

"My arm's just fine," Ralph grumbled as he stood and headed for the door. "It doesn't seize up."

"Right. Call it whatever you want, but after you went fishing last time you were whinier than a three-year-old without a nap." Delores walked to the door and turned around and winked at me. "Good night. You call us if you need anything."

"I don't whine," Ralph said as they went out.

I smiled after them, locked my door, and set the alarm. I called Deputy Biffle and told him what had happened at the Breeze. He played things close to vest, so I didn't know if he already knew that Perry had been down here for a conference or not. Or if he knew that Perry had been the one behind the banner, flowers, and wine. I also mentioned Perry's car.

"Have you found a car like that?" I asked him. "Maybe caught it on a security camera?"

"This isn't Chicago, Chloe," Deputy Biffle said. "We don't have security cameras every two feet around here. But I appreciate the information."

After we hung up, I washed the Baked Alaska off the ring. I decided to hide it in a dresser drawer until I could mail it back to the Franklins. I stared down at the ring lying there with my socks, wondered why Perry would do this, and if it had anything to do with his murder.

CHAPTER 9

The sunrise Sunday morning was spectacular as I ran along the beach like I usually did. There were just enough clouds so sunbeams shot across the sky with oranges and pinks as their background. Today I'd headed east away from the coastal lake where Perry's body had been found. I ran past Vivi's house and turned back a half mile later.

I tried to concentrate on the crisp air, the firm sand under my feet, and the gentle lapping of the waves. Instead, I kept picturing Perry in the lake. So instead of turning up the beach at my house I ran on by, back to the coastal lake. When I was even with it, I jogged in place. The tide was low, so I was a hundred yards away from the edge of the lake. The trees surrounding the lake looked ominous this morning instead of welcoming, as they usually did.

There was a couple walking not far from me, heads

down, looking for shells. It was usually all for naught here. Locals had told me that most of the shells were trapped on the other side of the outermost sandbar of two that ran along this stretch of coastline. I'd found the occasional sand dollar or those tiny shells that look like angel wings, but not much more, and I spent a lot of time out here on my runs.

I girded my loins—whatever that meant—and ran up to the lake. My pace was slower and slower—not only because of my hesitation, but because the softer sand was harder to run on. I stopped about ten feet from the edge of the lake. Water lilies floated placidly. How did Perry end up here of all places? The only signs of what had happened was the sand churned up with tire tracks and footprints. There wasn't even any crime scene tape left to mark the spot. I wondered if the tourism board made sure it was taken down so as not to scare off visitors.

"Oh, Perry. If only you'd called me. What were you thinking?" If Perry had called, or if Rachel had told me what was going on, could Perry's death have been prevented? I said a quick prayer before I made myself take a good look around.

The water rippled here and there, hopefully from a frog and not an alligator. The lake was surrounded on three sides by tall loblolly pine trees and dense underbrush. Things grew so fast here that keeping nature at bay was a constant battle. This side of the lake was open to the beach. On the far side, to the north, on the other side of the trees, there were three houses. I could barely see them through the trees. Those three houses were my closest neighbors. Although they were a good quarter mile from me as the crow flew.

I shook my head and turned to head home. There were

no answers for me here. As I walked, I noticed I was parallel to a set of footprints. They followed the edge of the lake, then the woods heading toward my house. They didn't seem deep enough or wide enough to be from Deputy Biffle's boots. I put my foot next to one. My foot was smaller and narrower. The footprints were giving me the creeps.

I trekked alongside the lake to the path that led to my nearest neighbor's house. Instead of the footprints cutting up that path, they continued on. My anxiety rose as I approached my house. The prints led me to the window of my guest room. The curtains were pulled. I'd closed them myself last night when I got home from the Breeze. I shivered, wondering if someone had been out there when I did so.

I looked at the aluminum window frame and noticed some scratches around the edges. I couldn't tell if they were fresh or had been there for a long time. It was unnerving nonetheless. I followed the tracks until they ended on my asphalt driveway. I checked my car to make sure it was okay and then walked to the other side of my house, where the footprints picked up again.

Under my bedroom window it looked like someone had stepped forward and back several times. There were gouges in the aluminum on this window too like someone had tried to pry the window open. A cold gust of wind from the north hit me just then, and it felt like a portent of bad things. Could I get any more dramatic? It was probably just my restless night's sleep talking.

I had an alarm system, but it was only for the front door, back door, and slider into my bedroom. I might need to upgrade the system. I followed the footprints over the dune, feeling guilty for walking through the fragile ecosystem. I normally used the walkway from my back door to the beach. The prints ended abruptly at about the high tide line, probably washed away during the last high tide, which was overnight. I turned back and looked over at my house. I'd enjoyed its isolation, but now it looked small and alone, just the way I felt.

After I dressed I called the sheriff's department. Emerald Cove was too small to have its own police department. My optimistic side hoped that the footprints were left by someone from the department who for some reason had decided it was necessary to investigate my house. Deputy Biffle showed up a half hour later, uniform pressed, boots polished, and said otherwise.

"Chloe, no one from the department would try to break in through a window. They'd contact you before doing anything around your house. There was only me and a couple other deputies out at the lake. These prints don't match the tread of our boots."

"I figured as much, but the truth is scaring me."

Deputy Biffle looked at me with what I interpreted to be a look of sympathy, the aviator sunglasses keeping me from knowing for sure.

"I can understand that."

I'd been hoping for something more reassuring, but Deputy Biffle was always straightforward.

We retraced the path together starting where the footprints ended on the beach, over the dune, around to my house. As we walked, I discreetly compared the footprints Deputy Biffle was creating to the ones we were tracking. Like he'd said they weren't the same, but I needed to double-check because I didn't know him all that well.

Deputy Biffle had frowned when he looked at the gouges at the windows.

"Ever notice these before?" he asked.

As always, it was impossible to read his expression. But there was a small crease between his eyebrows. Worried. He was worried. That couldn't be good.

"No. But it's not like I've really taken a close look at them until now."

"Could be from someone putting up storm shutters in the past when we were expecting a hurricane."

I liked the sound of that. It was much less frightening than picturing someone trying to pry my windows open. And if they'd tried, what had stopped them? On the other hand, someone for some reason had trekked from the lake around my house.

"Did you contact Suni Weatherly last night after we talked?" I asked as we walked toward the lake.

"I did."

"What did she have to say?"

"It's not your business, Chloe."

CHAPTER 10

"It feels like my business. My ex-fiancé is dead and someone was roaming around my house."

"I understand how you'd feel that way."

I waited for more, but nothing was forthcoming. I wondered if Deputy Biffle had a degree in psychology because that sounded just like what I'd expect a psychologist to say. Agreeing to appease me, but not adding anything that would help me out.

When we got to the lake I tried another question. "Could it have been one of the EMTs?"

Deputy Biffle frowned again. His face was usually set to neutral. Two frowns in one morning was something. "Even if it was, they had no reason to be there."

"This isn't helping me feel better."

"Is that why you called? You wanted me to make you feel better?"

"A girl can dream."

He laughed a short bark of laughter. "Sorry I couldn't help you out. Be careful, Chloe. I can't think of any good reason this happened."

Back in my house unsettled by Deputy Biffle's opinions, I figured I had two choices. I could either play defense or offense. I decided to go on offense. I called a local TV reporter, Mary Moore. I'd met her last fall when I'd been swept out to sea on an abandoned boat. She was driven, smart, and capable. I think she had ambitions that went way beyond the Emerald Coast.

I didn't particularly like the idea of going on-air, but I wanted whoever had been creeping around my house to know I was on to them. Mary agreed to come over in forty minutes. After we hung up, I called the security company to arrange for an upgrade to my system, which would include alarms on the windows.

The guy at the security company sounded surprised.

"You want your windows wired?" he asked.

"Yes." It didn't seem like an unusual request to me.

"Well, we can do it, but it's going to cost you."

Of course it would. Did he think I wanted him to work for free? "I understand."

"You know, we usually don't do much business in Emerald Cove. Only the odd house where the owners don't live in town."

Ahhh. Now I understood what was going on. Emerald Cove was mostly populated with locals, unlike in Destin or Seaside, where lots of out-of-towners purchased homes that they didn't live in full time. Emerald Cove, I'd found out, was a we-know-everyone-so-why-lock-your-doors-or-car kind of town. I always locked everything, but that was what living in Chicago my entire life had done to me. Of course, my first few months here hadn't been crime-free either. The man said he could come over at eight tomorrow morning.

After we hung up I checked my phone to see what, if any, news coverage there was about Perry's death. If Deputy Biffle wouldn't tell me anything, maybe the press could.

I found several articles. They all reported the same thing: that one Perry Franklin of Chicago had been murdered and his body found in a coastal lake in Emerald Cove. One article said Perry was attending the Midwest Accountants Association's annual winter conference, and that he'd been shot three times. Head, heart, shoulder. That was new information. And to me, it sounded like someone was angry with him. If it had only been one shot, it would make me think it was a professional hit. Who was angry at Perry and why?

I took a quick shower, styled my hair, put on more makeup, and dressed in leggings along with an aqua sweater as I pondered that question. Vanity thy name is Chloe, but hey, if I was going to be on TV I wanted to look okay. I realized that I didn't know enough about Perry's life over the last year and a half to know who would be mad at him. During the time we were together I couldn't remember anyone ever being mad at him either. Sure, he bickered with his siblings sometimes, but nothing that even came close to crossing a line. Perry had once told me that when he was growing up, his mother quickly squelched any strife by saying a "sick headache" was coming on. It had always bothered me how she manipulated all of them.

But as far as I could figure, that had nothing to do with this mess. I hadn't met a lot of his coworkers because he always said they were boring—which was saying something given my thoughts on Perry—and that he liked to keep his work and his personal life separate. Which, now that I thought about it, was odd. He'd wanted his coworkers at the restaurant last night for his proposal. Was he trying to prove a point with one of them? Suni perhaps? Or did he think he could pressure me into another yes with a group of coworkers around. What did that say about Perry that he assumed I'd say yes to a proposal after not seeing him for so long? Maybe that he was delusional.

My doorbell rang and Mary stood there with a camera-woman. Mary was blond, charming, and professional, in a pink, knee-length dress with a pink blazer one shade darker than the dress. She also had on black tights and sensible pumps. I didn't really trust reporters, but if I had to choose one, and I had, it was her. We'd seen each other socially a few times, but our busy schedules made it hard to get together.

After some pleasantries we settled on filming on the beach behind my house.

"I don't want to put my house in a shot," I explained. Mary's station covered a broad area of the Panhandle and I didn't want to invite trouble. I already had plenty. "You can get shots of the footprints after we talk." As in the fall, filming behind my house seemed safer than filming my actual house. Although in a small town like Emerald Cove, you could probably ask almost anyone where I lived and they would be able to point you here. Of course, they would say I lived in Boone's house.

The three of us traipsed through my house and down the walkway over the dunes to the beach. The view behind me could be almost anywhere on the Panhandle—a large expanse of white sand ending at the emerald-colored water. Although again today the northern wind was whipping up the waves enough that they had small whitecaps on them. And the water had a gray tinge to it.

My hair ruffled as I stared into the camera, bracing myself for the first question. Mary did a quick on-camera intro before she turned to me.

"I understand that the body found in the coastal lake was your ex-fiancé. What do you know about his death?"

It was like being punched in the gut. In fact, I actually sucked it in. And as with a good punch in the gut, my eyes filled with tears. My oldest brother had punched me in the gut when I was ten when I'd taken his dare. I'd never forgotten how that felt. I'd bloodied his nose before my mom pulled me off him.

"It's a tragedy, but I haven't had any contact with Perry for over a year and a half." Long enough to birth a whole new life. I hadn't had any idea what was in store for me the day I gave the ring back to Perry. I blinked away the memory of that day, along with my tears. Maybe calling Mary hadn't been such a great idea. "Listen, can we keep that quiet for now?"

Mary tilted her head to the side for a moment. "Why?"

"I don't want to be dragged into the middle of this. How did you even find out?"

"I saw that he was from Chicago and remembered you were. I did some digging and found your engagement announcement."

If Mary could figure it out, others would too. We stared at each other.

Mary gave a brief nod. "I'll hold that back for now but will update the story with your comment when it gets out."

"Thank you."

The camerawoman readjusted the camera on her shoulder. She looked too small to hold its heft, but it didn't seem to bother her. If anything, she looked bored.

I gazed straight into the camera. "Someone's been lurking outside my house. If you're trying to scare me, it didn't work." Yes, it did. I was on freaking TV because I was so scared.

"Lurking? Did you see someone?"

"No. But there are footprints in the sand, and someone tried to jimmy the window."

"Do you think the footprints are from the killer?" Mary's voice was low, intent.

"They led from the coastal lake to here." I shrugged. "I don't know for sure, but it seems likely."

"Has the sheriff's department been here to investigate?"

"Yes. Of course."

"And do they think there's a connection?"

"They weren't very forthcoming with their opinions." That was Deputy Biffle for you.

"This next bit will be off the record for now."

This time I nodded. "Okay."

"It seems strange that you haven't had any contact with Perry for over eighteen months, yet he was found murdered so close to your house. Do you have any ideas about what he was doing down here?"

"I don't." None that I was willing to share on TV or with a reporter anyway. "All I know was that he was here for a convention. I had no idea he was going to be in the area."

"Anything you want to say to whoever was around your house?"

"Don't come back." The short interview had been way more draining than I'd imagined. I turned back to Mary. "No further comment."

She did some wrap-up commentary and then the camerawoman shut things down.

I sighed. "Let me show you the footprints."

After Mary and her camerawoman left I looked up where the Midwest Accountants Association conference was being held. It was at the same place Suni was staying. That made sense. I'd be cutting it close driving there and getting back to work on time. Perry's murder so close to my house felt personal. Add in the fact that someone was creeping around my house and it made me realize I wasn't content to leave things to the sheriff's department. Oddly enough, Mary's questions put that in perspective for me.

I decided to drive over and talk to Suni Weatherly. She must have heard the news about Perry by now. And to be perfectly honest, I wanted to check out her shoe size. Maybe she was the one who was out here last night. Her behavior at the restaurant had been strange.

Thirty minutes later I waltzed by the front desk, the bar, and the restaurant, and hopped into the elevator. I knocked on the door of room 224. Suni opened the door, and I took in her tear-stained face. Her puffy eyes were bloodshot and tears streaked down her face. She grasped a couple of tissues in her right hand. Her grief punched another hole in my heart. I wanted to run back down the hall and out of there.

Instead, I did what I'd come here to do and looked down at her feet. She was barefoot. Toes painted a sky blue with gold fleur-de-lis on the big toes. Tiny toes, on impossibly tiny feet. I was amazed they held her upright. Unless she'd borrowed a friend's much bigger shoes, which was unlikely, Suni hadn't been tromping around my house.

"You knew last night at dinner, didn't you?" Her voice was low and tightly controlled.

I snapped my head up and took a step back at the venom in her voice. "I did. I'm—"

"You are one coldhearted witch to sit there in the restaurant like nothing was wrong while you ate your dinner."

I'd put my "show no pain" motto to good use last night, although inside I'd been a wreck. I wouldn't try to explain that to Suni because she was obviously suffering too. Maybe from across the dining room it had looked like nothing was wrong, but I'd mostly pushed my food around or given it to Joaquín.

"I wasn't at liberty to tell you." Ugh. I sounded like an uptight, prissy librarian I used to work with. A woman who took more pleasure in shushing people than finding someone the perfect book.

"I'm sorry." In reality, I could have told her last night. Perry's family had already known by that time, but I certainly hadn't wanted to tell her, and especially not in a crowded restaurant.

"He deserved better than you." She yelled it so loud that a door opened down the hall and a white-haired woman stuck her head out.

The woman took one look at the two of us and slammed her door shut. If I was going to find out anything from Suni, I'd better hurry because I had a feeling a visit from hotel security was in my near future.

"You're right. He deserved someone more suited to

him than I was." I paused, thinking again about how wrong we were for each other. "I wasn't right for him."

Suni jerked her head back in surprise. I think she expected an argument, not my agreement.

"Do you know anyone who was angry with him? Someone at work maybe?" I asked.

"You probably killed him yourself. I watched you at the parties he brought you to. You thought you were better than everybody."

"That's not true."

Had I come off that way? My memory included me laughing and talking with people. I frowned. When we did go to parties Perry often found us a table in the corner and kept me there as much as possible. Maybe he was trying to keep me from his coworkers, but why? I'd only gone to a couple of parties with Perry because of his whole keep-work-and-personal-life-separate policy. And I only went to those after I'd pestered him to take me. I wanted to know what his whole life was about if we were going to be married.

I didn't remember ever seeing Suni before last night. Perry had worked for a midsized accounting firm. It was well known in the Chicago area and probably employed one hundred people if you included all the support staff. I'm sure he'd never introduced me to Suni. I'd remember such an unusual name.

"I'm the one who helped pick up the pieces after you broke his heart, and then he comes to Florida. Determined to win you back." She shook her head. "Over my dead body." Suni slammed the door closed.

I stared at it for a moment. Or maybe over Perry's dead body.

CHAPTER 11

When I got to the Sea Glass I told Joaquín what had happened with Suni as we took barstools off tables in preparation for opening. Joaquín wore a pale blue Hawaiian shirt with light pink tropical flowers on it.

"Do you think I should call Deputy Biffle and tell him?"

Joaquín tilted his head to one side and tapped his index finger on his cheek as if he was thinking it over. Then he straightened. "For goodness' sake, of course you should tell him." He waggled that finger at me. "Not that anything will likely come of it, and I'm guessing he's not going to be happy you went over there to talk to her."

"You're probably right."

"I usually am." Joaquín grinned at me.

He unlocked the sliding doors that opened onto the deck. We both stepped through them and stood in the sunshine. The building blocked the north wind. The sun soaking into my skin felt marvelous. If there were such a thing as past lives, I'm sure I was an Aztec sun worshipper.

"Chloe, what were you thinking going to talk to Suni in the first place?" Joaquín's eyes looked extra-dazzling with the sun hitting them.

"This morning I found footprints that led from the coastal lake to my house. There were some scratch marks around a couple of the windows. I think someone tried to break in."

Joaquín's beautiful eyebrows popped up. "Chloe, that's terrible."

"It made everything seem even more personal if that's possible. I wouldn't put it past Suni to be the one lurking around my house after our conversation last night." I went back inside and lifted the last barstool off a table. "I wanted to see how big her feet were."

"Her feet?"

"To see if they matched the footprints around the house."

"Did they?"

"No. She has the tiniest feet I've ever seen. It's amazing she can walk."

Joaquín shook his head with a bemused smile on his face. "Just be careful. I don't like that someone killed your ex-fiancé after he spent the day declaring his love for you. Or that someone came to your house." He paused by my side. "You could come stay with Michael and me."

Vivi swept in just then in a turquoise twinset, skinny jeans, and brown knee-high boots. A turquoise designer handbag dangled from the crook of her arm. She had as many handbags as Joaquín did Hawaiian shirts. "Why do you need to go stay with Joaquín and Michael?"

Vivi wasn't going to like this, but I explained the foot-prints around the house to her.

"If you need somewhere to stay, come stay with me," Vivi said.

I was surprised she was so calm about this. I was afraid she'd call the governor, like she had last October when I'd been swept out to sea on a boat. "I appreciate the offers, but I'll be fine at the cottage." I needed some privacy right now. "I'm having the security system up-graded tomorrow morning."

They both protested, but I waved them off.

"At least come over for dinner tonight," Vivi said. "I'm having some old family friends over. I'm sure they'd love to meet you."

Vivi didn't ask me over all that often. "That would be lovely, but I'm working." I waved a hand around toward the nearly empty bar.

Vivi looked over at Joaquín.

"I'll be fine here alone. If it gets busy, I'll call Michael."

"Thank you, Joaquín." Vivi turned toward me. "Cock-tails are at six thirty."

"What can I bring?" I asked.

"Just yourself."

I called Deputy Biffle and filled him in on my conver-sation with Suni. As predicted, he wasn't happy. Amaz-ingly, he told me Perry's Trans Am had been found in the public parking lot not too far from The Diner.

"Why was it there?" I asked.

"We don't know."

Shocked that Deputy Biffle told me that much, I pressed

on. "Did you find his cell phone? Were any of the women on the list I sent you in his contacts?"

"Thanks for the information about the car and your conversation with Ms. Weatherly."

"You're welcome, but—" I realized Deputy Biffle had hung up. Just when I thought I was making progress with him.

After a busy day I walked out of my house to drive to Vivi's at six twenty. We lived closer via the beach, but it was dark out. I was spooked enough that roaming around outside on my own didn't seem like a good idea. Plus, I didn't want to trek across the sand with a bottle of wine and the flowers I picked up on the way home from work. Before I'd left my house I closed all the curtains I could. I'd even dropped the blinds across the windows that separated the living area from the screened porch. It was the first time I'd done that, and I had some serious dusting to do when I got home. After that I'd turned on the TV in my bedroom and left lights on. I also made sure that my security system was set. I'd gotten a little slack with using it after Christmas.

As I drove down my drive, I realized doing all that was probably for naught because my car wouldn't be parked at the house. Anyone who had any familiarity with me or my schedule would assume I was gone. Maybe I should have called a ride share. I gave myself a little shake. *Don't let whoever was at the house get to you. You're fine.*

Ten minutes later I was knocking on the door of Vivi's big Victorian house. The pleasing yellow paint, gables, and large covered porch said *come on in and sit a spell.*

Vivi's front yard was done in native plants to save on mowing and water. I could hear laughter and music as I waited. Part of me wanted to run away. It was like sadness for what had happened to Perry wafted around me like a cape from *The League of Secret Heroes* book, *Cape*.

The door opened and a man I'd never seen before stood there. He looked like he was around my age and was a few inches taller than me, with sandy brown hair and eyes to match. He wore black dress slacks and a button-down, long-sleeve shirt in a pale pink.

"Hi, I'm Chloe," I said. I left off my last name just in case he'd seen the airplane fly over with its banner about me.

"Garth Havers." He smiled, and a cute dimple appeared on his left cheek. Garth stepped back so I could enter.

Garth had a thick Southern accent and smelled like a delicious combination of lime and coconut.

"Everyone is out on the back veranda. Let me take those for you." He gestured to my wine and flowers, so I handed them over. "After you," he said.

I was still getting used to the whole Southern gentleman thing. It's not that men in Chicago wouldn't hold a door open for you. It's that here they might hold a door for you if they saw you a half a block away. It was too cold or too hot in Chicago to do that for most of the year.

As we walked down the hall Vivi's cat, Pippi Longstocking, came trotting out. She was black, with long, white stockings. I'd rescued her last fall from a sailboat that we'd been swept out to sea in. Pippi meowed when she saw me and rubbed against my ankle. I bent down to scratch her head for a moment.

"Looks like you have a fan," Garth said.

Pippi walked over to Garth and rubbed against his pant

leg. He shifted the flowers and wine so he could reach down. Pippi rolled over for a belly rub. Garth laughed and complied. When Pippi wandered off we went through the family room and out onto the large back screened deck. Another fifteen people were out there and I didn't recognize any of them. Everyone was dressed up, so I was glad I'd chosen a long-sleeved black dress that was fitted at the top but ended in a swirl just below my knee. It hid my thick thighs, but showed off my toned calves. At least all that running did something for me.

I took the flowers and wine back from Garth and we went our separate ways. I found Vivi and gave her the flowers and wine.

"Thank you, dear. I said you didn't need to bring anything."

Wade Thomas showed up at Vivi's side. He owned the Briny Pirate restaurant next door to the Sea Glass. I'd figured out in June that he was madly in love with Vivi. I knew she was fond of Wade and probably even loved him, but I wasn't sure it was the same kind of love.

"Hi, Wade," I said.

He kissed me on the cheek. "Want me to take those for you?" he asked Vivi.

"Yes, please." Vivi handed off the wine and flowers. "Let me introduce you," Vivi said.

She led me around the room and introduced me as her business partner, which surprised me. We still had things to work out, but I was content with how things were. I also didn't want to push Vivi. I knew she was still grieving over Boone.

"And this is Garth Havers," Vivi said.

"We met at the door," he said. "She's prettier than a newborn's skin."

I could put that in the strangest compliment—and I've had a lot of strange ones—I'd ever gotten column. I laughed. "Well, don't you just have a way with words." A weird way, but a way nonetheless. I turned to Vivi. "Can I help you with dinner?"

"No. You stay and enjoy yourself. Wade and I will finish things up in the kitchen."

I'd probably enjoy myself more in the kitchen but conceded.

"Let me get you a drink," Garth said. "What would you like?"

A bar was set up on the left side of the porch. "I'll go with you."

We edged our way around everyone. There was a bottle of sparkling wine chilling in an ice-filled bucket.

"That looks perfect," I said. Normally, I'd serve myself, but Garth was in the way and I didn't want to make a scene in a place where chivalry wasn't dead. I didn't even think it was dying or a little bit ill. My adopted home took some getting used to.

After Garth poured a glass of sparkling wine and handed it to me, I decided it was time to move on to the niceties part of the night. "Did you grow up here?" I asked.

"I did. But I've only recently moved back. It's an adjustment after living in Atlanta."

"Big city life is certainly different."

"I can tell that you aren't from around here," Garth said.

What did that mean? I certainly didn't have a Southern accent and I wasn't as put together as a lot of Southern women, but did I stand out that much? Maybe it was wearing black. Women down here dressed in brighter colors.

"Where are you from?" Garth asked.

"Chicago."

"Ah, so you really do understand adjusting to small-town life. How'd you end up down here?"

"Vivi's grandson, Boone, and I were best friends."

"Boone was a great guy. He was five years younger than me, so I didn't know him well."

I wondered if I'd always feel the stab in my heart at the mention of Boone's name. "Boone asked me to come down here and help with the bar if anything happened to him during his tour in Afghanistan." I paused to take a deep breath. Tears were unexpectedly close to the surface all of a sudden. The same thing had happened when Mary interviewed me. Maybe coming hadn't been a good idea. I'd thought it would be a distraction from thinking about Perry, but here I was, close to tears in front of a stranger. "And, as you probably know, the worst did happen."

"I am truly sorry for your loss," Garth said.

"Dinner," Vivi called from the doorway.

CHAPTER 12

Thank heavens. Garth held out his elbow for me to take. There wasn't anything I could do to get out of taking it without being rude. I didn't want to embarrass Vivi, so I slipped my hand in the crook of Garth's elbow and we walked to the dining room. The buffet had platters of steaming fried chicken, grilled shrimp, and the trinity of greens, grits, and gravy with mashed potatoes. It couldn't be more Southern if it tried, and I was thrilled with that.

I let go of Garth's arm and loaded a plate with everything. It was a hill of food, and I couldn't wait to dig in because I'd hardly eaten since Delores had fed me last night. I carried my plate and sat down next to a woman who would make a picket fence look fat. She reminded me of a line from *The Bonfire of the Vanities* by Tom Wolfe. He called the overly thin women of New York City X-rays. She had a deep tan and bleached-blond hair.

The woman had three pieces of shrimp and a spoonful of grits on her plate. She tried to raise an eyebrow at the sight of my plate, but her face was Botoxed into place. I didn't think her expression was because she was impressed with my ability to pile food on a plate and not spill it.

Garth sat on the other side of me. His plate was the middle bear of food—not too much and not too little. He looked around me to the woman on my right. "Chloe, this is my mother, Savannah Havers."

Perfect. "It's nice to meet you," I said.

She swept her eyes over my plate and dress. "You have quite the healthy appetite."

I heard Garth sigh. "I do. It's why I run, so I can eat."

"I run too," she said.

She sniffed a little, but the man on the other side asked her something, so she turned from me.

Garth leaned in close to my ear. "The only place my mother runs to is the spa or Destin Commons, and that's in her car."

Destin Commons was a big, outdoor shopping area. It was filled with pricey clothing stores, restaurants, and a movie theater. I grinned, picked up my fried chicken, and took a bite. Heaven. I could hear the angels singing and the harps accompanying them.

"Do you like it?" Garth asked.

I looked over at him. He was cutting a bite from his piece of chicken with his fork and knife. That was no way to eat fried chicken. "I do. How did you know?"

"You made this little noise that was half sigh and half moan."

"At least it was a little noise." I paused. "This time."

Garth laughed. I took a furtive look around the table. It

was half and half, with part of the crowd using a fork and knife on their chicken and part their hands. Vivi and Wade were eschewing their utensils, so I didn't feel so bad. Garth and I chatted between bites. He was a doctor and starting up a new practice. Dermatology. I guess that explained the weird "newborn skin" compliment.

"Good luck." Down here it would be lucrative, with all the people who spent so much time out in the sun.

"Thank you. It's good to be home." He leaned close to my side. "Parents and all."

When I'd whittled the hill to a small slope, I pushed my plate away,

"I guess my eyes were bigger than my stomach."

Garth's mom looked from my plate to my stomach. "Not by much."

I laughed. "Good point."

Savannah looked taken aback. Maybe she was used to getting a different kind of reaction from people. But what did I care? It wasn't like I ever had to see her again.

Vivi stood. "We'll have dessert out on the veranda."

Garth stood and moved my chair back for me. "Thank you," I said.

"Thank you for tolerating my mother."

"I used to be a children's librarian. I've dealt with way worse than her. She wouldn't even make the top ten list."

"You will have to tell me about that list if my mother didn't break the top ten. And please don't tell her that. She'd be devastated."

I chuckled. Garth took his mother with a healthy side dish of humor and tolerance. "We don't get to pick our families," I said.

"We sure don't."

"Do you have siblings?" I asked.

"A sister who lives here in Emerald Cove."

"That's nice."

"We don't see each other often. Different life choices."

I hoped that didn't mean she'd been in trouble. I knew how hard that could be on a family. "I don't see my family as much as I'd like."

"That didn't come out exactly right. She's a doll. She's married, had a baby, all highly mother-approved things. But she's into Roller Derby, and that drives my mother and her husband right up the wall and over it."

Roller Derby? How interesting, considering Perry was also into Roller Derby. "How long has she done that?" I asked.

"For a few years. She got fed up with being part of the Junior League and country club crowd. She always loved to roller-skate. I think instead of rebelling as a teen she decided to rebel at thirty-two."

We walked back onto the veranda where someone had set up a table with coffee, aperitifs, and a dozen different pies and cakes. Key lime, pecan, which I pronounced pee-con while everyone down here called it pee-can, and chessboard cake, which was another Southern thing I wasn't familiar with but now loved. Garth's mother wandered over to us.

"It's so hard to choose just one," she said. She had on a clingy, low-cut dress that showed she didn't have an ounce of fat on her.

"I could never pick just one," I said. I turned to Garth. "I think I'm going to need a bigger plate."

His mom's eyes widened and then narrowed. She flounced off to the side of another woman.

"I'm sorry," I said to Garth. "That was rude of me."

"It's kind of nice to see someone one-upping my mom.

I love her, but she's a piece of work. She does have a good side and does a lot of charity work. Do you want me to get you a bigger plate?"

I shook my head. "No." I held up my dessert plate. "I think I can wedge at least three pieces on this." In the end, I only took a small piece of Key Lime pie. As much as my eyes wanted more, my stomach said, *don't do it*.

I drifted over to a quiet corner of the veranda and sat in a chair where I could observe the crowd. Garth's mother flitted about. She smiled, laughed, and was way more warm and charming than the woman who'd sat next to me. Maybe she was awkward with strangers. Although Savannah didn't really seem like someone who would be a friend of Vivi's. However, I didn't know Vivi socially for the most part. And I didn't think I recalled any of these people showing up at the bar. I wondered what their connection was. Maybe it was through charity work.

Garth joined me, which I wasn't sure I was glad of. He'd been at my side almost constantly since I'd arrived. He was nice enough, but I hoped he didn't think I was interested in anything more than just a friendship. Then I chuckled inside. Gawd, my head had gotten big. Maybe it was just his polite Southern side being kind to the outsider. His company had made the evening less stressful for me.

Garth had wedged three pieces of pie on his plate. "I decided I'd better join you in this dark corner so my mother wouldn't spy my plate."

I laughed. "If she comes over, you can say you're holding it for me."

"Deal. I always did have a sweet tooth." He paused. "And you seem very sweet."

I almost choked on the bite of pie I was in the process

of swallowing. Thank heavens I was using my best manners and had only taken a small bite. Having to have the Heimlich maneuver pulled on me would have been embarrassing. I looked at Garth. "I think that's perhaps the first time in my life anyone has called me sweet." I'd been called a lot of things—scrappy, kind, determined, pigheaded, and a lot of other things that couldn't be mentioned in polite company—but never sweet.

"May I call you sometime?" Garth asked.

Awkward. "Sure," I answered. "I always love to have a new friend. I'm seeing someone."

A disappointed look flashed across his face. I'm sure if his mom was privy to this conversation a corresponding look of joy would flash across hers.

"Understood," Garth said.

I gave him my number. Garth and I chatted away and after I finished my pie, I told him I was going to head out. He stood when I did but didn't follow me when I made my way to the kitchen. I rinsed my plate and stuck it in Vivi's dishwasher. I noticed the sink full of dishes and went over and started washing them.

Vivi came in. "Oh, no. Don't do that."

"I wanted to help out."

"That's nice of you, but one of the things I love about a party is putting things back to rights after the evening is over and the house is quiet."

"Really? It's one of the things I hate about parties."

Vivi came over and took the sponge out of my hand. "That's what makes the world so fascinating. Did you have a good time?"

"I did."

"Garth's a nice man, although his mother can be something else. But she does a lot of good around Emerald

Cove. We went to the same church growing up." Vivi set down the sponge on the sink.

That explained how they knew each other. "Thanks for having me. I'd be happy to stay and help clean up."

"You're a lovely woman, Chloe," Vivi said. She brushed a kiss across my cheek, but then someone called to her.

I stood there for a moment, surprised. Now part of me didn't want to go home. I wanted to plunge back into the crowd of laughing people. Probably because I was worried I'd find more footprints around my house. But I gave myself a shake and left.

CHAPTER 13

I pulled up to my house ten minutes later. No one had followed me home. The floodlights set on motion detectors went on. I took that as a good sign because once, last summer, they hadn't and I'd had a very scary experience. I sat in the car a moment, looking around. I didn't see anyone, but suddenly all the trees I'd grown to love, which sheltered the house and gave it so much privacy, seemed to lean in toward me. Threatening.

I grabbed my purse and slung it over my shoulder crosswise. My old Volkswagen Beetle, didn't have the luxury of automatic locks or key fobs to click. I made sure all the doors were locked, leaped out, locked the driver's side door, put my keys between my fingers so they stuck out like a weapon, and ran to the front door. I didn't look behind me. I unlocked, rushed inside, slammed the door, locked it, turned off the alarm, and leaned back against the door. Breathing hard not from exertion but fear.

This was no way to live. I had to find out two things. Who'd been outside my house and who'd killed Perry. I couldn't imagine the two weren't connected and I couldn't wait around hoping the sheriff came up with an answer.

I grabbed a beer, threw on my puffy coat, and went out on the screened porch, trying not to feel vulnerable and scared. The flimsy screens weren't much protection if someone was out there. But sitting out here at night was one of my favorite things to do. I didn't want to cower in my house. I refused to cower.

I sat on the wicker chaise lounge looking out at the Gulf. I loved to paddleboard at night, but tonight the persistent north wind pushed at the waves, trying to keep them back. The waves fought to land on shore, white caps formed, and the accompanying noise was almost a roar.

Some thought it was foolish for me to go out at night on my own. Rip for one. But I took precautions, I stayed on this side of the first sandbar, where the water wasn't deep. It would be hard for trouble to find me under such circumstances. I was kind of surprised that Rip wasn't out there waiting for me, but maybe he knew me well enough by now to know that I'd never go out on a night like this.

I swigged some beer and took out my phone. I hadn't looked at Perry's social media accounts since I'd given him back his ring. It had been a promise I'd made myself on the way over to end our engagement. If, I told myself, I wondered what he was up to, I must still have feelings for him. And I didn't, at least not beyond our shared history. I didn't care if he dated, I didn't care who he dated.

I wanted him to be happy. To find his person. Because I knew it wasn't me.

I started with his favorite app. And scrolled down, looking for old photos. There were only a couple of pictures of us. One from the night of our engagement. One from the first night we met. In the first one I looked panicked, like a trapped bunny. In the second Perry had his arm slung around my shoulder. We were both holding shots and he was laughing at something I'd said. I did like to make people laugh. It was eerie that that moment had led to this. Perry dead and me wondering why and who'd killed him.

Staring at those two photos was getting me nowhere. I decided to try to match the list of first names Rachel had sent me with pictures on his social media. I started scrolling forward from our engagement photo. A month after we broke up there was a picture of him strapping on roller skates. He had on a helmet and other protective gear. He said this was going to be awesome. There were pictures of him skating, low, with a fierce, determined look on his face. A look that was unfamiliar to me. There were short videos of him careening around and then later bashing into someone to knock them out of his way.

That was a whole new side to Perry that I'd never seen. He came out bruised in some of the battles and fell and slid, but he always got back up. It was almost inexplicable. Then there was a picture of his cast. He was smiling and holding it up, like it was a badge of honor. And I guess for the quiet, sheltered life he lived, it was.

Next there was a picture of him in a sleeveless tank top at the trapeze school. Pictures of him in midair as he flew from one bar to another. His arms were sculpted, but they'd have to be to do something like that.

It looked like fun. I wondered if he'd suggested something like that when we were dating it would have changed the outcome of our relationship. But I shook my head. It was inevitable that we wouldn't end well, even if he'd tried different activities to please me instead of to please himself. That was no way to live your life.

Then there was the next cast. He was still smiling, but this one looked more determined and less happy. The next set of pictures were ones of him playing poker. He wore a black leather jacket and a baseball cap turned backward.

Again, this was a Perry I'd never seen. Although I did recognize that blank expression. He was great with the poker face when he was mad. He'd had a lot of practice when we were together when I wanted to go do something and he wanted me to stay home. I'd hated that expression, and it was a sharp contrast to his happy puppy face, but it gave him the face he needed for poker.

There were pictures from tournaments around Illinois—Urbana, Springfield, Normal. Then he started playing games farther afield. And finally ended up in Vegas. He'd won tournaments along the way, but he'd lost plenty too. How his mother must have hated that. I can see why she blamed me when she had to watch her beloved boy do all these things that were so out of character for him. Or maybe he'd found out who he really was. I hoped these last months had made him happy.

I got to the most recent pictures. He was down here. Walking on the beach, on a Jet Ski, even parasailing. I'd tried to get him to go with me on Lake Michigan when we were together, but that had been a big no. He'd given me examples of the dangers. Showed me photos of people bashing into buildings and falling when ropes broke. Even one of someone almost landing on a shark.

But I'd told him how seldom anything like that ever happened. That it was safe. That the odds were with him. It hadn't ever mattered. He wouldn't go. Now there were pictures of him with Suni and other people who must also be down here for the conference. And then there was a picture of a woman from a distance who didn't look very happy. It was captioned, One of my Roller Derby heroes. I looked at the picture closely. Holy Harvey Wallbanger! The woman looked a lot like Garth. Was she his sister?

I searched for and found Garth's account, and from there his sister's. Her name was Lori Clemens. There were lots of pictures of her at different Roller Derby events. She'd been in Chicago for a couple of derbys. *Chicago!* Interesting. Then pictures of her announcing she was pregnant and putting her career on pause. After that there were pictures of the gender reveal and, lastly, of her and the baby. I made the picture bigger. The baby looked just like Perry.

CHAPTER 14

I stared in disbelief, but I knew it was true. Perry's baby pictures, along with those of his siblings, were plastered over every wall and empty surface at his mom's house. I scrolled back through and looked at dates of various posts on her social media and his. Two weeks after Perry and I broke up, she'd been in Chicago for a big Roller Derby event. Perry had one of himself in the audience. Maybe that explained his obsession with Roller Derby. It didn't really have anything to do with me.

A bit stunned by all I'd just found out, I set my phone aside and looked out toward the Gulf. I became aware of the rustle of the palmetto fronds and shivered. Maybe from cold, or maybe from fear. I didn't think anyone was out there, but I wasn't going to take any chances. I finished my beer and went inside.

I set the alarm, got in my pajamas—plaid, long-sleeved flannels with matching bottoms—grabbed *Red Widow* by

Alma Katsu, and snuggled under my comforter. My
phone buzzed, I hoped it was Rip. Instead it was Garth,
asking me to meet him for coffee in the morning.

I didn't respond right away. On the one hand, maybe I
could find out more about his sister. On the other, I didn't
want to get his hopes up and just use him as a means to an
end. But I'd made it clear that I wanted to stay in the
friend zone. He couldn't have misunderstood. He might
need friends, having just moved back to town. I texted
back an okay and told him it would have to be quick because the security company was coming at eight and then
I had to go to work. Vivi had insisted I could come in late
to accommodate the security people, but Garth didn't
need to know that. We agreed to meet at nine thirty at the
coffee shop in Emerald Cove.

I read until my eyes drooped and I found myself reading the same page three times.

Monday morning I rushed around getting ready so I'd
be dressed before the security company came. Even with
the rush, I took some extra care with my hair and makeup. I needed to feel confident if I was going to pump
Garth for information. Usually after I ran I had some
leisure time before I had to get ready to go to work. Rush-
ing around this morning was more like my life in Chicago
had been, even though the cold north wind had changed
to a warm southern breeze. As much as they said wait
five minutes for the weather to change in Chicago, I was
beginning to think that held true here in the winter too. I
put on a long, lightweight turquoise turtleneck sweater
and black leggings. Comfortable black flats would work
for footwear. I always admired how Vivi managed to

wear heels or wedges every day. But my feet hurt after an hour if I tried that.

I dabbed some more concealer under my eyes. I hadn't slept well last night. The picture of Garth's sister's baby had haunted my dreams and turned to me having babies—too many to take care of. Some of them looked like Perry and some like Rip, although one had Joaquín's beautiful eyes. Go figure. I wasn't ready to have a baby yet.

While I waited for the security people, I checked the news to find out if there were any updates on Perry. Maybe overnight they'd found his killer and I could rest easier. No such luck. Fortunately, no one had connected me to Perry yet. I said yet because this was a small town and news traveled faster than a northern jet stream.

Thankfully, the security company had proven to be very efficient, so at precisely nine thirty I walked into Grounds For, the local coffee shop. The owner named the store after she divorced her cheating husband and used her alimony to finance the business. She smiled at me when it was my turn at the counter. "The usual?"

"Yes, please," I answered. How fun to have someone know what I wanted. The coffee shop I went to in Chicago had rotated baristas more quickly than the moon orbited around the earth. My roots went a little deeper into the sandy soil here, and it made me happy. After I got my drink—a coffee with light cream—I found a table by the window and waited for Garth. He swung in five minutes later, came over, and started apologizing.

"I'm so sorry I'm late," he said for the third time in the space of a couple of minutes.

"It's fine. Like I said the last two times. Why don't you get a drink?" And take a breath. It was only five minutes. I'd waited longer for almost everything in my life.

Garth grinned. "Yes, ma'am. It's just that—"

"I got it, you're sorry." I made a shooing motion with my hands. He stood and made his way through the tables, stopping now and then to say hello to someone. A couple of women giggled after he'd left their table and bent their heads together, whispering. He might have been gone from town for a while, but he certainly wasn't forgotten.

The two women followed his progress from ordering to doctoring his drink with cream to returning to our table. That was when the frowns came out.

"I think you have some fans," I said. His head started to turn. "No! They're still looking over here. Do I have any daggers in my chest?" Oh boy, why did I say that?

Garth swept a not-so-Southern-gentlemanly look over me. "Everything looks just fine to me."

Warmth crept across my pale Irish face, which made the two women frown even more. I drank my coffee in hopes of covering my embarrassment.

"I've known them both since we were all in diapers. They were mean girls in high school and I'm not sure they've changed that much now, but let's forget about them. I want to get to know you. You said last night you were a children's librarian. Do you miss it?"

"I do. I guess maybe I never grew up all the way. I still love reading children's and young adult books. There's such honesty to them. But I also love working at the Sea Glass. Are you a reader?"

"I am. I love a great mystery."

A woman knocked on the window and waved. She was

with a man in a Florida State University baseball cap, black slacks, and a short-sleeved, button-down shirt.

"Hey, that's my sister, Lori Clemens." He smiled at her.

I recognized her from the pictures I'd seen last night but acted nonchalant. She wore black capri-length leggings, an oversized pink shirt, and a jacket.

"She meets up with other parents and their kids almost every morning over by the tot lot on the town circle." He pointed across the street, where a group of people with children stood. "Looks like she's coming in."

He sounded disappointed, but I was relieved. This coffee felt more like a date than two friends hanging out. The man kissed the baby's head and walked off.

"Great." He had no idea how interested I was in meeting his sister. I recalled the names of the women Perry dated that Rachel had sent me. I didn't remember anyone named Lori being on the list. Of course, Lori was married, so it didn't seem like he would advertise that relationship. There was, however, the picture of Lori on his social media app, so he'd seen her since he'd arrived. At least from a distance.

Garth stood, kissed his sister's cheek. The baby hung in some kind of snugly thing. Garth patted the baby on the head and pulled out a chair for Lori. He introduced us, asked Lori what she wanted, and headed off to get her the requested herbal tea.

Lori was thin like her mother, but more muscled, which probably helped out with the whole Roller Derby thing. Her face had the same shape as Garth's and she had the same sandy brown hair and eyes. There were dark circles under her eyes, but she had an infant, so maybe that wasn't too surprising. The baby was nestled against her, so I could only see hair and a peek of her cheek and chin. Lori shrugged off a light jacket before she sat down.

"It's nice to meet you, Chloe."

Her answer seemed perfunctory, not sincere. She must have heard about Perry's death. This was too small a town not to. If I was right and Perry was the father of her child, it must be taking a terrible toll on her. Or could she be relieved?

"It's nice to meet you too."

"I heard a lot about you from our mother this morning."

Oh boy. This was no way to start a conversation. "I'm sorry. I should have held my tongue."

She laughed. "I always admire someone who can get my mother's dander up. It's not easy to do. She pictures herself the queen bee and she loves to sting. Most of her drones do her bidding. You made quite the impression."

"Probably not the one I should have made." I'd always thought Southern women were famous for their backhanded ways of getting things across. But it certainly wasn't the case with Lori and Garth's mom. I looked over at Garth. They were handing him Lori's drink so we didn't have much time to talk. "How old is your baby?" I asked.

"Olivia is five months old."

I did some math in my head. If Perry had slept with Lori, it was after I'd broken off our engagement. But not very long after. Olivia woke just then. Lori pulled her out of the snugly thing. Olivia yawned and looked around, grinning at me. It was Perry's grin. I was sure of it. It took me a moment to find any words. "She's adorable."

"Would you mind holding her for a minute while I go

to the bathroom?" She shoved Olivia in my arms before I had a chance to answer.

It didn't bother me. I was used to holding my nieces and nephews. One of the pure joys of the world was snuggling a baby. She came to me without a protest. I jiggled her up and down, staring into eyes so much like Perry's it was unnerving. When Garth returned with his sister's tea I finally managed to break eye contact.

"I see you've met my niece."

"I have. She's so cute."

"I guess she got those looks from some ancient relative on her father's side because Olivia doesn't look like the rest of the family."

I smiled, trying to cover my discomfort. "Well, no matter who she looks like, she's a doll."

Lori rejoined us and sipped her tea while I held Olivia. "Garth told me you're from Chicago originally."

I was uncomfortable with how much this family had discussed me since they'd only met me last night. "I am."

"I know some people from Chicago."

I'll bet you do. There was a trace of something in her voice—sadness or relief? Was it possible that Lori had killed Perry? I tried to keep a neutral expression on my face because that idea had me recoiling in horror. I grasped Olivia to me. Part of me wanted to run out of there with her. Was she safe? Lori had handed her off to me quickly, but maybe it was just the exhaustion of being a new mom.

"I'm not sure Garth told you, but I used to be in Roller Derby. When Olivia gets old enough, I'll rejoin my club."

Lori reached for Olivia so I handed her back, missing her warmth.

"Roller Derby started in Chicago back in the Depression." I'd read up on it last night.

Lori nodded. "It's changed a lot over the years. We use flat tracks instead of banked ones."

"I had a friend who was interested in Roller Derby until he broke his ankle."

Lori's eyes widened for a moment and her face turned a light shade of pink. "It can be a rough sport, although it's better now than it was in the sixties." She took a drink of tea.

I didn't know what to say. Fortunately, Garth spoke up. "Mom was hoping you'd give up Roller Derby," he said.

"Well, she can hope all she wants, but I love it."

"Did your club come up to Chicago?" I asked.

"Yes. We traveled all over the place."

"That must be so much fun. Do you go to Chicago often?"

"Just a couple of times, and I quit traveling once I found out I was pregnant." She kissed the top of Olivia's head. "I miss the thrill of racing around the track, but for now Olivia is keeping me busy."

"No kidding," Garth said. "Their schedule is so packed I almost have to make an appointment to get some uncle time in with Olivia."

Lori grinned at Garth. "It's not that bad."

"Almost. And then I have to fight Mom for time."

"It's nice she's so loved." I looked at my watch. "I have to apologize, but I need to leave for work."

Garth stood when I did. "It was nice to see you."

"You too," I said.

It looked like he was going to kiss my cheek, so I ducked my head, searching my purse for keys. When I looked back up the moment had passed. "It was nice to meet you, Lori, and your sweet little girl."

Lori nodded but didn't manage to say anything.

When I got to work Joaquín was already there. "You're early," I said. Since Joaquín fished every morning, some days he was later than others, depending on how the fishing went.

"I wanted to make sure you were okay," he said.

"Why wouldn't I be? Did you already hear about last night?" Had I messed up that bad at Vivi's house with Garth's mother that the whole town was already talking about it? Did I care? Ugh. The answer was yes to that. I didn't want to hurt Vivi or the bar by doing something to one of her guests.

"What are you talking about?" Joaquín asked.

"What are you talking about?" I countered.

"Rip was taken to the sheriff's office to be questioned in Perry's death."

CHAPTER 15

I collapsed on the nearest chair. Plopping down like a stone thrown into a well. It felt like I was drowning for a moment. I shook my head. "Are you serious?"

"Yes."

"Saturday Deputy Biffle asked me if there was anyone interested in me who might feel threatened by Perry."

"Did you mention Rip?"

"No. Perry and Rip don't know each other. Questioning Rip doesn't make sense."

"They might know each other."

I gawked at Joaquín. "Why do you think that?"

"A video of them arguing in the town circle emerged. It was from a few hours before Perry was found in the lake."

That meant Perry had been alive while I was at work. I couldn't help but feel a bit of relief mingling with my worry for Rip. "What happened?"

"Perry pushed Rip and Rip decked him."

This wasn't possible. I shook my head. "That can't be true. How would they even know each other?"

"I've seen the video. Someone posted it on a social media site."

"Show me."

Joaquín pulled out his phone, scrolled, and then handed his phone to me.

I watched in horror. Perry was thinner and more muscled than when I'd last seen him—not at the lake—in Chicago. At the lake I'd only focused on his face and only long enough to know it was him. He had a buzz cut and looked unlike the man I'd been engaged to. Different even from the pictures I'd scrolled through last night. I'd never seen him in skinny jeans. He wore a denim jeans jacket over a tight T-shirt that showed defined pecs. Pecs that weren't there when we dated.

In the video Rip was sitting on a park bench drinking a coffee with his back to the camera. Perry charged over to him. Rip stood after Perry said something to him, but whoever filmed this was too far away to catch the conversation. Rip shook his head and put out his hands in a calm-down kind of gesture. But Perry got even closer. They were about the same size. Perry said something else. Rip moved to get around Perry when Perry shoved him and spoke again. Rip slammed a fist into his jaw. Perry stumbled back and Rip spoke. Perry said something back before Rip turned and walked away. That was the end of the video.

Why hadn't Rip told me about this? I watched the video a second time. I stood there staring down at Joaquín's phone for a minute before handing it back to him. "Why would someone even take this video?" I asked

Joaquín. "It's almost like they knew both of them were going to be there and something was going to happen."

"I hadn't looked at it that way. But you're right because it starts with Rip just sitting there minding his own business."

"I think someone set this up to point the sheriff at Rip. Someone egged Perry on to go after Rip so that person could film it." I'd never seen Rip angry before. He had a gentle, easygoing demeanor for the most part. I'd seen him annoyed, even frustrated a couple of times, but never anything close to lashing out physically at anyone. I'd never seen him slam a door and I wondered what in the world Perry had said that would make Rip punch him even after being shoved. I took out my phone and sent Rip a quick text, asking him to call me.

"Who would set Rip up like that?" Joaquín asked.

I thought about Garth's sister, Lori, and Olivia, who looked so much like Perry. Maybe she'd killed him to keep it quiet, or maybe her husband had if he'd realized the baby wasn't his. But I didn't want to say any of that out loud. Yet. I could be wrong about Perry being Olivia's father. My oldest brother had a son who didn't look like either of his parents. And maybe I was grasping at straws to get it out of my head that Rip was being questioned in the murder of my ex-fiancé.

"I'm not sure. Who posted this?" I asked.

"It's been posted and reposted. I don't know who put it up originally."

That was frustrating. "It won't look good that Rip and I are, um, friends." That sounded awkward. "Close friends."

"In a relationship?"

"Sort of."

"Sort of? Chloe Jackson, I can't believe you just said that." Joaquín wagged a finger at me. "Are you seeing anyone else?"

"Not really." No. No, I wasn't.

"Is Rip?"

"Not that I know of, but we never said we'd be exclusive."

Vivi came in just then. "Garth sure took a shine to her last night."

Thank heavens. At least now we would quit talking about my relationship with Rip. But I couldn't quit thinking about that video, and that Rip hadn't told me about the altercation with Perry.

"Garth Havers?" Joaquín asked.

Vivi nodded.

"I didn't know he was back in town." Joaquín turned to me. "His mother is a piece of work."

"I know. I found that out last night," I said.

Joaquín looked over at Vivi. "I thought you couldn't stand that woman."

"She's not my favorite, but I've always liked Garth. I decided to invite them over along with other friends. Building bridges never hurts."

"You'd need a bigger bridge than the Mid-Bay Bridge in Destin to reach that woman. But whatever. Are you going to see Garth again, Chloe?" Joaquín asked.

Ugh. Why couldn't someone come in or the phone ring right now? "I made it clear to him last night that we could only be friends."

"And," Joaquín said, "I feel like there's an 'and' in there."

"We had a friendly cup of coffee this morning before work."

"Huh. Well, that explains this." He swept his hand in an up-and-down motion at me.

"What?" I asked.

"You look mighty fine this morning."

"Are you saying I don't usually?"

"No. I'm saying there's something extra there today. Hair carefully done. Your makeup is perfection and your outfit says va-va-voom."

"I have on a turtleneck."

"Oh, please. You know you look hot."

I gave in then. "Okay. You're right. I made an extra effort, but not because I'm interested in Garth." I couldn't blurt out that I wanted to get information from him. But I needed to get off this topic. "I met his sister, Lori. She was heading to the park with her baby but spotted us at Grounds For and came in."

"She's a lovely woman," Vivi said.

"She seemed very nice."

"She has a wild streak. Always did since she was little. Jumped off their speedboat when she was six because she was convinced she could fly. Almost drowned when she was eight because she'd decided she was a mermaid and got caught on the boat they sank for a man-made reef." Vivi shook her head. "Her mother was beside herself and signed her up for cotillion and kept her in it through her senior year. I always admired that rebellious streak.

"At the debutante ball she came down the stairs of the country club in the traditional white dress. At the bottom she ripped off the skirt, and she had on these tiny, black-leather shorts. Savannah looked like she was going to faint, but Lori's dance card was full that night. Much to the chagrin of the other mothers who wanted her tossed out." Vivi smiled at the memory.

Last night Garth had said his sister rebelled not as a teen, but when she took up Roller Derby. Did Lori embarrass him? Maybe having a fling with someone wasn't out of character for Lori, but I didn't think I could broach that subject without having to answer a lot of questions. And I didn't want to make trouble before I had some solid answers. I checked my phone. Nothing from Rip. A claw of doubt and worry tore across my stomach. But it was time to unlock the doors and get going for the day. A light yet firm knock sounded on the back door.

"I'll get it," Joaquín said.

One of my dreams for the bar was to reconfigure things someday so we could have a patio that overlooked the harbor on the backside. I hadn't brought it up yet because just adding shelves for a lending library had created a small stir last fall. Baby steps. There wasn't anything I could do for Rip in the moment.

Joaquín came back with two women. One on his arm and one trailing behind. I did a double take. It was Rip's grandmother, Melanie, and another woman I didn't recognize. This couldn't be good.

CHAPTER 16

Because of the feud between Melanie and Vivi, I'd only seen Melanie in here once. It was last June, for a memorial service for a mutual friend. A man who'd been part of the reason the feud started in the first place. That night she'd been on Rip's arm. I glanced at Vivi. She stood stiffer than the wood planks that the walls of the Sea Glass were made of. Her dark green eyes were alert and narrowed slightly. Melanie's silver hair was piled in a sleek topknot bun.

"What do we owe this pleasure to?" Vivi asked.

If sarcasm could drip, it was in Vivi's voice.

Melanie dropped Joaquín's arm. He went and stood behind the bar.

"I'm not here to deal with you," Melanie shot back. "I'm here to see her." She raised a cane I hadn't noticed and pointed it directly at me.

"It isn't her. Her name is Chloe Jackson. But you know that," Vivi replied.

"How can I help you, ma'am?" I asked, walking over to stand nearer to Vivi. The "ma'am" didn't trip off my tongue the way it did for the natives, but for Rip's sake I wanted to show her some respect. I swear I heard Melanie mutter "Northerners" under her breath.

"You are to leave my grandson alone." She pronounced it like she was a queen uttering a decree or like Lady Catherine de Bourgh in *Pride and Prejudice* when she warned Elizabeth Bennett to stay away from Darcy. Melanie didn't like me seeing Rip any more than Vivi did.

The woman behind her, who seemed to be some kind of companion—I recalled Rip mentioning her at some point—mouthed, *I'm sorry*. She had light blond hair and dark eyes, surrounded by laugh lines.

I opened my mouth to speak, but Rip's grandmother held up her hand. My parents had taught me to respect my elders, so I waited. Let her say her piece and leave before Vivi tossed her out.

"Because of you, he's been dragged into the sheriff's office. You've brought shame to his honorable name and that of our family."

Melanie was on quite a roll here. And it wasn't like Rip's father had been a shining example of what a good man was. I'd found that out last fall.

"That's quite enough," Vivi said. She sounded as imperial as Melanie did. Vivi moved over to me and put an arm around my shoulders. She raised her chin and looked right down her nose at Melanie. "Rip's being questioned has nothing to do with Chloe and everything to do with losing his temper and punching a man."

"Miss Melanie," I said, using the Southern polite address, "I think someone set him up."

She straightened her spine as only a true steel magnolia would. "What are you talking about?"

I glanced at Vivi, who looked surprised, as did Melanie's companion. "Let's sit down."

Vivi nodded. Whew.

After Melanie, the companion, and Vivi had taken a seat at one of the tables, I asked, "Would you like something to drink? A coffee or sweet tea or water?"

Melanie looked at Vivi. "I always did love your mother's sweet tea when we were girls. Do you still use her recipe?"

Vivi's face softened at some distant memory. "I do. And that sounds good to me too."

I looked at Melanie's companion.

"I'll have the same." She sounded relieved that Melanie had calmed down.

"Do you want some?" I asked Joaquín as I went to the kitchen.

"No, thanks. I'll just stay back here in case anyone needs to call the sheriff."

He said it softly and I grinned at him. "Excellent."

I walked to the kitchen and got the pitcher of sweet tea that was always in the refrigerator. We also brewed regular tea every morning for those foolish enough to want it. I poured four glasses, put some mint leaves and lemons in bowls on the side just in case someone wanted either, and took it out to the table.

As I passed Joaquín, he said, "I'll do the prep work. Maybe you can mend some long-ago torn-down fences. Be funny if a Yankee pulled it off." He winked at me to soften the insult.

I passed out the glasses, some cute napkins with flamingos on them, and put the bowls of mint and lemon on the table. Melanie sniffed when she saw them, like they were something vile instead of citrus and an herb.

Melanie took a cautious sip. She smiled. "This is just as good as I remember. Not all things are."

Vivi beamed. Beamed! She hadn't in my experience been a beamer. Vivi had gone through a lot in her life, and although I'd seen her happy and laughing more and more over the past few months, I'd never seen her look quite like this.

Melanie set down her glass after a few moments. "Now tell me about this theory of yours about my grandson."

Melanie never referred to Rip by his nickname, one he'd gotten from his job as a volunteer fireman in Emerald Cove. Last fall when he was saving a cat, it had ripped his shirt to shreds. The cat's eighty-year-old owner was quite impressed with his abs and told the other fireman he was ripped. They'd had a good laugh, and the nickname had stuck.

I explained that the angle of the video seemed off. "It looks to me like someone got Perry all riled up, pointed out Rip, and then stepped back to film the whole incident. Otherwise why would the video start before the argument did and end just when Rip walked off?"

"That's an excellent observation, Chloe," Vivi said.

Melanie tilted her head like she was agreeing.

"Maybe Rip saw someone filming and that person might be the key to getting him out of trouble." Rip's back was to the camera, but maybe when he walked off he'd noticed something.

"I'll bring that to our lawyer's attention," Melanie

said. "And while it may be true, that doesn't mean you are any less responsible."

I might have won a battle, but I certainly hadn't won the war.

She looked over at Vivi. "I suppose you are still keeping it a secret how you make this sweet tea?"

"Yes," Vivi said. "It will be passed along to someone one of these days."

"Why don't you just tell me?" Melanie's voice had a wheedling note to it.

"I heard that tone from you a thousand times when we were young. It doesn't work on me anymore. I won't tell you."

"You are just as stubborn and obstinate as you've always been. Stealing my boyfriend and my land." She stood and her companion leaped up.

"If he was your boyfriend, he couldn't have been stolen. And as for that land, it was my family's and not yours. Your family is the one who tried to steal it. Thankfully, now it's preserved, so you or any developer won't get a chance to build on it."

The land in question was the state park to the east of the Sea Glass. It had saved acres from development. I shuddered at the thought of it full of houses like so many other tracts of land here in the Panhandle.

Melanie eschewed the arm her companion put out and stomped out. Her companion glanced over her shoulder and mouthed another *I'm sorry.*

Vivi flounced off to her office and the door closed more firmly than usual. I picked up the glasses and took them to the kitchen before going back out to finish helping with the opening tasks.

"That went well," I said to Joaquín.

"You can't win all battles, and this war has gone on far too long."

"I had hope for a minute."

"Me too. At least I didn't have to call 911."

I unlocked the sliding glass doors that spanned the front of the bar. Light sparkled off the emerald-green waters, making it look like sea glass. I spotted some dolphins frolicking out beyond the second sandbar and wished I was as free as they were. Although their frolicking was probably the hard work of finding food for the day. But it looked like fun.

I checked my phone. Still nothing from Rip. I hoped his grandmother would share my concerns about the video with him and his lawyer. My information might come to naught, but I hoped it wouldn't. A flood of people rushed in taking my mind off anything beyond making sure our customers were happy.

At noon, Rip finally walked in.

CHAPTER 17

I was busy helping a group of customers but took a moment to smile at him. He smiled back but lingered near the sliding glass doors. It was so rare to see him here, and it felt like the sun had come in to warm the place. I realized now how worried I'd been and that maybe I liked him more than I was willing to admit to anyone. If he was here, that must mean he hadn't been arrested.

I took the orders up to Joaquín. Poured two beers from the tap, while he made a Bloody Mary and a Peach Bum Fizz. One of his original concoctions. I put everything on a tray.

"Why don't you take a break?" he said, nodding his head toward Rip. "Take your time."

"Want me to go pick up some lunch from the Mexican food truck?"

Joaquín clasped his hands together and looked upward. "You have just made my day. Go on and get out of here before Vivi comes out of her office."

I picked up the tray of drinks and dropped them off.

"If you need anything, Joaquín is there to help," I told the group. "I'm going to take a break and be back in a little while."

They nodded their thanks as they started in on their drinks. I returned the tray to the bar, untied my apron, stuck it under the counter, and picked up my purse. Then I hurried over to Rip. I grabbed his hand, pulled him out and around the side of the building. Then I pushed him up against the wall, reached up, and kissed him. He wrapped his arms around me and pulled me closer. After I broke off the kiss he rested his cheek on the top of my head.

"What was that about?" he asked.

I wasn't one for public displays of affection and was embarrassed. "Relief, I guess. I was worried about you." I tried to pull away, but he held me tight.

"You look gorgeous and feel even better," Rip murmured into my hair. "Maybe you should be worried about me more often."

I wanted to purr like Vivi's cat, Pippi Longstocking. "Let's go get some food at Maria's. You can tell me what happened on the way there."

"Okay."

We walked over to Rip's black Mercedes. I loved riding in it. While I wouldn't give up the vintage VW Beetle my grandmother had given me, the smooth ride of the Mercedes was like being cradled in leather luxury.

Rip didn't say anything right away, so I pressed. "How did it go with the sheriff?" I tried to keep my voice calm.

Rip shrugged. "I told them what happened."

"Did you have a lawyer with you?"

"Yes. Of course."

"Why didn't you tell me about punching Perry?" We'd seen each other since Perry was murdered.

"First, I was embarrassed for losing my temper like that." Rip shook his head. "It's not like me."

"And second?"

"I was afraid you wouldn't think of me the same way. You had enough on your plate and I didn't want to add to it." Rip glanced at me. "I called Biffle after Perry died and told him what had happened. I'd thought that would be the end of it."

That made me feel a little better. "How did you happen to end up tangling with Perry?"

Rip had both hands on the steering wheel, gripping it like it was a last tenuous hold before going over a cliff. "It was so strange. I was sitting there sipping my coffee, enjoying the sunshine while I was on my break from the fire department like I do most days." He glanced over at me. "Then this man came up and started yelling at me about ruining his life. I asked him to calm down and tell me what he was talking about."

"Had you ever seen him before?" I asked. It was possible if someone scrolled far enough back in my social media accounts, they would find pictures of Perry and me. Or if someone did an internet search like Mary Moore had, they'd find a link or two to our engagement announcement. Not that Rip was likely to do that.

"No. I'm sure of it. Asking him to calm down was like throwing water on an oil fire. He just flared up even more. He said some terrible things about you, Chloe. One I refuse to even repeat, so please don't even ask me."

Terrible things? The same day he had the banner fly

over, the flowers and wine sent, and dinner for two? That didn't make any sense, but really none of this did. I wouldn't press Rip for more. Not now anyway. Maybe never. I didn't care what Perry had said about me.

"When he pushed me, I was so mad that I just struck out at him. I don't think I've thrown a punch since second grade, when Billy Bixler cheated during the spelling bee."

"The spelling bee? That's what got you riled up in second grade?"

"Yeah. I was a bit of a nerd back then and not in a cool, hip way."

I smiled at that. It was impossible to believe. I reached over and took his hand and kissed his knuckles. Rip turned over his hand and grasped mine, setting our joined hands on his thigh. He drove around the town circle. I'd heard that from above, the town looked like a starfish with the circle its center and the five streets that peeled off from it, its arms.

"I'm not the only one holding things back," Rip said. "I saw the piece on the news about the footprints around your house. Why didn't you tell me?"

"I'm sorry. There's been so much going on, I just didn't think about it."

"Okay, but I'm here if you need me. Being concerned about each other works both ways."

That made me warm up almost as much as Maria's spicy food would. Rip took the street that veered toward the beach. A few minutes later we pulled up to the food truck.

Maria and Arturo owned the truck. Arturo fished in the morning and Maria turned his catch into the best fish tacos and burritos on the planet. My stomach rumbled loudly as we walked toward the counter. Rip laughed and pulled me to him, putting his arm around my waist. I think he was getting used to what used to embarrass the heck out of me. My brothers had teased me about having monsters in my stomach that were always grumbling.

We placed our order. I chose the fish tacos for me and asked Maria if she could make a batch for Joaquín in fifteen minutes. I ordered a burrito too in case Vivi wanted it. If she didn't, I'd eat it for dinner tonight. We sat side by side at a picnic table. The sand dunes were low here, so we could see peeks of the Gulf.

"I heard my grandmother paid a visit to the Sea Glass."

"She did. It was going so well. I thought I saw white flags being run up poles to end the feud. But between your grandmother and Vivi they managed to reignite the war. Over sweet tea, of all the stupid things."

Rip kissed my cheek. "Honey child, sweet tea is worth fighting over down here in these parts. I'm not sure a Northerner such as yourself could understand that."

I laughed at his gentle, mocking tone and his exaggerated Southern drawl. "Up in Chicago we fight over deepdish pizza. Some people just don't get it either."

"I'm one of those people."

I looked at Rip with mock horror. "Then I'd better make you one so you'll understand. That's a hill any true Chicagoan will die on."

"I guess you'd better."

Maria called and said our food was ready.

After a few bites I realized I had more questions than appetite. I put down my taco. "Did you see anyone in the park with Perry before he came over to you?"

"I didn't even see Perry before he came over to me."

"How about after you punched him? Maybe he walked over to someone?"

Rip shook his head. "I don't even like to think about punching him. I can't believe I did it."

"That didn't answer my question."

"After I punched him I apologized."

"Did he say anything?"

Rip considered that for a minute. "Something like you'd better find a lawyer because that was assault. I turned and walked off."

"And then did you see anyone?" I prompted him again.

"No. I kept my head down and walked back to the fire department. What's with the interrogation?"

"I'm sorry. I didn't mean to come off like that. I'm convinced something is wrong here. It's just too convenient for Perry to show up and for someone to film the whole thing from start to finish. I could see someone recording part of the fight. People do that all the time. This was different. Unless there's some creep out there who is always filming people in the park. But if that were true, someone in town would have noticed it by now."

People around here were very observant about what went on. Maybe I needed to drop by The Diner to see if Delores Harrison knew anything. The Diner was situated right across from the town circle. Maybe she'd seen something or someone.

"I get that, but again, why the interrogation?" Rip looked concerned. "You don't believe me?"

"Of course I believe you. I care about you. It's just all whooshing out of me in a big rush of anxiety. I know you'd never hurt Perry." I believed that even though there was evidence to contradict that. But a punch and bullets were two different things.

"You care about me, Chloe Jackson." Rip cupped my face in his hand and ran his thumb across my cheek.

I shivered noticeably. I can't believe I'd blurted that out with everything else I'd said. I hated feeling this vulnerable. Up to now we'd kept things light and easy between us. I think I just pushed us a step forward. And what if he didn't feel the same way? I hated myself. Although he didn't leap up and run away screaming. That had to be a good sign, right?

I sighed. "Yes, I care about you." I almost held my breath waiting for an answer. I moved my face and picked up my taco. Rip took it and put it back down and turned my face back to him. We were so close. And my heart was doing a mambo. While my face was warm, other parts of me were counteracting that with shivers of fear waiting to hear what he had to say.

"Do you care about me in a he's-a-great-guy, good-friend way?"

I'd gone this far, I might as well lay it all out there. "No. I care about you in a woman-who-is-very-attracted-to-a-man way. Who wishes she didn't feel this way and is scared to feel anything."

Rip stared into my eyes, but for the life of me I couldn't read that expression. I'd had a lot of expression-reading experience as a children's librarian. Why did that skill have to fail me now?

"I care about you in a man-who-is-very-attracted-to-a-woman way. But I'm not scared. I want to explore all those feelings with you."

"The rest of your food's ready," Maria called.

It was probably for the best or I might have jumped Rip right there. Instead, I grinned at him, pulled back, and turned to the food truck. "Be right there." I packed up the rest of my food to take with me. When I stood Rip grabbed my hand.

"This conversation isn't over," he said.

Thankfully, it was for now, before any "l" words came tripping off my tongue. Even though my body was all in with that, my heart still had some reservations. I planned to rush nothing.

Back at the bar, Joaquín and Vivi took their food to Vivi's office to eat. I tripped lightly around the bar, smiling like a fool. And I must be one if I could feel so happy that the man suspected of murdering my ex-fiancé had said he cared about me. How weird was that?

When Joaquín finished eating and came back out, I called his husband Michael, who had mad computer skills.

"Hey, Michael. Can you look into the video of Rip fighting that was posted to see if you can find out where it originated and who is behind the account?" I explained about the video of the altercation between Perry and Rip.

"I'll see what I can do, but it won't be easy. I'm trying to think if I know anyone who works for that social media company who might have more specific information."

"That would be great. I can't believe they dragged Rip in for questioning. He would never hurt anyone." After exchanging a few more comments we said our goodbyes.

Vivi was standing there. Her expression wiped any lightness out of my mood because it was grim.

"Don't be so sure about that."

CHAPTER 18

"What?" I asked.

"That Rip wouldn't do anything. He got in some trouble while he was in high school."

"He did? For what?"

"Beating someone badly."

I shook my head. "That's not the man I know. Whatever happened couldn't have been too bad or he wouldn't have gotten into law school." Rip hadn't mentioned anything other than the incident in second grade.

"You saw the video, Chloe. How much more evidence do you need?" Vivi asked. "A good lawyer and a lot of money make things go away. I won't say more, but if you want the facts, go see Quinn Olsen in DeFuniak Springs. Then you'll know what kind of man Rip really is."

* * *

I was so shocked it was hard to get much done. By the time we closed it was too late to go see whoever Quinn Olsen was. Instead, I sat on my back porch and did an internet search for Rip. There was no hint of scandal, just accolades for his football prowess, his community service, and his scholastic ability. But as Vivi said, a good lawyer and money could make things disappear. The man I'd grown to know over the past months was like the boy in the articles—smart, good at what he did, and served his community by volunteering with the fire department. He certainly wasn't a snob with money or he wouldn't be dating me, a waitress and part owner of a bar.

Thinking about Rip made me think about our talk today. It was lovely and warmed me just remembering it. I was glad he was working tonight, though, because I didn't know what would happen next with us. Part of me liked the anticipation and part of me felt like I was on the verge of one of those nightmares you have as a kid, where you step off a cliff and just keep falling, never hitting bottom.

I looked up Quinn Olsen next. I found an article about the opening of his computer repair shop and recycling center in DeFuniak Springs. The article was from four years ago. A man who was about my age stood under a sign in front of a store with Quinn's Computer Repair and Recycling above him. He leaned on a cane, grinning. A fancy one with a silver knob on the end. Why did he need it? Could it have been because of Rip? I just didn't believe Vivi. There were a few earlier articles about him in high school. He was also a football player. Maybe that was his connection with Rip.

Tomorrow was my day off. I'd go see him. I had to, to prove Vivi wrong.

*   *   *

After my run Tuesday morning I showered, ate breakfast, and puttered around the house before driving to De-Funiak Springs. It was the county seat of Walton County and had a historical district. In the late eighteen and early nineteen hundreds it was the winter home of the New York Chautauqua, which had cultural enrichment programs like lectures, music, and dramas.

DeFuniak Springs was an easy thirty-minute drive up highway 331 and across a long bridge over Choctawhatchee Bay. There wasn't much traffic. I decided to drive around the historic district on Circle Drive before heading over to see Quinn. Yes, I was chicken to approach him and just start blurting out questions. Part of me felt like I was being disloyal to Rip too.

Circle Drive went around an unusual lake that was almost a perfectly formed circle. I'd read it was fed by a natural spring. The houses were amazing with turrets, double verandas, gingerbread, every house slightly different but equally intriguing. There were also some beautiful old churches. But all too soon I'd made it around the entire circle. I pulled over and stared out over the lake for a few minutes. It was now or never. I had to go see Quinn or just drive home.

At ten forty I parked in front of the strip mall where Quinn's store sat. There was an "Open" sign on the door. Drat. I guess part of me hoped he wouldn't be there. And who knows, maybe he wasn't. He could just have an employee in there. I walked by and tried to peer in but couldn't see more than a foot beyond the window. I walked on by and got a Coke at the convenience store at the end of the strip mall.

I walked back by, slowing in front of the window again. I shook my head and continued on. There was a cute gift shop, so I went in and browsed, talking to myself as I moved through the store. I bought some cards, straightened my shoulders, and headed back to the computer shop. I slowed a third time, chickened out, and turned to go to my car when the door of the shop opened.

A man with a cane stood there. The man from the picture in the newspaper. Quinn Olsen. I took a few steps toward my car.

"Can I help you with something?" Quinn had a slow, good-old-boy voice. "Or are you casing my shop to rob it?"

I froze. I was an idiot. I turned toward him. "I promise I'm not casing your shop."

He held the door open. "Why don't you come in and tell me what's going on."

A couple of minutes later we settled on stools on opposite sides of a counter littered with computer parts and paperwork. Quinn pushed some of it aside so there was a clear spot in front of me.

"Do you need help with a computer or phone and don't have the money?" he asked. "I could help you out with that."

Wow. Not what I was expecting, and what a nice man. "No. It's not that." I shook my head. "It's incredibly personal and awkward."

"Don't tell me you've had my child. I was drunk and don't remember." He winked and smiled to show he was joking.

I laughed. "Not quite that personal. I heard you were in a fight with Rip Barnett in high school."

His smile disappeared. Not a good sign, but I pressed on. In for a penny, in for a pound. I'd heard my grandmother use that phrase even though I wasn't ever quite sure what it meant.

"Someone was spreading rumors about him. I—I care about him and it doesn't seem to be a part of his character. But if it's too painful to talk about, I'll just go."

Quinn rubbed a hand over his face. "It was a long time ago, but my leg is a constant reminder of that day."

That didn't sound good. "I'm sorry."

"Don't be. It was my own damn fault."

Quinn was full of surprises. "How so?"

"We played for rival football teams and always thought the kids on the coast thought they were better than us country boys. Our coaches fed that to us to get us riled up before the game." He looked above my head toward the window, like he could see the past. "I'd been taunting Rip all night, calling him a wuss and a pretty boy."

Rip certainly was pretty.

"I dirty tackled him a couple of times, brought up his dad disappearing, got up in his face and said some insulting things about his mother. He pushed me and I fell over one of our players. Ended up with a double fracture that never healed right."

"I'm sorry." That was a vastly different story from Vivi's. Relief for Rip and sorrow for Quinn washed over me.

"Don't be. Like I said, I brought a lot of it on myself by playing dirty and trash-talking him. 'Sides I might never have realized how good I was with computers if it wasn't for Rip."

"How's that?"

"A couple of days after my surgery he came to see me

in the hospital and brought me a laptop. My family couldn't afford one. I told him to get out and I didn't want anything from him. But he left it.

"He showed back up the next day and every day after that. Even when I was at home. He taught me how to use it, but after a couple of weeks I was doing stuff he didn't know how. At least he said he didn't." Quinn looked at me. "Rip taught me more than just about computers. He taught me not to judge people. We've been friends ever since."

"Then why do people think badly of him?" I asked.

"Because they don't know the real story. They only know what they saw in the newspaper. The pictures of Rip pushing me and me being hauled off in the ambulance. My parents wanted to sue, but I talked them out of that. Rip's family paid all my medical bills. Even for the physical therapy after."

Vivi might not be a big fan of Rip's family, and with some good reason, but that was a decent thing of the Barnetts to do. "Thanks for telling me."

"Can't have people bad-mouthing my boy Rip. But now I need to ask you something."

"Sure."

"Rip never wanted anyone to know about the computer or money for the bills, so will you please keep that quiet?"

"If you won't tell Rip I was here." I felt a little stab of guilt and a stab of frustration. Maybe I should tell Rip that I'd come here. I wanted to have an open, honest relationship with him. But I didn't have to decide right now. The frustration came from not being able to correct Vivi, but maybe even if I did tell her, she wouldn't believe it.

Quinn stuck out his hand and I took it.

"It's a deal," he said as we shook. "Besides, how could I tell him? You never told me your name."

I was tempted not to tell him and just run out of the store, but he'd been honest with me. "I'm Chloe Jackson."

"Pleased to meet you, Chloe."

On the way home I parked up the street from The Diner and set off to walk around the circle. I was hoping to find Garth's sister because we needed to talk. Confronting someone I barely knew about who the father of their child was didn't exactly sound like fun. But talking to Quinn had gone better than I hoped. I'd been lighter and freer as I'd driven back to Emerald Cove.

It was a great day for a walk. The sun was warm on my back, the palm trees rustled in the light breeze, and people were out enjoying the day. Kites flew, kids were on swings, and a group of women sitting at one of the picnic tables were laughing their heads off. It made me smile. I took out my phone and checked my weather app. It was minus one in Chicago, with a windchill of minus twenty-five. It made my day even better.

I stayed on the sidewalk, going past shops, art galleries, and the kiosk for the Redneck Rollercoaster. I kept glancing over at the people in the park but so far hadn't caught a glimpse of Lori. It was much later in the morning than when I'd seen her before.

I crossed the street when I spotted a group of women and a couple of men over by the tot lot. Maybe Lori was with them, but I couldn't see her from here. Kids squealed as they went down the slide, moms and dads jounced babies up and down in their arms. A lot of the parents looked my age or younger. That was another problem with Perry and me. I wanted to live life for a while—travel to Croatia or China and have some adventures. Perry had already started talking about mortgages, babies, and college funds. That thought had made me shiver more than Chicago's famed winds.

I drew closer to the parents and kids and realized Lori wasn't in the group. While I was disappointed, approaching her in a crowd wouldn't make for an easy conversation. I passed on by them and headed to The Diner for lunch.

I slipped onto one of the bright-red-and-chrome stools at the counter instead of taking up a table or booth when it was just me. Delores ran the place, but she was nowhere in sight. She must have been at the 911 call center. That was disappointing because I knew she heard a lot of gossip both at the call center and working here.

I took the large menu. It wasn't *Schitt's Creek* Café Tropical large, which was gargantuan, but big enough that it was hard to manage with people sitting on either side of me. I placed an order for a burger with caramelized onions and blue cheese. I knew it would come with a healthy side of fries. I asked for a glass of water to make up for the sins of eating I was about to commit. Maybe I should take another run this afternoon, after all my food digested.

The good thing about eating alone was the chance to overhear things without being too obvious. I always had a book with me in case things were boring. It either kept me busy or was a good cover for eavesdropping. The two people to my right were locals from their conversation about kids in school and after-school sports.

I wasn't sure about the two women to my left—one with smooth, light brown skin and the other with sunburned skin paler than mine, and that was saying something. They were thin, lithe, and muscular all at the same time. The woman next to me had beautiful, natural hair that fell to her shoulders in a cloud of curls. Salads sat in front of them with none of the good stuff on them. No dressing, croutons, or cheese. No Craisins or fried chicken tenders. Garth's mother would approve. One added a sprinkle of pepper. Wow, I bet that made a huge difference in the flavor.

The waitress put the burger and fries in front of me. The woman who'd peppered her salad glanced over at me. *Maybe I should offer her some of my fries.* But she looked at my food and grimaced. Then turned slightly, so her back was to me, but she leaned over to her friend and whispered something. I took out my phone and scrolled through more of Perry's social media photos.

I stopped when I realized the two women next to me attended the trapeze school Perry had attended in Chicago. There were photos of Perry with them. What were they doing down here? The one sitting beside me was Kellye. I was so shocked I dropped my phone onto the counter and it slid over in front of Kellye. The noise made her look down. She picked up my phone and glanced at it. Oh boy, this was going to look bad.

CHAPTER 19

She stared at the photo for a moment, showed it to her friend, and then looked down her nose at me. "Are you stalking us?"

"No. I was a friend of Perry's." I hoped that would give me some kind of in with them.

She swept her eyes over me again. "Roller Derby?"

What was that supposed to mean? I'd like to skate on out of here after that comment, but I kept my rear end right where it was and didn't let it squirm. Interesting that she knew about his interest in Roller Derby. "No. Like I said, we were friends. I used to live in Chicago. Were you in Roller Derby too?" I added it just because she'd gotten under my skin.

"Obviously not if you were looking at this picture."

I took my phone out of her hand and squinted at it like I hadn't had a good look. She was standing by Perry. Both wore leotards. Hers a pale purple and his black. I almost laughed out loud at the sight of Perry in a leotard but managed to refrain. There was trapeze equipment behind them. They had their arms wrapped around each other's waist and gazed into each other's eyes.

For someone who was supposedly grieving over our breakup, Perry was certainly getting around. The woman looked at me again. Her eyebrows lifted, not in surprise but recognition. Darn.

"You're Perry's ex-fiancé, Chloe, not his friend. The one he came down here to see."

"How do you know that?" I could have tried to finesse an answer out of her, but I just blurted out my question.

"I helped pick up the pieces of Perry's shattered heart after you left him."

Whoa! That was almost to the word what Suni had told me at the hotel. "I'm glad he had someone there for him." Now I was saying almost the same thing I'd said to Suni. I was glad, but I was starting to wonder just how many women were picking up pieces of Perry's supposedly shattered heart. Not only that, but I was wondering if his heart was shattered, or if anything I'd ever thought about him was true.

She leaned away from me, startled. "I wasn't expecting you to say that."

I wasn't expecting me to either, but it was true. I didn't wish Perry any ill. I had wanted him to get on with his life. He'd made a few initial attempts to contact me after we'd broken up. He'd even reenacted the scene from the movie *Love Actually*, where the guy comes to the door, holds his finger to his lips, and holds up cardboard signs saying he loved me. I'd asked him to please leave me alone. It was harsh, but letting him in would have made things worse.

"Why are you in town?" I asked.

"We're headed to Venice, Florida, to an advanced trapeze school. We knew Perry was here for a conference and it wasn't too far out of our way to stop here. I wanted to surprise him."

I wondered why they were still here. "You heard the news about Perry?" I couldn't bring myself to mention his death.

"We did." Kellye's lip quivered just a little.

I narrowed my eyes at Kellye. "Did you come here looking for me?"

"Maybe."

"How would you know I'd be here?" The more logical place to look for me would be at the Sea Glass. I knew it was on a lot of my social media posts. Although I had a lot of pictures about eating here too. I liked to support our local businesses and posted about them as much as possible. Everyone needed a boost.

"Once we got down here we realized that you lived in the area. We stopped by the Sea Glass and found out it was your day off."

The other woman leaned around Kellye. "Perry told us you liked to eat here. It's the fourth time we've eaten at The Diner." She didn't sound happy about that. "There's not even a view."

Perry must have been following my social media closely and had been talking about me in intricate detail to people I knew nothing about. I didn't like that one little bit. It was all so odd given the relationship with Kellye, maybe Suni, and the apparent one with Lori.

"You two are the ones doing the stalking, not me."

" 'Stalking' is such a harsh word," Kellye said. "We were just interested in you."

"Why?" I asked.

Tears formed in Kellye's eyes and trickled down over her high cheekbones. Ugh. A beautiful crier. I resented that, and until now had thought that beautiful criers were only in fiction.

"I still care about him. We were in love. After he broke his arm and gave up the trapeze I was devastated. He didn't only give up the trapeze, he gave up on me too. Perry had a natural talent for the trapeze and could have been great."

I was starting to wonder if we were talking about the same man. If it weren't for the photographs, I wouldn't believe it.

"He's a loser if he gave up after one injury," her friend said. She went on to list the number of breaks, sprains, and contusions each of them had had over the years.

"I'm sorry he hurt you," I said. But I wondered if that side of hurt came with a side of revenge so big that she'd killed him.

"Oh, we got back together not long after his injury. We were very happy. He was going to Venice with us after his conference was over. At least I assumed we were until I got down here." Another couple of teardrops rolled down her cheeks.

I was still amazed that Perry had inspired such passion in someone. I wasn't going to burst her bubble by telling her about the flyover, the flowers, the wine, and the dinner. The more I found out about Perry, the less I recognized the man I'd been engaged to.

"What made you think he wasn't happy once you got here?"

"I saw him with another woman."

I kept my face neutral, while inside I was going wild. That ruled me out because I hadn't seen him. A third woman? Maybe it was Lori. It must have been her. Perry was no Casanova.

"Did you know her?" Did she have a baby with her?

"I don't know her, but I saw her once at an office party Perry took me to. They worked together. She was definitely flirting with him that night. Right in front of me." Kellye stopped and frowned at the memory.

That ruled Lori out then. It must have been Suni. At least I hoped it was because if it wasn't, that meant there was someone else too. My stomach was starting to splash around more than the waves on the beach. "Perry talking to a coworker here doesn't seem so bad."

"You're right," Kellye said. "I didn't mind the talking part. It's when he kissed her." She looked at me and held up a hand to stop me from speaking. "It wasn't just some little kiss-on-the-cheek kiss. It was an I-need-to pry-your-tongue-out-of-my-esophagus kiss."

I rocked back on my stool. Perry had told me he'd had one longtime girlfriend all through middle school, high school, and college. Then me. I guess he decided he wanted to be a player. Although there were a lot worse names to call him. There wasn't anything wrong with dating around as long as each of the women knew that's what was going on. But it didn't sound like Kellye had any idea there was anyone but her. Plus, he was planning to propose to me and still running around? How did he think that was going to work? My mind was truly boggled.

"What did she look like?" I asked.

"Petite. And she had this blue-black, board-straight hair. Tiny feet."

The perfect description of Suni Weatherly.

"I'm sorry you've gone through all this."

"Thank you." Kellye took a napkin and dabbed at her eyes.

Maybe I should make my excuses and get out of there. Deputy Biffle would probably want to talk to Kellye. I glanced at my barely eaten burger and fries with regret. But before I left I needed more information. "When are you leaving for Venice?" I asked.

"We're staying for a few more days," Kellye replied. "I feel like Perry's spirit is restlessly roaming and needs me here to be free."

Wow. She saw him kissing another woman and she was still sticking around? Maybe he'd taken up hypnosis after we broke up because these women were devoted to Perry. I kept my face neutral, something I was very used to doing from the demands of the patrons of the branch of the library I had worked at in Chicago. Honestly, that had been the best preparation for my life as a bar waitress. Ask me something outrageous and I'll answer with a smile and can-do attitude. Having Kellye here for a few more days would be a good thing.

"I'm sure Perry and his spirit truly appreciate that."

Kellye gave me some side-eye, but I ignored it. "Where are you staying?"

"We're moving to a house we rented for a couple of nights on the beach, near the lake where Perry was found. I wanted to be near his spirit."

That meant they were staying way too close to me for comfort. I pictured the footprints around my house and tried a subtle look down at her feet. They looked too narrow to be the ones that made the tracks around my house. Although they were long enough.

"Take care of yourself. I'm so sorry for your loss."

And I'd be reporting it to Deputy Biffle as soon as I got out of there.

"You don't seem all that upset," Kellye said.

"Yeah," her friend added, "Seems kind of suspicious."

Back at you on the suspicious behavior. "We all grieve in different ways." I put some cash on the counter and stood. I grabbed a couple of French fries and left.

As if this day couldn't get any worse, Savannah Havers was walking down the street right toward me.

CHAPTER 20

She was looking down at her phone. Here was the thing I was still getting used to about small towns: Once you met someone, it seemed like you saw them everywhere. Soon I'd see her at the grocery store, the beach, and Grounds For. She was between me and my car. Mrs. Havers hadn't noticed me yet, but there was nowhere to hide, so I plastered on a smile.

"Hi, Mrs. Havers."

She jerked up her head. "Chloe."

Interesting. She didn't sound repulsed.

"Please call me Savannah. And I have to apologize to you."

My eyebrows wanted to pop up, but I managed to give her a tilt of my head in a *you do?* gesture.

"I was not my best self the other night and I took it out on you." She put her hand on her chest. "Bless your heart. I had a headache and it got the best of my manners."

A headache. Shades of Perry's mom. I never could decide if a "bless your heart" was to be taken at face value or an insult, which I'd heard it could be. "I understand." I wasn't going to tell her it was okay, because really it wasn't. On the other hand, if she was making an effort, maybe I should too. "Headaches can be debilitating."

Savannah hooked her arm through mine. squeezing me to her like she was a blood pressure cuff pumped to its fullest. "Walk with me. I'd really like to get to know you better."

I pulled away my arm but walked with her. Okay. This was interesting, but I couldn't help being curious. Savannah's words didn't feel genuine to me.

"I heard you lost your fiancé. That he was the young man who was murdered. You must be devastated."

Hmmm. Where was she going with this? "He was my ex-fiancé. I'm very sad, especially for his family, but I hadn't seen him in over a year and a half."

"Oh. Did you flee down here to escape him?"

I shook my head. "No. I came for other reasons." I was surprised she didn't know the story of Boone leaving me part ownership of the bar. Or that Garth hadn't told her. Although maybe he avoided her, which would be completely understandable.

"He wasn't a violent man?"

"Certainly not when I knew him."

"But to die the way he did. Someone must have been provoked."

Was she accusing me? Or did she somehow know that Perry was Olivia's father and she was trying to suss out what kind of man he was. "I wouldn't know about that."

"Garth has had his heart broken recently too." She sighed. "He's in no shape to start a new relationship."

That was an abrupt, not-so-subtle change of subject.

And there were more than this town's fair share of broken hearts going around. "I'm sorry to hear that. It took me awhile to recover from my broken engagement, but I'm seeing someone now and it's healed all the old wounds."

"Oh, I didn't know that." She sounded delighted.

Your precious boy is safe from me.

Savannah's phone rang. She glanced at it. "I apologize, but I have to take this. I hope we can do this again soon." With that, she turned and hurried away.

What was that about? Because I was certain it wasn't about being friends with me. I stared after her. Savannah certainly was concerned enough about the reputation of her family. Concerned enough to kill over?

As soon as I was settled in my car, I called Deputy Biffle and told him about my encounter with Kellye and her friend. I didn't mention my conversation with Savannah because it was all subtext and speculation. "A broken heart could be a motive for murder," I added when I was done talking about Kellye and her friend.

"Lots of things are motives for murder, Chloe," Deputy Biffle replied. "Don't believe all that business about the only motives are love and money."

"You aren't going to do anything about them?"

"That's my business, not yours," Deputy Biffle answered.

He had a point, but he was wrong if he thought Rip did this, and I told him that.

"Chloe, you can speculate all you want, but I deal in facts. And the fact is Rip was seen in an altercation with Perry Franklin not long before Perry was shot and killed. He was one of the last people to see him alive."

"So was the person who filmed the whole thing. That's who you need to be looking for."

"Not that I need to explain any of the workings of the sheriff's department to you, but we are looking at all aspects of the investigation. It's not like I'm Barney Fife from *The Andy Griffith Show*. This is serious and it's being treated as such. I don't like the implication that it is otherwise."

Ouch. "I apologize." I sighed. "I know you're good at your job."

"You should have told me that you were involved with Rip. I asked you about that the day we found Perry."

"I keep giving you information and you don't tell me anything."

"That's the way policing works, Chloe. Now, why don't you tell me about your relationship with Rip."

It sounded so seedy put like that. "We're dating. That's it. We're nowhere near being so passionate about each other we'd be jealous, and neither of us would ever kill someone."

"Like I said, we have to consider everything at this point. And maybe you aren't jealous, but how do you know Rip isn't?"

Okay, so I'd be jealous if Rip was seeing someone else, but Deputy Biffle didn't need to know that. "Rip wouldn't do this," I insisted again.

"I'm sure he appreciates your faith in him. And thank you for the tip about these two women. I'll follow up."

I went home because I was still hungry. I fixed a quick salad, thinking longingly of the burger and fries I'd left behind. Why didn't I get it packed up to go? After I ate I made three batches of chocolate chip cookies and shoved them in the oven. Two for neighbors and one for the guys at the fire department. I hadn't ever met my closest neighbors because they were to the west and a wooded area separated my house from theirs. Cookies were an excellent way to introduce myself and get some information. The house smelled delicious of vanilla, chocolate, and brown sugar.

While I waited for the cookies to bake, I whipped out my phone and looked up vacation rentals in the area, trying to figure out where Kellye was staying. She said it wasn't far from the coastal lake where Perry had been found. I opened a maps app and found my house. I scrolled over and spotted my nearest neighbors' house. There were two houses to the west of it on a courtyard. Each of the houses were on large lots surrounded by trees offering them a lot of privacy. It didn't take long to figure out which house was the rental by comparing the street-view shots of the houses and the photos on the vacation rental website. It was the middle house.

From the description and the pictures, I ascertained that it had two bedrooms, one bath, and was rustic, with dark wooden siding. It did have a nice view of the trees surrounding the lake. It probably had glimpses of the lake and maybe even the Gulf. If someone had been staying there during the day Perry had been shot, they might have some information. My eyebrows popped up. They might even be the killer. I shot off a message to the owner, saying I had some questions for them. It wasn't exactly a lie. I did have questions for them. It just wasn't about renting their house.

I divvied up the cookies. Putting each batch on paper plates and wrapping some clear wrap around them. I drove so I didn't have to tramp through the woods and underbrush worrying about snakes, poison ivy, and any other critters who might be around. Five minutes later I climbed out of my car and knocked on my nearest neighbor's door.

CHAPTER 21

It was a one-story house like mine, but it was a wood frame unlike my cement block. Sun glinted through the trees making patchy, interesting shadows. An older woman answered the door. She was in a house dress of red plaid. She reminded me of my grandmother.

"Can I help you?" she asked.

I held out the cookies. "I'm Chloe Jackson and I moved into Boone Slidell's cottage. I feel bad that I haven't been over to say hello before now."

"It's okay. I had a hip replacement last fall and haven't been out as much as usual. I'm Helen. Would you like to come in and have a cup of coffee and a cookie?"

"I'd love that." More than she would ever know if they had any information about Perry's murder.

The house was darker inside than mine. As we walked along I saw a kitchen to the left, dining room beyond it, and then a small living room. All the rooms were walled off from one another and had low ceilings. The furnishings were simple and worn. The living room had a couch with a faded tulip pattern. A man sat in a brown leather recliner.

"Henry, this is Chloe Jackson. She moved into Boone's place."

She set the cookies on the oak coffee table. "She brought cookies. I'll go get some coffee. How do you like it?"

"With cream if you have any. Otherwise black is fine," I said. "Thank you."

"I believe I've read about you in the paper, Chloe. Saw that piece on the news too," Henry said, gesturing for me to sit on the couch. "You found a body and a couple of months later got swept out to sea. That's no good." Henry was a big man who filled the chair. He had long, silver hair that swooped away from a broad forehead. He reached over and snagged a cookie. After he took a bite he closed his eyes for a moment. "Um, um. These are delicious. We don't eat many sweets anymore."

"I'm glad you like them."

Helen came back in with three cups of coffee on a tray, passed them around, and sat next to me on the couch.

"I suppose you heard about the body they found in the lake," I said after sipping the hot coffee. It was a little weak for my taste.

"We did," Henry said. "Just a terrible thing."

"Were you home that day?" I asked.

"We were," Helen said. "The deputy came by and questioned us. I never thought I'd be questioned by a sheriff's deputy. Scared me a little."

Henry snorted. "She wasn't scared. If you ask me, the deputy was the one who was. Helen's always been a flirt."

Helen blushed. "Oh now, that just isn't true."

"It's how we ended up together." Henry turned toward me. "She couldn't keep her hands off me. I decided I'd better marry her and make an honest woman of her."

They were so cute. But I was here for information and didn't want to forget that. "Did you hear gunshots that day?"

"Why are you asking?" Henry said.

"I knew the man who died. We were both from Chicago." I didn't want to go into more detail than that if it wasn't necessary.

"We're sorry for your loss, then," Helen said. She pursed her lips for a second. "I did hear something that afternoon. But I just assumed it was some firecrackers. People seem to shoot them off any old time now."

"Do you know what time it was?" I asked.

"Well, I'd just lay down to read," Helen said.

"That's code for taking a nap," Henry commented.

I laughed. "I love a good nap."

"Anyways," Helen said, "it was about one thirty. I remember because I was thinking it was a little late for reading. If I drift off that time of afternoon, I can't get to sleep at night."

"I'm the same," I said. "Did either of you see anyone that day who isn't usually around?"

"Hard to tell," Henry said. "Ever since the Joneses moved to Tennessee to be closer to their daughter there's been a lot of strangers around."

"Oh. Because of the vacation rental?" I asked.

"Yes. Their daughter talked them into it. Convinced them they'd practically be millionaires if they did," Helen said. She shook her head and her curls bounced around. "I think they pay more in upkeep and cleaning fees than they can possibly be making."

"I did see some people going back and forth that day on the path. It leads from the Rivers' house, then behind the Joneses' and ours. Of course it goes through the woods to the beach."

"No one stood out that day?" I asked.

"Sorry. I've just gotten used to the situation and don't really pay any attention to who's out there," Henry said.

"Well, we didn't pay attention until that handsome Deputy Biffle stopped to talk to us. Believe me, we are paying attention now."

"I think she's writing down all the comings and go-ings," Henry said.

"Can't be too careful," Helen said. "Besides, I wouldn't mind helping out that sheriff deputy."

"Could I see what you've written down?" I asked.

Helen got up. "Sure. Give me a minute. I don't move as fast as I used to." She came back a few minutes later with a pink-covered spiral notebook. "Here you go."

I took it from her and ran my finger down the list. Only about five people had gone by. None of the descrip-tions were very helpful. She had written about seeing two women who matched Kellye and her friend walk by. Had Kellye been out here before she moved in? I was hoping for more, for something like—obvious killer, carrying a gun, sweating, and confessing. I handed it back. "Thank you." I stood. "I hope you enjoy the cookies. Give me a call if you ever need anything." I wrote my number in the notebook and left.

My next stop was the vacation rental. No one was around, so I went for a walk around the house. Like the pictures showed, it was a little worse for wear, but a great location, with a short walk to the beach. I followed the path from the house, behind Henry and Helen's house, and down toward the beach. I went slowly, looking from side to side to see if there was something that had been discarded. I got to the beach and hadn't seen a thing. Of course Deputy Biffle and his team had probably already been through here.

I retraced my steps. This time, with the sun to my back, I noticed footprints that looked eerily similar to the ones around my house. I stopped for a moment and took in my surroundings. From where I stood on the path Henry or Helen wouldn't be able to see me. Nor would anyone else. A woodpecker started hammering on a tree and I almost jumped out of my shoes. I snapped a couple of pictures, but the footsteps ended or just blended with all the other prints in the sand in each direction.

Back at the vacation rental, I got in my car and drove to the next house. I grabbed another plate of cookies and walked up the flagstone path. Everything was neatly trimmed. An American flag flew on a flagpole and two white Adirondack chairs were on the small front porch. The house was a dark-red brick and looked much newer than the other two houses. I wondered if there'd been an old cement block house here that had been torn down. It happened a lot in this area. Many of the cement-block houses were on big lots, but the houses themselves were small. People just tore them down and rebuilt newer, more modern homes. Frankly, it made me sad. The little cement houses were a piece of the Panhandle's history and obviously held up against hurricanes.

No one answered my knock, and I noticed there were several newspapers on the porch, so maybe the occupants were out of town. Drat. I glanced at my phone. I'd spent an hour here and hadn't learned a thing. On to the fire station next. I guess they were getting two plates of cookies instead of one.

The newish fire station sat next to an old schoolhouse that had been converted into the library. I volunteered there, sometimes reading at story hour or shelving books. I missed my life as a librarian and it filled a little gap in my life.

The big doors on the firehouse were open and there were two men standing beside one of the big engines. I flushed a little when I saw that one of them was Rip. I wasn't sure if he'd be here or not. It was the first time I'd ever stopped by and I was feeling a little shy.

"Knock, knock," I called out when I stood at the entrance.

"Chloe." Rip smiled a huge smile.

"I brought by some cookies." I held up the plates like a fool.

Smoke came over and stood by Rip. He had broad shoulders, blue eyes that were almost violet, and long lashes that were blond on the tips. Smoke took the plates out of my hands. "These look delicious. How've you been? I haven't seen you for a while."

"Good. I mean I'm good, not that it's good I haven't seen you for a while."

"We were just discussing the Super Bowl and where to watch it," Smoke said. "Rip's boat is too small. My place is too far. So that leaves a bar and they are always so crowded."

I laughed. Midwesterners were the champions of the passive-aggressive. Smoke was originally from Minnesota. None of us liked to ask for anything directly. "Why don't you come to my place? Only there's one condition."

"What's that?" Smoke asked.

"You have to bring your famous wings."

"Done deal. I'll take these cookies to the kitchen. Good to see you, Chloe."

When he left I turned to Rip. He pulled me in for a hug. "If I didn't know you so well, I'd be jealous."

I couldn't say I wasn't a little flattered that he was jealous. It made me kind of warm and gooey inside, just like those chocolate chips had been when the cookies came out of the oven. "You don't have anything to be jealous about. Smoke is strictly in the friend zone."

"Good."

I smiled at him like a goofball. "I'd better go."

The fire alarm blared. "It looks like I have to get to work."

I waved and headed out. I loved that Rip helped people, but thinking about him fighting fires made me nervous. I never knew when real danger would be right around the corner.

CHAPTER 22

Back at home I put on my wet suit, grabbed a paddleboard and paddle, and went out on the Gulf. People walked along the beach, fishermen fished, the north winds had died down. This was my own little slice of heaven.

Without thinking about it, I realized I'd ended up directly across from the coastal lake where Perry's body had been found. I paddled to shore and carried my board and paddle up the beach, dropping them at the high tide mark. I could see from here that a little memorial had been set up. I went closer to see if I could figure out who'd set it up.

There was a white wooden cross, candles that had burned out, and several bunches of flowers, very typical things for a memorial. A stab of sadness swept through me. Even though I'd seen Perry floating here with my own eyes, it didn't seem possible that he was dead. It sounded like he'd found a passion for life after I gave him back the engagement ring. Or if not a passion, at the very least a curiosity to try new things. If that was what my breaking up with him did, I was glad. But all I'd found out about Perry the last two days was so confusing. He wasn't the man I thought he was.

I swept my eyes over the memorial. There was a worn roller skate. A mini-trapeze. An ace of hearts. A calculator. There was a stuffed brown teddy bear. Someone had hung a necklace on the cross. The kind you gave one half to a friend or loved one and kept the other half for yourself. And there was a corked green glass bottle with a note rolled up inside it. Curiosity made me itch to want to find out what it said, but I shouldn't touch any of this. Maybe the killer had been back. Maybe this was evidence. Something gold glittered in the sand. I pushed it with my toe. It was a bullet casing.

I whipped out my phone and called Deputy Biffle again. My calls to him were becoming so frequent I should put him in my contacts under favorites. I guess I could call the sheriff's department directly, but I trusted Deputy Biffle. He'd shown himself to be competent in the seven months I'd known him. Why risk getting hold of someone I didn't trust when I could talk directly to Biffle?

"Chloe." Deputy Biffle had a combination of weariness and wariness in his voice.

"I'm sorry to bother you, but you need to get over here to the coastal lake where Perry was."

"Why?"

I wish we had the kind of relationship that would mean

Biffle would just jump when I called or, even better, ask how high, but we obviously didn't and I'm guessing we never would. "There's a memorial set up here."

"That's not so unusual."

"I know, but there's a bottle that looks like it has a message in it. But, more importantly, there's a bullet casing. That could be something, right? I'm not sure if it was disturbed when the memorial was set up or if someone left it there on purpose." The last scenario was unnerving. I swept my eyes across the lake and into the woods surrounding it. Plenty of places for someone to hide.

"Okay. Can you stay there until I arrive? Only if you feel safe. I don't want anyone messing things up. It will take me about twenty minutes to get there."

"No problem," I said. I wished my voice didn't sound quite as hesitant as it did.

I didn't just wait, I looked around some more, circling the cross to see if there was anything else that had been left behind. There wasn't. I studied the lake, picturing Perry lying there with my photo clasped in his hand. I'm not sure any of this made much sense. In some ways it sounded like he'd moved on with his life with Kellye and Suni. But in others it seemed like he was obsessed with me and winning me back.

I wondered what he was planning if I'd said yes when he proposed. Did he think I'd return to Chicago with him, start on that family, and become a stay-at-home mom like his own mother? I'm not saying I wouldn't ever choose that path, but it wasn't right for me now. It made me realize that Deputy Biffle or someone must have gone to his hotel room. Maybe they'd found something that would give me some answers about Perry. However, it was unlikely that Deputy Biffle would tell me anything even if he did find something.

I walked back in front of the memorial and studied the footprints. Some went off toward the public beach access to the west, which was about a quarter of a mile from here. Probably from the emergency people and sheriff's personnel or whoever had set all this up. Some went down toward the beach. One set led toward my house. It was a different imprint than had led to my house the last time. But the foot size looked about the same. It could be the same person in a different pair of shoes.

I decided to follow the footprints for as far as I could without letting the memorial out of my sight. I stayed a couple of feet down from them to make sure I didn't mess them up just in case they became important. I walked a couple of hundred feet when the footprints turned and started up a thin path that went to Helen and Henry's house.

I turned and walked back to the memorial. Ten minutes later Deputy Biffle came from the direction of my house. He had some other people with him who were carrying equipment in what looked like toolboxes. One of them was tall and thin, the other average. Both wore coveralls, and as they arrived they set down their boxes and pulled on gloves.

"Thanks for waiting," Deputy Biffle said. "You can go."

I'd been hoping for an introduction and some information. "When was the last time someone saw Perry alive?"

"As far as we know, it was at the town circle after the fight with Barnett."

Wow. He'd answered my question. "That lets Rip off. He went back to work right after the fight."

"So he says."

"What's that supposed to mean?"

"It was slow. People came and went from the fire station that day. There's a big window where he could have been gone and no one would know it." Deputy Biffle gestured toward the memorial. "I need to get to work."

"But I have more questions."

"Not now. I parked at your house. I'll stop before I leave if I can."

Arguing with him was useless and would just make him mad at me. "Okay. I'll just head home, then." I stood there a couple of beats, but Deputy Biffle turned away. That was my signal to leave.

"Wait."

I turned. It was the tall, thin man.

"Where's the casing?"

I trotted back over and pointed it out. I looked at Deputy Biffle. "See, you do need my help."

I'm sure Deputy Biffle rolled his eyes behind those mirrored aviators.

"I appreciate the call," he said.

I walked off, mentally patting myself on the back. That was a lot coming from him.

I had to choose between carrying my paddleboard and paddle home or going back out on the water. The air had cooled and the wind had kicked up a notch. But wearing myself out on the water would be a lot more fun than carrying everything back home. By the time I got back to the house my arms were so tired I could barely drag the paddleboard up to the house, much less carry it.

I stowed my equipment, went through the house, and looked out front. A sheriff's SUV and a crime scene van were still parked out front. I took a quick shower to soothe my overworked muscles, blasted my short hair with the hair dryer, and slapped on some eye shadow, mascara, and lipstick.

I slipped on leggings and a comfy sweatshirt that had Da Bears on the front. It was one I'd stolen from my dad years ago and was still a favorite. It was from the Bears glory days. The ones I'd heard stories about from my dad, my grandpa, and my grandma at the dinner table—Walter Payton and the Refrigerator. I'd worn it through thick, which was rare, and thin, which wasn't.

I grabbed a stiff-bristled broom out of the closet and took it outside, along with my phone. I snapped a few pictures of the mysterious footprints and then used the broom to obliterate them, working my way from the back to the front of the house. When I was done on each side, there was smooth sand so I'd know if someone came back around.

As I put the broom back in the closet, I heard car doors slamming. I tossed the broom in. It bounced off the water heater and smacked me in the face. I shoved it back in and raced to the front door, yanking it open only to see Deputy Biffle driving off, lights flashing. Darn. The crime scene van trundled after him.

What to do? Rip was working at the fire station tonight. I could take another turn around the town circle to look for Lori or I could call Garth as a way to get to her. But I didn't want to encourage him, so using him to get to his sister was out. I looked up Lori's address. She lived a couple of blocks from the town center. But this was such a delicate issue that I didn't want to march up to her house and knock on her door. What if her husband was home? I couldn't do that to her.

Thoughts like ghosts swirled around my head. Maybe Kellye wasn't wrong. Maybe Perry's spirit was still around. I shook my head at that. I'd never been one to believe in woo-woo stuff. However, the threat to Rip was real. The video damning. I went into my bedroom, threw on a nicer sweater, grabbed my purse, and headed out. Sitting here stewing wouldn't solve anything.

CHAPTER 23

I pulled into the small parking lot by the Sea Glass. There were two reserved spots. The one Vivi usually parked in was empty. There were lots of people out on the beach waiting for sunset. I slipped in the back door of the Sea Glass.

Joaquín was busy making drinks, Michael, his husband, sat at the bar across from him. Almost every table was full. I grabbed an apron and went to work.

"Thanks, Chloe," Joaquín said.

When all the drinks were served I sank on a stool next to Michael.

"Joaquín, you should have called me," I said. "I thought Vivi was going to be here."

"She looked tired and it was slow, so I sent her home."

It was a reminder of Vivi's age. She was so youthful in spirit and energy that I'd forget she wasn't as young as me.

"Then the sunset viewers started streaming in, so I called Michael to come give me a hand."

I gave Michael a quick kiss on the cheek. "You're the best."

"He is," Joaquín hummed the Tina Turner song *The Best*.

I smiled at his *Schitt's Creek* reference where one character had sung the song to the other. I'd watched the show over and over because it made me happy if I was feeling blue.

Joaquín leaned over the bar so he was closer. "What did you learn today?"

"What are you talking about?"

"Come on, Chloe, I may only have known you for seven months, but that's long enough to know if someone you care about is in trouble, you're going to move heaven, hell, and earth to help them."

My eyebrows popped up. I blustered for a minute trying to deny it. It's not how I pictured myself, but he had a point. I narrowed my eyes. "And who is it you think I care about?" I thought I'd been playing it so cool with Rip. Well, maybe up until yesterday anyway. I'd been flirty when other men came in.

Joaquín laughed and Michael joined in. They were starting to annoy me.

"I thought you were going to burst into flames when Rip walked in here yesterday," Joaquín said.

I turned to Michael. "Do you have anything you want to add?"

He held up his hands. "Not me. I only know that every time Rip's name comes up you get one of those dreamy looks on your face like starlets did in fifties movies."

"Now I'm Gidget?" I'd loved watching those movies and the TV show with my grandmother. Gidget liked to be out on the water as much as I did and I'd always admired her dogged determination, along with her taste in men. Ah, Moondoggie.

"If the shortness fits," Michael said with another laugh. "And you do kind of look like a short-haired Sally Fields when she played Gidget."

That wasn't the first time I'd heard that comparison. However, if they could tell I liked Rip, I must be losing my ability to not show my emotions.

"Come on, what'd you find out?" Joaquín asked again. "I'll make you a happy drink."

"The happy drink first and then I'll talk." I never knew what Joaquín's happy drink would be, but it was always fruity, refreshing, and came with one of those little paper umbrellas. A few minutes later he put a hurricane glass in front of me filled with orange-colored liquid. It was called a hurricane glass because it was shaped like a hurricane lantern and was used for a Hurricane and other tropical drinks. The umbrella was blue this time, as was the eco-friendly straw, and blue represented how I felt.

A beautiful citrusy smell wafted out as I took a sip. It had slices of oranges floating in it and tasted of fresh orange, sparkling wine, and something I couldn't identify. I sighed. "It's delicious."

"Okay, so spill," Joaquín said.

I pretended to tip my drink like I was going to spill it. Joaquín arched his perfectly manicured eyebrows at me. "You know that's not what I meant. Talk to me."

"It's incredible. I've found at least two women who seemed to be in relationships with Perry. Both said they were picking up the pieces of his broken heart after I left him." I didn't want to throw Lori under the bus until I had more information.

Michael ooohed while Joaquín leaned back in surprise.

"That doesn't sound anything like the man you described," Joaquín said.

"I know. I'm flummoxed. It's making me rethink everything I thought I knew about him. Maybe all those times I went off and did things with friends he was off doing things too." Had Perry been a professional liar? Had he duped me like he had Kellye, Suni, and maybe Lori?

Joaquín and Michael exchanged a concerned look.

"Maybe you breaking up with him was some kind of awakening," Michael said.

"Exactly," Joaquín said, "he realized he had oats to sow. My mom used to say that about me when I moved from here to Los Angeles to dance. Before I met Michael of course."

I'd found old videos of him online and he was really, really good. But it was hard on his relationship with Michael. He'd chosen Michael over his dancing career.

"You can't do anything about the past, Chloe," Michael said.

"He's right. Try not to worry about what might have been," Joaquín added.

"I won't unless something from my past is what got Rip in trouble. Then I can't let it go." I stood before they could say anything else. "I'll check on our customers."

About an hour after sunset most of our customers cleared out. I ordered a Redneck special from the Briny

Pirate. It was a bowl of smoked, shredded pork with black eyed peas, corn, cabbage, greens, rice, and a dash or two of hot sauce. Joaquín and Michael ended up ordering too. It was slow enough that we sat at one of the high tops.

After we'd eaten most of our food I turned to Michael. "Have you had any luck tracing the social media account? The one that first posted the video of Rip and Perry fighting?"

Deputy Biffle may want me to stay out of it, but Joaquín was right. When someone I cared about was in trouble, I wouldn't sit back and hope that everything would turn out all right. I'd bust my butt to make sure it happened.

Michael shook his head. "I'm sorry, but I haven't found out anything."

"Do you know anyone who works there?" I asked.

"I wish I did, but I think that account is a dead end with a fake name."

"Maybe the sheriff's department will have some kind of pull with them," I said.

"I'm not sure even they will. Those companies are strict with their privacy policies," Michael said. "I haven't given up completely. I put out a few feelers to friends, but I also wouldn't count on me finding any answers for you."

That was disappointing. Michael had helped me out in the past, but sometimes things were insurmountable. It meant I'd just have to dig harder. Maybe another visit to Suni was the solution. And at some point finding a way to talk to Lori.

CHAPTER 24

I heard the back door open, and seconds later Vivi walked in with a tall, incredibly handsome black man. I had to remind myself to close my mouth. I don't think I'd seen anyone as handsome as him in real life before. He wore dark slacks and a dark, long-sleeved shirt. His hair was close-cropped.

"Chloe, what are you doing here? It's supposed to be your night off," Vivi said.

"I needed to eat and didn't feel like cooking." I wouldn't mention I'd been working too.

"This is Dale, my financial adviser. Of course his mother used to be my financial adviser, but she retired to travel with Dale's father. Imagine that." She made introductions.

"I remember when you played basketball here, Dale," Joaquin said as they shook hands. "I was in sixth grade the year you all took the state championship."

Dale smiled a beautiful smile. He had one of those chin dimples. His light brown eyes flashed with amusement and intelligence. "Those were fun times."

When it was my turn to shake Dale's hand, my hand felt dainty.

"Nice to meet all of you," Dale said.

He had a deep voice that thrummed through me. "I don't think I've seen you in here before," I said, because trust me, no one would forget Dale.

"It's been a while. I've been working in New York City for the past five years. But when Mom decided to retire, I decided I'd had my fill of the city. It made my parents happy and it's making me happy too."

Dale, Garth, and I had all left the city for Emerald Cove. At this rate Emerald Cove was going to become a city.

"Sounds like a win-win for your family," Joaquín said. "Can I get you a drink?"

"It has been. A gin and tonic would be great. Thanks."

The women of Emerald Cove would be happy with first Garth moving back and now Dale. I could definitely see the appeal of moving back here, especially if someone was close to their family. Once Joaquín fixed Dale's drink, we pulled more barstools up to the table. I ended up sitting next to Dale. He smelled of expensive cologne.

"If any of you need a financial adviser, Dale's taking new clients."

I wasn't sure what Joaquín and Michael's financial situation was. They owned two boats, one Joaquín fished on and one they lived on. Michael did some kind of computer work for various companies. He'd never really spelled it out and left it vague when I'd asked him.

"I've been using my parents' financial adviser," I said.

My parents had made me start saving part of my allowance when I was five and had always emphasized the need to not rack up debt and save part of anything I'd earned. I'd been diligent about it.

"Don't think I'm pressuring you to change," Dale said. He glanced at Vivi. "Family connections are important. So, what's the fun thing to do around here? I've only been back a couple of months and it's been all work as we transferred Mom's business over to me."

"Usually this is the place to be, but it's quiet tonight," Joaquín said.

Vivi and I had never really talked about how she ran the business. In the beginning she wasn't happy I'd turned up. Then she accepted me, and in the fall she'd mentioned turning the bar over to Joaquín and me. I couldn't imagine this place without her and was glad she hadn't followed through.

"Quiet can be good," Dale said.

"Family or kid activities?" Michael asked.

Dale wasn't wearing a wedding ring, but not all men did.

Dale chuckled. "Never had time in New York. It's one of the reasons I decided to come back. A job isn't going to keep me warm at night. I'm only thirty, but my mom thinks it's time for grandkids. I told her maybe finding someone to love might be an important first step." Dale looked over at me. "Chloe, you have any friends who are single?"

I guessed he wasn't interested in me, not that I was available. "I don't have a lot of female friends yet." It was true, and something I intended to work on. The summer and fall had been so busy that it had been all work and little play. My friend circle came from the bar and the heritage business owners, most of whom were close to Vivi's age. They were a hardworking bunch of people.

"I know a TV reporter who's single. I could have her swing by sometime when you're here."

"That would be great. For the record, Vivi told me you were in a relationship or I'd be asking you out."

I flushed a little and looked over at Vivi, surprised that she'd told someone. "I guess I am."

"Well, if you ever guess you're not, let me know." Dale stood. "Great to meet all of you. Vivi, I'll go over those numbers we talked about and get back to you."

We all sat in silence as we watched Dale walk out the back. Joaquín fanned himself.

"Mmm, mmm, that man is hot," Joaquín said.

"Hey, I'm right here," Michael said.

"He's not as hot as you, and I meant for Chloe," Joaquín said.

Thankfully, a group of couples came in and put an end to that conversation.

At nine thirty Vivi and I walked out to the parking lot together. "We really should have a conversation about the business one of these days," she said. "You haven't ever asked me a single question about it and just took my word for the profit you get."

I felt like I was walking over a bunch of those little cockleburs that were so common in the grass around there. They hurt like heck if you stepped on one.

"I trust you," I said.

"Do you not want to be a part of the business?" Vivi asked. "I know the whole thing was thrust unexpectedly on you."

"It's not that," I said.

"Then what?"

"It was forced on you too. I wanted to give you space."

"Thank you. I know I was prickly when you first got here. I apologize for that."

"Prickly" might be a wee bit of an understatement, but I let it pass. "You don't need to apologize. You were grieving and I wasn't upfront about why I was here."

"Because Boone asked you not to be. It was an untenable situation for you."

It had been. I was glad Vivi and I were growing closer.

"Why don't we meet at Grounds For, not tomorrow morning, but the day after, and start discussing things?" Vivi said.

"Okay."

"I'll be late tomorrow. I have a hair appointment and a facial scheduled."

"No worries." I watched as Vivi headed toward her car. "Hey, Vivi." She paused and I jogged over to her. "I haven't seen Ann Williams around lately. Do you know how I can get hold of her?" Ann Williams was a local woman who was a fixer and a descendant of Jean Lafitte, the pirate and war hero. She'd helped me out in the past and maybe she could help me out now. Ann's ethics landed smack dab in the middle of the gray areas of life.

"She's in New Orleans. One of her family members is ill." Vivi climbed into her car.

Darn. Ann was just what this situation called for. I watched Vivi drive off. I wanted to head home but had things I needed to do.

* * *

I entered the lobby of the Sandpiper Hotel just after ten. As I headed to the elevator, I could hear laughter and conversation coming from the bar. I changed directions to see if Suni was perhaps down here mingling with her fellow accountants. If we were in public, the conversation might be more civil than it had when I went to her room.

The place was packed. Men and women stood shoulder to shoulder. Every table and barstool had someone sitting in it. It looked like a mix of businesspeople—conference attendees wearing lanyards—and tourists wearing shorts or sundresses. I went to the bar and ordered a glass of merlot so I'd blend in as I looked for Suni. Plus, after working at the Sea Glass, I was a firm believer if you entered a place of business, you did some business there.

As I waited for my wine, I looked up and down the bar to see if Suni was seated there. No luck. I started to go around the outer edges of the room when a man stepped in my path. Balding, pasty, with a rounded belly that overhung his belt slightly. His lanyard confirmed he was attending the Midwest Accountants Association conference.

"Haven't seen you around before," he said. A gold wedding band glistened on his left hand. Whiskey wafted from his breath. The rocks glass in his hand was empty.

"Haven't been around." I tried to step around him, but he blocked me.

"Want to come up to my room and see my etchings?"

What did that even mean? "No, thanks." I wasn't really concerned with this man, even though he continued to move every time I did. There were enough people around that he wasn't going to be a problem.

Another man came up. "Hey, if your wife finds out you want people to go up to your room, you aren't going to have a room to go to." He clasped the man by the shoulder and steered him away from me. He glanced back and winked as I said, "Thank you."

When I got to the far corner of the room I spotted Suni sitting tucked in a corner. The chair next to her was empty, so I slipped into it. She didn't look happy when she saw it was me.

"What do you want now?" she asked, her words slurring just a little.

"Some clarity," I said.

"You've come to the right place, then." She laughed, a bitter sounding laugh. "I'm feeling very clear about a lot of things right now." Suni held up a rocks glass with what looked like straight-up whiskey or bourbon or maybe scotch. Not even a twist of lemon or an ice cube to be seen.

"What was going on with Perry?" I asked. "I talked to a woman named Kellye—"

"The trapezist." She sounded disgusted.

"She mentioned that you and Perry, that she'd seen you and Perry, that maybe you and Perry . . ." Geez, just spit it out. In the end I couldn't mention them kissing. I tried a different tactic. "She said Perry was in love with her." My whole body wanted to lean in to see her reaction. Instead, I tried for casual and waited.

CHAPTER 25

"Ha, that's rich."

I was hoping for more. "How so?" I was also hoping the alcohol would loosen her lips.

"I told you that he had a months' long campaign going to win you back."

I nodded.

"What I didn't tell you was I assumed at the time, what he led me to think, that it was all for me."

"I don't understand."

She snorted. "I thought he was trying to win me back with all the new, adventurous Perry goings-on. But then we got here and poof! It wasn't. It was all for you."

"But Kellye saw you kissing." Might as well lay it all out there.

"It wasn't like it was the first time. Nope. No sirree. Wanted to remind him what he was missing."

I really didn't want to know the details. "The months' long campaign?"

"He kept telling me about all these plans. It was flattering. About winning his love back. We dated in high school and college. But then we got here, and he said it was all for you. That jerk." She choked back a sob.

So Suni was the girlfriend Perry had mentioned in the past. Had she been mad enough to kill him? "Was that before or after the reminder kiss?"

"He always came back to me. Always. So I put up with his little dalliances until you."

Perry had dalliances? "What was different about me? That made him," I searched for the right word, "faithful?" If he was.

"God, you are stupid. He fell for you and he was faithful. But I was stupid too. He took me to the jewelry store with him when we got here. I thought he was going to ask me to marry him, but no, he wanted my opinion on *your* ring." She almost shouted the last, but the bar was so noisy no one even looked over. "I didn't let him know how hurt I was."

I'd been clueless to all the nuances of Perry's life. I believed who he showed me he was. Suni was right, I was stupid, at least when it came to Perry. "But you didn't give up?" That was kind of weird. I wondered if she knew he was planning to go to Venice with Kellye. Or had he really intended to? Propose to me, kiss Suni right before that, and lead Kellye on. The man had been busy, and Lori played into all of this along the way too. The more I heard, the less I was surprised that he'd been murdered.

"He would have come around. Like I said, he always did."

I kept wondering about the video—who had shot it, how that person knew about Rip. "Do you know Rip Barnett?"

"Your 'little side fling'? That's what Perry called him."

"How did Perry even know about him?" Honestly, I didn't think there were any pictures of us on social media. We'd been so low-key, *I* barely knew we were seeing each other.

"Some local told him. It made me like you more and hate you more." She pointed her drink at me.

"Why?"

"You were the one that got away. That was catnip to Perry."

"Were you in the park when Perry confronted Rip?"

"Yes."

"Did you go with him?"

Suni took a gulp of her drink. She set the glass on the table and looked directly at me. "No. I followed him there. I saw the fight, and when Perry was storming back to his car I confronted him."

"That must have been hard."

"You have no idea. He told me to leave him alone. So I did." She shook her head. "Maybe if I hadn't, he'd still be alive."

Or maybe she was so mad she'd killed him. It wasn't the first time I'd suspected her. This gave her more reason, not less.

"And if you're wondering, I've told all this to that hot deputy."

The bald man with the etchings showed up. "Hey, honey, how are you doing?"

Ugh. Was I never going to get rid of him?

"I'm fine," Suni said. "Chloe, this is my husband, Roy."

After I got over my shock I mumbled some excuse and got the heck out of there. I almost ran out to my car. When I got in I locked all the doors. All I wanted to do was go home and take a shower. But I was frozen in place, thinking about Suni and Roy. How twisted were they?

Suni was married, yet ramming her tongue down Perry's throat and hoping he was buying an engagement ring for her. Ugh, ugh, ugh. But that gave me another suspect. Roy. How did he play into all this? I realized I was cold, started the car, and headed home. I'd have to call Deputy Biffle in the morning and tell him all this. I was willing to go a long way to help Rip, but this was getting to be too much for me to deal with. Way too much.

After I took a long, hot shower I made a cup of hot chocolate and took it out to the screened porch. I grabbed a throw and wrapped it around me, listening to the whoosh of the Gulf, trying to let it calm me.

After a busy morning Garth came into the Sea Glass around noon. I wasn't happy to see him. Although with the restless night's sleep I'd had, I wasn't too happy to see anyone. I'd called Deputy Biffle before I'd come in and told him what I'd learned last night. His only comment was a brief "Thanks."

"Any chance you can take a break and go to lunch?" Garth asked.

Thank heavens we were so busy. The sun was warm

and the tourists were thick. The deck out front was packed
and the overflow was inside.

"I'm sorry, we're just too busy for me to leave right
now."

Garth looked disappointed. "I'll sit and have a drink.
Maybe you'll free up in a few minutes."

Not if I could help it. It wasn't that I didn't think Garth
was a nice guy. I just didn't want to encourage him. Even
though he'd agreed to the whole friend thing, I worried
he thought he could win me over. And while that was flattering, I didn't want to be won. I was happy with how
things were going with Rip. In fact, I was fixing him a
late dinner. That Chicago-style, deep-dish pizza we'd
talked about. That perked me right up.

"What can I get you to drink?" I asked.

"Blanton's neat, please."

"I'll be right back with that."

Blanton's was a Kentucky bourbon that was supposedly exceptionally smooth. I'd never tried it because of
an incident in high school when my brothers—who
thought they were hilarious—got me roaring, sick-to-my-
stomach drunk on cheap whiskey. I'd avoided it ever
since. I went around the bar, grabbed the Blanton's, and
poured a jigger full into a rocks glass. Neat meant no ice.
Feel the burn, baby.

I sidled over to Joaquín. "If things slow down, you go
to lunch first. You have something to do that's important."

"Why?" Joaquín asked, his voice low.

"I'll tell you in a minute." I took Garth his Blanton's
and then checked at various tables, writing down orders
as I went.

One of my favorite groups of ladies were sitting out on

the covered deck. They'd started coming in last fall and were drinking their way through a book called *The Ultimate A-To-Z Bar Guide*. They were on the Fs when they first came in, and now they were on H. They came in a couple of times a month. Today they'd ordered a Hula Hula, a Hunter cocktail, a Huntress cocktail, and a Huntsman.

The last three sounded like a metaphor for my life. "How are the cocktails?" I asked.

"We'd like another round," one of them said.

"They must be good," I said.

"It's hard to go wrong with Joaquín's drinks, but these were exceptional," another one said.

"I'll tell him you said that," I said.

"If you can lure him out here, we'd love to tell him ourselves," the woman with the huge diamonds said.

"Oh, pshaw," the big-haired woman said. "She just wants a look at his rear end when he walks away. A good tip will tell him you liked the drinks."

The woman with the huge diamonds laughed. "You're on to me." She looked my way. "I can't get away with anything with these old broads."

I laughed and left as they argued about who was old and who was broad.

When I took Garth's third Blanton's to him he grabbed my wrist. "Don't cha like me, Chloe?"

I yanked my wrist back and he looked surprised. Oh brother. Just what I needed, a slightly loopy man who thought he liked me. "I don't like you when you grab me. I'm not some carnival prize you just won."

"My apologies," Garth said. "I was absolutely out of line."

"I accept." He wasn't a bad guy. He just wasn't the guy for me. "There's plenty of attractive women in here." I swept my hand around.

"Most of them are tourists. I'm not interested in a fling. I'm ready to settle down."

"Then I'm definitely not the one for you, Garth. I'm so far from being ready to settle down I'm an outer galaxy."

Garth nodded, but I'm not sure he was convinced.

"And sometimes flings turn into something more. Long-distance relationships can work. Besides, from the accents, most of them are from the South anyway, so they probably don't live that far away."

"Whatever, Chloe."

He didn't sound like he was going to give up.

"Look at the woman over by the sliding glass doors. I think even your mom would approve."

The woman had thick, glossy brown hair. Her lips matched her nail polish and her purse matched her very expensive-looking hot-pink sandals. She wore a Lilly Pulitzer dress in a bright pink-and-green-floral pattern.

"She's been looking over here since you walked in."

"She has?" He looked over and smiled at her. "You're right, my mother would definitely approve. Not that it matters."

He sighed, a sigh that made it sound like his mother was a burden, and I was 99 percent sure Savannah was.

The woman lifted her drink and winked at Garth. That perked him up. Ugh. I didn't think Garth's mother would approve of the winking, but maybe she'd overlook it to have a daughter-in-law like that woman. She and her friends were nice enough. They were Deltas on a sorority reunion trip and had been in a couple of times this week. They tipped well, left before they couldn't stand, and were loud but not disruptive. Although one had tried to go back behind the bar and help Joaquín make drinks.

"Want to send them a round of drinks or a bottle of sparkling wine?" I asked. "I know their favorite."

"I think I do. How about a bottle of sparkling wine? And thanks, Chloe. You're amazing."

"I am. As a friend." I smiled to tone down the dig.

He laughed. A few minutes later I'd taken over the sparkling wine and the women had asked Garth to join them. My work here was done. I looked over the crowded and getting-more-crowded bar. Well, not really, but I could tick one thing off my to-do list: Find Garth a suitable woman, check, check, and check.

At three I took a much-needed break. I'd brought some hummus and pita bread with me and took it out to Boone's boat—my boat—to eat. I unsnapped the tarp that covered it and climbed to the front bench, stretching out my legs and wiggling my tired feet. The sun heated my skin, and if I wasn't so hungry, I'd nap.

As I ate my hummus, I thought about hunters, huntresses, and huntsmen. Had someone been hunting Perry? Even if he was a scoundrel, killing him wasn't okay. Had it been planned or an impulse? I still needed to talk to Lori to try to figure out how she fit into this whole chessboard of players. But I wouldn't have time until after my meeting with Vivi tomorrow morning. At least I had Rip to look forward to as a distraction tonight.

* * *

By eight p.m. the pizzas were almost done, the small dining room table was set, and I had candles ready to light whenever Rip arrived. The house smelled of Italian sausage, tomato sauce, basil, and cheese. My stomach growled in anticipation. I'd put on a slinky black sweater with a sweetheart neckline that clung to my curves. My necklace was a silver lasso that dangled just above my cleavage. I had on comfy black leggings because I intended to eat too much and didn't want to have to undo any buttons, hooks, or snaps.

Blues music played as I chopped romaine lettuce. The singer wailed about how miserable her life was. I guess that was the thing about the blues—misery loved company. Although tonight I wasn't miserable. I was excited. I chopped fresh tomatoes, basil, and put it all in a wooden bowl that had been my grandparents'. Then I made a quick vinaigrette, drizzled it over the salad, and tossed in the croutons I'd made from a stale baguette. They smelled like garlic and olive oil. The last touch was some fresh shaved parmesan. I pictured Rip eating it across the candlelight and fanned myself a little.

I poured myself a glass of red wine and took a sip just as I heard a knock on the door. I set down my glass on the kitchen counter, ran over, lit the candles, and hauled myself back over to the door. I took a couple of deep breaths, straightened my sweater, and opened the door. Two men stood there. I took a step back, recoiling in horror.

CHAPTER 26

"What? You aren't glad to see us?"

It was my brothers—Randy and Kenny. I blinked. I must be hallucinating. Maybe I'd picked up something other than basil by accident. Maybe I'd fallen asleep waiting for the pizzas to finish and for Rip to arrive. They brushed by me into the house. Nope, this was worse than a nightmare. This was real.

"What are you doing here?" I asked.

They were both tall—around six two, with dark brown hair and eyes that were similar to mine. Everyone always said they could tell we were related. I just ended up being a scrub oak to their loblolly pines. They looked around the house. I watched their progress taking in the living room, kitchen, and dining room table with candles burning. The pizza smell wafted around as Randy sniffed the air.

"I smell a date," Randy said.

Kenny looked me over. "Yep. I do too."

I whipped out my phone and sent a quick text to Rip. **I have to cancel. Sorry. Something came up.** Two somethings. I hoped I caught him before he left his boat. I hurried over and blew out the candles. Then I turned to them, planted my hands on my hips, and glared. "What. Are. You. Doing. Here?"

"We really thought you'd be a lot more excited," Randy said. He was the slightly taller of the two and fifteen months older than Kenny. Kenny was three years older than me. Yeah, I was the afterthought. The accident, but always assured the best accident ever by my parents. Not so much by my brothers.

I softened. "I am happy to see you. I'm just shocked."

"Mom and Dad were worried about you with Perry being killed. Then our wives started in on you not being safe," Kenny said.

"Next thing you know, we're taking time off work and driving down here to save you," Randy said. "And this is the thanks we get."

"Yeah, well, you wouldn't be so happy if I showed up and caused date-us-interruptus back in the day," Kenny said, punching Randy on the arm.

I just shook my head. These two never changed. I don't know how their lovely wives put up with them. I went over and hugged each of them. "The sentiment was nice, but I'm fine. You didn't need to drive all the way down here. A call would have worked."

"We said the same. But like Randy said, we didn't have a choice." Kenny stretched. "Man, Randy, you really need to get some new shocks. A thousand miles in that old beater doesn't cut it."

"That old beater is two years old," Randy retorted. "It rides like a pillow. It's you, man. You're falling apart."

"Where are you staying?" I asked.

"Here," Randy said.

"With you," Kenny said. "How else are we going to protect you?"

With me? Just when things were heating up with Rip. No, thank you. "I don't need protecting. I can take care of myself." I gestured around. "It's only two bedrooms and I'm not giving up mine."

"This couch looks comfy," Randy said. "Kenny won't mind sleeping on it."

It was a big sectional and incredibly comfortable. I'd slept on it more than once when I'd fallen asleep in front of the TV. Either of them would fit on it with no problem. But that wasn't the point. I'd been looking forward to this date with Rip—*I needed* this date with Rip. There was no way it was going to happen with them hanging around.

"It's a really nice place," Kenny said. "Boone did you a solid."

"Yes, well, I'd rather have Boone alive than own this house."

Kenny came over and wrapped his arms around me. "I know. I'm sorry. Show us around and tell us about who was supposed to be here for dinner."

As if I was going to tell them about Rip. The tour was short because the house was small. We all stood out on the screened porch for a few minutes. The moon made dazzling patterns on the Gulf. The water whooshed gently. The air was tanged with salt.

"You'll have to come back in the summer and bring your families," I said. I did love spending time with my nieces and nephews. Randy's three and Kenny's five. It would be crowded, but I could deal.

"That would be awesome. But enough procrastinating. Who is going to show up for dinner?"

"No one. I told him I was busy." And boy, was I.

"Yeah, well, you look dressed up for a no one," Randy said.

"I don't recall her ever putting out candles for a no one. Do you, Randy?" Kenny asked.

The timer dinged inside. Saved by the bell. "He's just a friend," I said as I headed back inside. A very hot friend who I cared about. "Let me get the pizzas out of the oven." Thank heavens I always made two—one for now and one for later. "I assume you're hungry?"

They were always hungry. They could have had fast food ten minutes ago and they'd still want to eat. How they stayed so thin was a mystery. They weren't out busting their butts running all the time. Although they both worked as plumbers and were active dads, always out playing ball or riding bikes with their families.

They followed me in and watched as I grabbed hot mitts, opened the oven, and took out the pizza.

"Yum. Your deep-dish pizza is the best," Kenny said.

"It has to cool for five minutes before we cut into it," I said.

"Let's go get our bags," Randy said. "We'll be right back."

I took the candles off the table and set them on the kitchen counter. The blues singer was singing about missing her man. I knew how she felt. I set a third place at the table as my brothers came back in with overnight bags.

"Look what we found out there," Randy said. They stepped back and Rip stepped in.

*   *   *

Just kill me now. That's what my head said, but the rest of me was screaming *oh yeah* at the sight of him in worn jeans, a purple V-neck sweater, with a white-collared shirt peeking out.

"Rip." Well, that was brilliant. I'd get an A for being a stunning conversationalist. "These are my brothers. They just got here. From Chicago."

"Yes, we met outside." He had a slight smile and his eyes were sparkling. He held out a bottle of red wine. "I brought this for dinner."

"I take it you didn't see my message."

"He did," Kenny said. "He thought it sounded odd."

"Rip was worried about you," Randy added.

"I was," Rip said.

"He came over to check on you." Randy clapped a hand on Rip's shoulder and gave it a squeeze. A big squeeze, like a don't-you-dare-upset-my-little-sister-if-you-want-to-live squeeze. I'd seen it intimidate many a date back in high school.

"That makes him okay in our book, so we invited him in," Kenny said.

If they hadn't approved, trust me, Rip wouldn't be in the house now. Rip was slightly shorter than them, but broader and more muscular. I needed to avoid thinking about his muscles because it was starting to feel a little warm in there, like it always did when Rip was around.

"I'll set an extra place," Kenny said.

Mr. Helpful. I'm not sure I trusted that.

"And I'll pour the wine." Randy held out his hand and Rip passed him the bottle.

They moved away and Rip leaned down, brushing a

slow kiss across my cheek. One that blazed a trail so hot I could relight the candles with it.

"Are you all right?" he murmured.

"I'll let you know later. You don't have to stay. They can be a lot."

"Bring it on."

"Okay, you two lovebirds. We're hungry," Randy said.

"See what I mean?"

Rip just grinned. "What can I do?"

"Run," I said. "As far as you can."

Rip laughed. "That's not going to happen."

We settled at the table, which was crowded with three big men sitting around it. Or maybe it was just this particular group of men that was making me feel emotionally crowded.

Kenny cut slices of pizza. Cheese and tomato sauce oozed from the sides. "Our sister makes the best deep-dish pizza in Chicago."

"She does," Randy said. "She has some secret ingredient we always speculate on."

"Don't say it," I said. I knew what was coming because I'd heard it often enough.

"What do you think it is?" Rip asked.

"Spit," they said in unison.

"You don't have to stay," I told Rip again. "And I swear I didn't spit on it."

"I'm not passing up the best deep-dish pizza in Chicago no matter what ingredients are in it."

"You two have probably already swapped spit anyway," Randy said.

I picked up my knife. "Do you want to live to see your wife and children again?"

He put up his hands. "I'll be good."

"I won't count on it," I said. I put down my knife and remembered Perry dead in the lake and felt guilty for threatening my brother even if I was joking. I grabbed the salad and passed it. For a few minutes my brothers were blessedly quiet while they ate.

"What do you do for a living, Rip?" Kenny said as he reached for a second piece of deep-dish pie.

The quiet didn't last long. "You don't have to answer, or you can plead the fifth," I said. This could complicate things even more.

CHAPTER 27

"I'm a volunteer fireman," Rip said.

"Correct me if I'm wrong, but I believe that 'volunteer' means you don't get paid," Randy said. His tone was light, but there was an edge to it.

"It would be nice to have a girlfriend with her own house, boat, and part ownership of a bar, don't you think, Randy?" Kenny said.

I gripped my knife again. I'd heard that tone before, and while they might sound like they were joking, they weren't.

"I do," Randy replied.

Rip laughed.

Thank heavens he didn't get riled up easily because I'd have been out of here by now. "Rip used to be a criminal defense attorney. If you two don't knock it off, I'm going to have to hire him."

They all looked at my hand grasping my knife. I let it

go for a second time. "Seriously," I said, "it's none of your business." Although I had to admit I too was curious about how he supported himself even though he did come from a wealthy family.

"It's okay," Rip said. "You're lucky to have brothers who care about you."

"No more questions," I said. I looked each of my brothers in the eye. Mine narrowed, theirs widened like they were completely innocent.

"You're both plumbers?" Rip asked.

They nodded, wary. They'd been defensive in the past when boyfriends of mine who'd gone to college had looked down on my brothers who worked their butts off. Those boyfriends never lasted.

"I've dabbled with disastrous results," Rip said. "It didn't take me long to realize I needed a professional."

The rest of the dinner passed with Randy and Kenny trying to top each other with sewer backup stories. I'd bet Rip's family never told poop stories at their dinner tables. I, on the other hand, was used to it. And I was so grateful that my brothers weren't questioning Rip anymore that for once I didn't try to shut them up.

After everyone had had their fill of pizza and salad there were only two pieces of pizza left.

"That was the best deep-dish pizza I've ever had," Rip said.

"We miss you, sis. You need to come back and make pizzas," Randy said.

"Did you make your cannoli cake?" Kenny asked.

All three men looked at me hopefully. "Sorry, I didn't

have time. But I picked up some cannolis from this great local market, Russo's."

I didn't see how any of them had any room to eat anything. "Go sit on the porch while I clear the table."

"Naw," Randy said. "We'll clear. You and Rip go sit. If it got back to our wives that we didn't help out, there'd be hell to pay."

My parents had raised us right. There were no "girls did this" and "boys did that" rules in our house. Everyone did everything, from mowing the lawn, to laundry, to shoveling snow.

Rip poured me more wine and stood up. "I'll help Randy and Kenny while you relax."

I shot my brothers a warning look. Who knew what was going to happen if I stepped away, but I was happy to sit out on the porch. When I got out the temperature had dropped so I grabbed a throw from the back of the love seat and snuggled in it. I could hear the three of them laughing as they worked. That had to be a good sign, right?

Fifteen minutes later they came out. Randy had a plate of cannolis and napkins. Kenny carried a carafe of coffee and Rip carried the cups. They set everything on the wicker coffee table. Rip sat next to me on the love seat while my brothers settled in chairs on either side of us.

I poured coffee and passed cups around.

Randy ate a cannoli in three bites. "It's never going to work between you two."

Oh boy. Here we go again. "Why's that?" I asked.

"He's not a Bears fan."

Rip looked at me. "For the record, I said I didn't have a favorite professional football team."

"Doesn't matter," Kenny said. "You either are a Bears fan or you aren't."

This was what happened when a family never left the city they were born and raised in.

"And he had no opinion on the White Sox and the Cubs," Randy added.

"It's the Cubs," I said. "The White Sox are imitators. We don't even say their name in our house."

Rip picked up my hand. "Every couple has their obstacles."

I was glad it was dark out there because if my hot face was any indicator, I was bright red. We were a couple apparently. I restrained myself from getting up and doing a happy dance. I took a big bite of my cannoli so I couldn't say anything mushy.

Thirty minutes later Rip stood. "Thanks for the delicious dinner and great company."

I wasn't so sure about the company, but I was glad he'd liked the dinner. "I'll walk you out."

My brothers stood and shook Rip's hand. They said their "Nice to meet yous."

I looked at them. "Stay."

They gave me their innocent, wide-eyed look, like what else would we do? At Rip's car he pulled me close.

"I'm never going to see you again, am I?" I asked.

"You can't scare me off that easily," he answered, tucking my hair behind my ears. "I didn't get a chance to tell you how fabulous you look."

"You can now," I teased.

"You look fabulous." He nipped my earlobe. "Delectable." He brushed his thumb from my ear to my collarbone. "Come home with me."

I was shivery and hot all at once. "You have no idea how tempting that is."

He kissed me. "Be tempted."

I sighed. "I can't."

Rip rested his forehead against mine. "As much as I don't like that answer, I understand."

"Thanks. They're a lot."

"They love you and have your back."

I sighed again. "They do." I peeled myself away. Suddenly very cold. I wrapped my arms around my waist. "Have you heard anymore from Deputy Biffle?"

"He called me back for more questioning. And yes, I had my lawyer with me." He pulled me back to him. "I was going to tell you tonight, but I didn't want to ruin the evening with your brothers."

"What did he ask you?" I looked over Rip's shoulder at the stars and felt small and scared.

"He just wanted me to go over what happened again. I think he was trying to see if I'd changed my story or if he could trip me up. Since I wasn't lying that didn't work."

Or Deputy Biffle might think his story was too rehearsed. Having my brothers here was going to complicate things, but I had to investigate.

Rip kissed me again. "Good night, Chloe Jackson."

"Bye, Rip." I hurried back into the house. I heard Rip's car start up once I was inside and wondered how the night would have turned out if my brothers hadn't shown up. My brothers were still out on the porch, long legs stretched out.

"'Chloe and Rip sitting in a tree . . .'" started Randy.

"'K-i-s-s-i-n-g," Kenny chortled.

"Will you two ever grow up?" I asked as I sat down.

Randy shrugged.

"I'm guessing that's a no," I said.

"Why change now?" Kenny asked. "Rip seems like a good guy."

Well, that was a surprise. None of my boyfriends had ever measured up. If my brothers had teased Perry like they had Rip, Perry would have gone all stiff and frowny.

"He does, doesn't he," I said. "But I'm taking things real slow."

"How long have you known him?" Randy asked.

"We met last June."

"Seven months ago," Kenny said.

"You always were a math genius," Randy said to Kenny.

"Yes and no." I picked up the throw and tucked it around me again. "We met seven months ago, but Rip was gone for four of those months. He left in June the day I was supposed to move back to Chicago." At the time I'd only planned to be down here for a few weeks, helping Vivi after Boone's death. But while I was here the library in Chicago cut a lot of jobs, and mine was one of them.

"Where was he?" Randy asked.

"Out having an adventure on his boat," I said. I took another cannoli from the plate and bit into it. I was going to have to take a long run tomorrow to make up for all I'd eaten tonight.

"I do wonder about his income," Kenny said. "You don't think he's up to no good, do you?"

"I don't. What he didn't tell you is that he comes from a very wealthy family. I'm sure there are trust funds at his disposal."

"He doesn't have to work, but he volunteers at the fire

department to keep busy?" Kenny asked. He nodded to himself like he approved.

"Yes. As far as I know, but I haven't really asked him. It's none of my business at this point."

"What if it gets to that point?" Randy asked. All serious older brother all of a sudden.

"Then we'll have a conversation. But who knows? With you two big louts here, that might have been the last of him."

"I don't think so," Randy said.

I hoped he was right. I finished my cannoli and stood up, suddenly weary. "Who is sleeping where?"

"We flipped for the bedroom," Randy said. "I won."

"Heads I win. Tails you lose," I said. They pulled that one over on me way too many times when I was a kid.

"You were always a good sport," Randy said.

"I didn't have a choice with the two of you ganging up on me."

"I suppose not," Kenny said.

We picked up the rest of the things on the coffee table and carried it all to the kitchen. I ran soapy water in the sink, but they nudged me out of the way. Instead, I grabbed extra blankets and pillows and put them on the couch for Kenny.

I locked the doors and set the alarm.

"What's on the agenda for tomorrow?" Kenny asked.

"You guys can relax. There are a lot of water toys under the house out back. Or you can take the boat out if you want."

"We're down here to protect you," Randy said.

Great. Just what I needed. "I go for a run at six," I started.

They looked at each other.

"I'm sure she'll be fine for her run," Kenny said.

"Yeah," Randy said, "who is going to be out at six?"

I laughed. "Chickens. Then I'm meeting Vivi at nine at the coffee shop in Emerald Cove for a business meeting."

"We're available for that," Randy said.

"No. You aren't," I said. I was really hoping Lori would be around in the morning and that I'd have a chance to talk to her. "It's a business meeting, as in 'none of your business.' Then I work from ten thirty to sevenish." It was the slow season, so I'd been working an early shift, with Vivi and Joaquín taking turns coming in at noon and working until we closed at nine. It didn't work out that way every day, but it did most days. We covered for one another as needed. My bartending skills still weren't such that I was confident being there alone for long periods of time.

"We'll meet you at the bar, then."

That I could handle. "Okay. Good night." I headed to my room. It was kind of nice having them here. This was the first time in my life I'd ever lived alone. First, it was home, then college roommates, then rooming with Rachel in the apartment/condo her grandmother had left her. After brushing my teeth and putting on my jammies, I settled into bed with my book. I could hear my brothers chatting, but I didn't hear them for long.

Wednesday morning, after using my phone to turn off the alarm system, I slipped out through the sliding glass doors in my bedroom so I wouldn't wake up my brothers. They didn't get to sleep in often, what with jobs, and wives, and kids. I planned to make them French toast when I got home. It would be fun to have someone to cook for. When I lived with Rachel I cooked all the time, but since I'd moved here I hadn't cooked as much. I missed it.

It was still dark out, but birds were starting to stir in trees, and I could hear the far-off noise of boat motors as fishermen made their way from the harbor by the Sea Glass out to the Gulf. It was just me and the ocean so far this morning. I often ran into another woman out here. We were usually running in the opposite direction. I was glad because I didn't like to run with other people. I wanted to set my own pace, depending on my mood. Today's mood was leisurely as I headed west.

I'd like to talk to Kellye again. To see inside the house where she was staying. There was a possibility that Perry had been killed there and then tossed in the lake. But there were a lot of possibilities. Too many. Plus, she could have killed him in a jealous rage, but why stay here if she did? Maybe she wanted to get caught? I was tempted to turn up the path and go knock on her door, but it was early and no one knew where I was. Maybe I'd find a chance to talk to her in public. That would be much safer.

When I got even with the coastal lake I shivered. The lake was like a black hole, surrounded by evil woods. I picked up my pace, breathing harder. That's when I heard footsteps pounding behind me.

CHAPTER 28

I pushed myself harder. Glancing back would waste precious time. But the feet pounded closer.

"Chloe."

Kenny. Thank heavens it was only him, although I wanted to throttle him for scaring me. I slowed and turned. I jogged in place until he caught up with me.

"What is wrong with you?" he asked.

"Me? What the heck is wrong with you, chasing me like that?" I set out again. Kenny's long legs paced easily next to mine.

"We're here so you won't be alone. I didn't mean to scare you."

"You didn't scare me." Ha. "But last night you said I'd be fine."

"Geez, we were kidding."

"I don't need bodyguards. It's nice to see you two, but you don't need to watch over me."

Kenny glanced toward the lake, which was twenty yards up the beach. "Is that where they found Perry?"

"Yes." I managed not to shudder.

"I didn't like the dude, but no one deserves that."

"Why didn't you like him?" I asked. "He was always nice to me. Devoted." I hadn't told my brothers all that I'd found out about Perry yet. Maybe I never would.

"Yeah, well, there's devoted and then there's cloying. He was cloying."

I thought that over as we ran.

"That whole engagement surprise was a little weird too. It was too early in your relationship." He shook his head. "He was so stuffy and you so aren't."

"Why didn't you say anything at the time?" I noticed Kenny was panting a little, so I discreetly slowed my pace. My family had always been polite to Perry but never warm. There was never any kind of jokey, teasing relationship with him. Last night I'd seen what they were like with Rip, and he took it well.

"You said yes and none of us wanted to interfere."

"Then what was that about last night with Rip because it seemed like interference?"

"Yeah? Well, I guess we learned our lesson with Perry."

I couldn't believe no one in my family had ever said anything. "No one said anything after we broke things off."

"We were all so relieved that we didn't want to rock the boat. You have a long track record of doing the opposite of what Randy and I suggest."

I was going to protest, but Kenny was right. If they'd suggested I avoid Boy A and go out with Boy B, I'd be dating Boy A before the end of the day.

"If the running shoe fits," Kenny said.

"Let's head back. I'll make breakfast." Even with the slower pace Kenny was panting, but I didn't want to point that out and embarrass him.

After we'd all eaten French toast and showered, the arguments started again. I'd thought we'd settled all of this last night, but my brothers not only looked like whippets, they had a dogged determination too.

"I'll be safe as can be today. First at the coffee shop and then at the Sea Glass. Why don't you play with the toys or take a drive? The beaches are stunning. You could drive over to Navarre and then to the National Seashore. There's an old fort at Pensacola. Hike around there, have some lunch at a restaurant on the beach, and I'll see you back here this evening. You can protect me again then." I didn't want them following me around when I had things to do and people to question. No one was going to say anything in front of those two.

They looked at each other and shrugged.

"You two deserve a vacation." I grabbed my phone and checked my weather app. "It's one above in Chicago. One. Here it's going to be in the seventies. You two choose. Follow me around to a boring meeting and sit inside the bar all day or get out there and have some fun."

"Fun sounds good," Kenny said.

"It does," Randy admitted.

"If you're feeling guilty, don't. I slept better last night with you here." I wanted to give them something to get them off my back.

"I'm glad someone did," Kenny said. "I forgot about your snoring."

"How could you forget that?" Randy asked. "I could hear her all the way across the house."

I didn't believe Randy, but I did have a reputation when it came to snoring. And my snoring is how Rip and I first met. I smiled at the memory.

Randy was standing behind Kenny and winked at me, mouthing, *I slept like a rock*.

"Okay, toys and touring it is," Randy said.

At nine I walked into Grounds For. I'd taken a circuitous route to make sure my brothers weren't tailing me. They weren't unless they'd added expert trackers to their resumes. Vivi had arrived ahead of me and sat at a corner table. She wasn't alone. A man sat with her, his back to the door. Maybe she'd brought a lawyer or an accountant with her. She was serious about this.

I'd worn a Kelly-green fit-and-flare dress and stuck a notebook in my purse in case I needed it to take notes.

Vivi smiled and waved when she spotted me. I wended my way through the tables as the man with her turned and stood up. He wore jeans and a red-and-blue-plaid western shirt with pearl buttons. A worn, brown leather belt fitted over slim hips and matched the worn brown cowboy boots that looked like they'd been ridden hard.

"This is Clay Walroth," Vivi said, introducing us.

"Nice to meet you, Chloe."

He had pale blond hair that fell over his forehead, light blue eyes, and a tanned, wind-buffeted complexion that screamed *I spend a lot of time outside*. His strong nose sloped over full lips and he had a day's stubble that wasn't the groomed, I'm-sexy statement. Instead, it was an I'm-busy-and-forgot-to-shave look. Clay looked like he was in his late thirties or early forties.

"I need to grab a coffee, then I'll be back for our meeting," I said.

Vivi held up a cup. "I already got coffee for you."

Clay held out a chair and I sat down. "Are you an accountant? Lawyer?" I wasn't sure why he was here for our meeting.

"No, I like to work outside," he said with an easy grin. "I happened to be in town and ran into Vivi."

Vivi's phone rang. She looked at it and rolled her eyes. "Excuse me, but I have to take this." She grabbed her purse and answered as she made her way outside.

"I'm sorry to crash your meeting," Clay said.

I tilted my head toward where Vivi was walking out the door. "Looks like you aren't the only one." Whoever called Vivi crashed too. I looked at Clay. Mentally, my lips were pursed, outwardly I was smiling. First Garth, then Dale, and now Clay. Was Vivi trying to set me up with someone? I did a mental headshake. I wasn't supposed to be at the Sea Glass when she brought Dale in and for all I knew Clay was happily married.

"Mind if I keep you company until Vivi comes back?" Clay asked.

Polite. I liked that. "Not at all."

"Vivi told me you're part owner of the Sea Glass now," Clay said.

"I am." I took a sip of my coffee. Hot with light cream, just the way I liked it. "I used to be a children's librarian so it's a whole new world. What do you do?" I pegged him for a cowboy, although his buckle was normal-size and not the kind you got on the rodeo circuit that came through this area every year.

"I have a small place near Milton with horses. We breed them and use them for therapy."

I'd ridden a time or two, but horses made me nervous. They were so big and strong. I'd gone to a camp in high school out in Colorado. The horse they gave me was called Widow Maker and I think it was determined to live up to its name. On the way home it had taken off and all I could do was cling on. Saying "Whoa!" had no effect on the horse at all. "What kind of therapy?"

"Mostly for kids. Riding and caring for horses helps with a world of hurt."

"Do you specialize?" I asked.

"No. We work with kids from troubled families, or with learning disabilities or psychological problems. However and whoever we can help is our motto."

"How do you know Vivi?" I asked.

"She's been riding with my parents since they all met in college. Vivi's made a lot of very generous donations to our programs too."

We chatted for a while longer until Vivi returned.

Clay stood up. "I'd best be on my way so you two can get on with your meeting." He picked up a big cowboy hat that I hadn't noticed sitting on the fourth chair of the table, but he didn't put it on. "Come by sometime if you get a chance, Chloe. Maybe you can give us some advice about books we can buy to get the kids reading."

He kept saying "us." There was no sign of a wedding ring or tan line from where there had been one. But my father and brothers didn't always wear theirs because of the work they did.

"I'd love that. It was nice to meet you."

"You too."

Vivi and I watched Clay stride off.

"He's nice," I said.

"He is. He's been through a lot because his wife died five years ago and he's raising twin twelve-year-old daughters.

"That must be difficult. He was telling me about his little operation out in Milton."

Vivi laughed. "He might call it little, but it's a thousand acres and sixty horses. Their program has been a model across the nation. Probably the world because of its success."

Vivi glanced at her watch. "Rats. I have an errand I have to run before we open. A quick meeting with one of our beer distributors. I'm sorry we didn't get down to business this morning."

"No worries."

"I'll see you back at the Sea Glass."

I watched her leave. She didn't seem that upset about not talking about the business. Maybe she didn't really want me to be a partner. She'd run things on her own for a long time so that wasn't completely unreasonable. Or maybe something else was up with Vivi.

I left Grounds For with another cup of coffee. Outside, I shaded my eyes and looked over at the town center, searching for Lori. This was about the same time of day as when I'd first met her with Garth. People tended to fall into routines. I hoped Lori was one of those people. I spotted her jiggling a big stroller. It looked like she was telling a group of men and women goodbye.

Lori started pushing the stroller this way. If I hustled, I could meet her before she crossed the street and after she left the group of people she was saying goodbye to. I dashed across, then slowed my pace, whipped out my phone, and studied it. A few moments later I looked up and put a surprised look on my face.

"Lori," I said. "Hi, how are you? Garth introduced us the other day."

Lori looked incredibly uncomfortable. Interesting. Maybe she heard the news about me being Perry's ex-fiancé.

"Hi. I'm in a hurry. Olivia isn't feeling well." She pointed into the stroller. It was one of those fancy ones that were more common in England than here.

I came around to stand beside Lori and looked at Olivia. She was cooing and staring at her hands. If this baby was sick, I was too. But I decided to go with it. "That's too bad. It can't be easy when little ones don't feel well."

I reaffirmed my earlier opinion that Olivia looked just like Perry and his family. She had the same narrow eyes, turned-up nose, and narrow lips. Plus her mop of dark, curly hair. I'd read once that babies resembled their fathers early on, so they wouldn't be rejected like they might be in the wild.

"You know, don't you?" Lori said.

CHAPTER 29

I jerked my head up, surprised. I thought I'd have to do a lot of fishing and it wasn't something I'd looked forward to. Or that I'd have to just blurt out my suspicions, which I looked forward to even less.

"Do you want to talk about this out here?" For a moment I'd toyed with lying. But quickly shed that idea because it was, after all, the whole reason I'd sought her out.

"Let's go to my house. It's only a couple of blocks north. Noah isn't home, so we'll be able to talk in private."

Noah must be Lori's husband. We walked along in a not-at-all companionable silence. It was awkward and uncomfortable. I had to remind myself more than once that I was doing this for Rip. And I guess for Perry and his family too. They needed to know the truth behind what happened. Lori turned up the sidewalk of a small

Craftsman-style house. It was painted a dark green with a silver tin roof.

A small but wide porch was lined with window boxes filled with pansies. Growing seasons were so different here than in Chicago. Pansies at home grew in spring and summer, but here it was too hot for pansies except for this time of year.

"It's lovely," I said.

"Thank you." Lori left the stroller at the bottom of the steps, took Olivia out, and opened the door. She gestured for me to follow her.

It wasn't until I was inside that I wondered about being in here. Lori was on my list of suspects, and her husband would have to be too, if he'd figured out this wasn't his baby. I hovered in the door, first listening to see if it sounded like anyone else was at home and then checking out the lay of the land. Living room, through to a dining room, and beyond it there was an open kitchen with a small island, two stools, and marble countertops.

The house was decorated in beach cottage chic, a spin-off of shabby chic, so there were lots of shell decorations and paintings of beach scenes. A large TV hung over the gas fireplace. Family photos filled the mantel. The house smelled of baby wipes and cleaner. Nothing was out of place.

"I need to put her down for a nap and then I'll be right back."

Lori took off down a hall to the left and I heard a door close. I went over and studied the photos. There were many with Lori, Olivia, and the man I'd seen Lori with outside of Grounds For the first day I met her. Olivia didn't look anything like him with his carrot-colored red hair, round face, and pale gray eyes. Did he know? Had he gone into a rage and killed Perry? The gentle, happy smile said no, but pictures never told the whole story and often weren't worth a thousand words.

I heard the click of a door and soft footsteps returning.

"Have a seat," Lori said.

I chose a hard-backed chair with easy access to the front door. Lori sat across from me.

"I couldn't get pregnant. After several years of trying the doctors came to the conclusion that my husband and I weren't able to have children. I'll spare you the medical details." She looked down at her clasped hands, one thumb rolling over and around the other repeatedly.

"That must have been terrible," I said.

"It was months of ups and downs. I went to Chicago for a Roller Derby tournament, drank too much, met and slept with Perry. I came home feeling guilty and then found out I was pregnant. Figures, doesn't it?"

I didn't know what to say to that.

"I told my husband what had happened. For a few weeks we were on the verge of splitting up, but we talked about it at length, decided to stay together, and raise the baby as our own."

"He must be a good man."

"He is for the most part."

I waited for her to go on, but she didn't add anything. "Did Perry know he was your daughter's father?" I asked.

Lori shook her head. "I never told him. No one knows but my husband and now you. And Perry wasn't her father. He was a sperm donor, just like all the others I tried in vitro with."

That was shocking to hear. Sperm donors knew what they were doing and Perry had no idea, but I guess Lori had to justify it all in her mind. "You didn't tell your family?" I recalled Garth's comment at Grounds For, saying Olivia must look like some long-ago family member. I guess Lori really hadn't said anything to them.

"You've met my mother. You can imagine how she'd take the news."

How sad. I imagined me in that situation and knew that my family would love and support me and the baby no matter the circumstances.

"Did Perry find out somehow?"

"I'm not sure, but I think he did." Her thumbs went around and around, faster and faster. "I was careful about not posting many pictures of us on social media, but there were a few. Maybe he saw one and figured it out."

Perry, as I learned, was many things, but stupid wasn't one of them.

"He called and asked me to meet him the afternoon he died."

"Did you?"

"Yes and no. I went to where he suggested we meet, but he never showed up."

"When and where was that?"

"The state beach east of the Sea Glass."

Not too far from where Perry had been found. "What time?" I repeated.

"We were supposed to meet at three."

Perry was already dead by then. I'd gotten to the coastal lake at around two thirty. I didn't know if Lori was lying or not. They might have met earlier and she shot him to shut him up. "Did your husband know that you were meeting him?"

"Heck no. I wanted to find out what Perry wanted first. Maybe it was this awesome mom bod." She cracked a small smile, but the joke fell flat.

Lori looked as fit as anyone I'd seen after having a baby. It looked like she was ready to roll, or in her case ready to Roller Derby. I stood because I needed to get to work, and I didn't think Lori had any other information that would help me.

"Please don't tell my family," she said as I walked to the door.

"I won't." But I wasn't about to say that I wouldn't tell anyone else. Despite Lori's story, either she or her husband could have killed Perry. I hoped not because I'd hate to see this lovely little home shattered.

Back at the town circle I headed to my car when I heard my name called. I turned to see Savannah waving at me from outside of Grounds For. Great. She was the last person I wanted to talk to right now, with my mind still whirling from my talk with Lori, but I walked over to her.

"Chloe, honey, how are you?" Savannah asked.

"I'm good. I need to get to work."

"I wanted to thank you because Garth said you introduced him to a young woman when he was at the Sea Glass."

Oh boy. Where was this going? "I did. She's been in a lot this week with her sorority sisters. They were having a reunion."

"And you think she's a nice person? Not one of those *Girls Gone Wild* types? A mother can't be too careful about who their children are with." She patted my arm. "I'm sure your mother feels the same."

My mother had always let me make my own decisions. "I wouldn't have introduced them if she was." That might not be entirely true. I'd been a little desperate to point Garth in someone else's direction.

"Turns out she's a lawyer who lives over in Niceville, and she went to Bama."

Niceville was twenty-five miles northwest of here and Bama was the University of Alabama. Apparently, both were Savannah-approved things. "That's fabulous," I said. I needed an exit strategy because standing here with Savannah was uncomfortable at the very least.

"Are you okay, Chloe? You seem a little . . . off-kilter?"

Here was my chance. "I didn't want to be rude, but I have to get to work."

Right then Garth came out of Grounds For with two cups in his hands. Just when I thought things couldn't get worse, they did.

"Hey, Chloe," Garth said. "Here's your coffee, Mother." He handed one of the cups off to Savannah. "Can I get you one, Chloe?"

"No, thank you."

"Are you all right?" Garth tilted his head to one side for a moment.

I did my best to smooth my face to neutral and rid it of whatever Savannah and Garth were picking up on. "I'm just running behind this morning. I had a meeting here earlier with Vivi and then ran into a friend. Please excuse me for hurrying off." I waved and hustled to my car.

CHAPTER 30

I tried to put my swirling thoughts aside as I went through the bar-opening routine of taking the stools down and chopping the lemons and limes that would be needed for drinks today. But it wasn't working very well. I kept thinking about Lori, her husband, and if I should call Deputy Biffle. Then the face of that sweet baby girl would pop into my head.

I needed to focus on the task at hand before I accidently chopped off a finger. The fresh citrus scent filled the air and mingled with the not unpleasant aroma of cleaner, beer, and beach. It was going to be a warm winter day and I was glad my brothers could get out and enjoy it.

At ten thirty I unlocked the sliding doors that ran across the entire front of the bar. I pushed them aside until they were fully opened and a warm, Southern breeze swept in. Too bad I couldn't hang with my brothers. Vivi hadn't returned yet, which made me a little nervous. I was good with basic drinks, but I still needed to work on the more complicated ones. Gin and tonics? I got you. Anything more complicated and I'd be searching through the book Vivi and Joaquín had put together of how we made our drinks. The book they hadn't told me about originally, which resulted in some not-so-great-tasting drinks prepared by me. I'd found out that the internet wasn't always the expert on how to make a drink. I could write a book about what I didn't know about the bar business.

Bam! Bam! Bam! Someone pounded on the back door. At least I'd locked it; now the only other problem was that I couldn't see who was on the other side. I decided to take my chances and opened the door. It was two of our regulars, an older man and an older woman. They came in almost every day and sat on opposite sides of the bar, sparring.

He usually ordered a whiskey sour but would occasionally ask for an old-fashioned just to keep me on my toes. The one day I hadn't asked him what he wanted and presented him with a whiskey sour, he'd ripped me a new one. If I recalled correctly, I'd been deemed an impertinent little twerp, an ignorant whippersnapper, and an intolerable cretin. There'd been more, but at some point I'd tuned him out and whisked away the offending whiskey sour. Then he complained loudly about wasting a drink. I'd dubbed him "the whiskey sourpuss" that day. Not that I ever said it out loud. But even with all his bluster, I got a kick out of him. More often than not he had a good story about his days as a merchant marine and the hearts he broke along the way.

The woman varied her morning drink. If it was me

here alone, it was something simple, like a mimosa or regular coffee or tea. If Joaquín was here, she might order a Bloody Mary—we didn't have any mixes and made everything from scratch—or something more complicated. While the whiskey sourpuss was telling his tales, she would roll her eyes, or challenge him on some story, saying he'd only been in kindergarten when that happened and he couldn't possibly have been involved.

Frankly, I thought they liked each other even though, according to them, they would never have anything to do with each other, after I said as much one morning. They called each other "old man" and "old woman," but it was done with great affection and camaraderie.

The old man grumbled at me as he brushed by. "Locking doors is what happens when city folks show up."

"I think it was more about the dead body behind the bar last summer than city folks," the woman told him.

"There was never a body behind the bar until the city folks showed up."

"Would you like your usual?" I asked him once they'd separated and gone to their normal sides of the bar.

"Usual? I don't have a usual."

When I first knew I was coming down here I pictured the bar like the one in *Cheers*, another favorite TV show of my grandparents. Where everyone would shout, "Norm" when a regular came in, and Norm would always want the same thing. Reality was so much different from TV.

"Of course you have a usual, old man," the woman said. "I'm the one who likes to shake things up."

"I do not." He slammed his fist on the tabletop. "I'll have . . . I'll have . . . a gimlet."

"Oh, a gimlet. Feeling fancy this morning, are you?"

the woman said in a mock British accent. "Well, as long as you're making gimlets this morning, Chloe, I'll have one too."

Great, just great. I wasn't sure what a gimlet was, although I had this vague notion of old movies, women in long gowns, and men in tuxes sipping gimlets. Oh, and I remembered reading about gimlets in *The Long Goodbye* by Raymond Chandler. In the book Philip Marlowe had said something about how they were better than martinis.

"Coming right up," I said, trying to sound sure of myself instead of terrified. I had no idea what was in a gimlet. If only I'd just asked what he'd like to drink. Lesson learned.

I hauled out the drinks book. Whew, only three ingredients. It was supposed to be served in a chilled martini glass and fortunately wasn't that hard to make. Although I'd had that thought before to disastrous results. I still had nightmares about martinis. Step one was taken care of because we always kept some glasses chilling in the refrigerator. I squeezed limes, mixed in a teaspoon of confectioners' sugar, added gin, poured it over ice in a shaker, and gave it a shake. But I didn't shake too hard so I wouldn't bruise the gin—wild that you can bruise gin. I strained the liquid into the glasses. I added a twist of lime to each glass and put them on a tray.

I took the first one over to the woman and then served the man, setting down the glass with a flourish. I knew better than to hover while he took the first sip so I hightailed it back behind the bar.

The couple saluted each other with their drinks held high and then took a cautious sip. I couldn't blame them. Joaquín would never let me forget the time I forgot to put

the lid on the blender when I was making frozen straw-
berry daiquiris, or the martini I made that turned out to be
a disgustini.

"It's excellent, Chloe," the woman said. "And rather
fancy for first thing in the morning."

"It'll do," the old man said. He surprised me with a
wink. "Reminds me of the time I was in the port of Le
Havre, France."

He was off and running with a tale that included can-
can girls, spies, and him saving the day. If only figuring
out who killed Perry and clearing Rip's name was as
easy. At least all seemed right in the world for a moment.
Vivi arrived and the bar filled up. She took over making
drinks until Joaquín arrived a little after noon. At three I
looked up and my brothers were standing in the door of
the bar.

I hustled over. "What are you two doing here? You're
supposed to be out having fun." They did both have slight
sunburns so maybe they'd had a little fun. "I told you I
don't need a babysitter. Or bodyguards. Or whatever it is
you think you're doing here."

"Chloe, slow down," Randy said.

"Take a breath," Kenny added. "We came by because
we wanted to take the boat out and you didn't leave a
key."

"Oh."

I looked around. Vivi was in her office and Joaquín
was in an intense discussion with a woman at the bar. My
purse with the boat key in it was under the counter. I gestured for my brothers to follow me, grabbed my purse
from under the bar, searched for the key, and came up
with it. I'd hustle them out the back and show them the

boat. That way I'd get them out of here without having to introduce them.

"Who's this?" Joaquín asked. He turned from the woman he was talking to.

Vivi popped her head out of the office. "Chloe, are these your brothers? They look just like you, only a heck of a lot taller."

Drat. Talk about bad timing. Vivi must have been looking at the security camera feed on her computer. It's not that I didn't love these two, but after last night with Rip, I didn't want to go through the same thing today.

I made the introductions. Hands were shaken. "They're heading out on the boat." It was still hard to call it mine instead of Boone's. I was always cautious about calling things mine in front of Vivi for fear of upsetting her. Our shared grief at losing Boone wasn't far below the surface. "Otherwise, I'm sure they'd like to stay and chat." I tugged on Randy's arm, trying to herd him out the door, but he didn't budge.

"It gets dark early here," I added.

"Why don't you stop back when you're done boating and we'll all have dinner together?" Vivi turned to Joaquín. "You can invite Michael and we'll just close up early. Tell Michael dinner will be at six thirty." Vivi turned back to me. "I can't believe you didn't tell us you had family in town."

She went back in her office and closed the door. Vivi could be very imperious at times, and this was one of them.

"Do you already have plans for dinner?" I asked hopefully, knowing the odds of that were small.

"Nope," Kenny said. "It sounds like we'll have enough time to take out the boat and clean up before dinner."

"Great," I said cheerfully. *Great*, I thought, moping. I led my brothers out the back, showed them the boat and how to get from the harbor to the bay. "Have fun. Take your time."

"Oh, don't worry. We'll be back in plenty of time for dinner," Randy said.

"We'll make sure we have time to shower and get presentable first too." Kenny grinned and waved at me as he said it.

I watched them putt out of the boat slip and turn left. I looked up at the sky. Why me? I'd shake my fist at it, but there were too many people around and I didn't want to look ridiculous. Dinner was going to mess up my investigative plans. I wanted to find out more about Lori's husband and his whereabouts the day Perry was killed. I hadn't explained the feud to Kenny and Randy so that they wouldn't mention Rip. Hopefully, I'd snag them before they came for dinner so I could fill them in. Life was complicated. But when I got back in I was surprised to see two new arrivals sitting at a table. Things were looking up.

CHAPTER 31

Kellye and her friend were sitting at a high top. Excellent. I could serve them drinks and ask them questions. Then I paused for a moment. What were they doing here? Did they want something from me? No matter. I wasn't going to lose this opportunity to talk to them.

I walked over. "What can I get you two?"

Kellye wore a floral sarong over a bikini. It showed off her toned shoulders and arms. Her friend wore a white cover-up over her swimsuit.

Kellye pointed to our drinks' menu. "What's this Peach Bum Fizz?"

"It's an original by Joaquín. If you like peach flavored drinks, you'll love this," I said.

"Sounds good," Kellye said.

"I'll have that too."

I checked a couple of other tables and took the orders

up to Joaquín. While he made the Peach Bum Fizzes, I poured beers.

"Are you doing okay, Chloe?" Joaquín asked.

"What's with everyone asking me that today?"

"You have this little line between your brows that isn't usually there and you're a lot quieter than usual. Not to mention you were a little weird about your brothers being in here."

"I'm sorry. I don't want me to affect your tips."

"I'm not worried about the tips. I'm worried about you. You should have taken some time off after you found Perry so you could grieve." Joaquín poured the two Peach Bum Fizzes into hurricane glasses and set them on the drinks tray with the beers I'd poured. "It isn't your problem to solve. I know you're worried about Rip. But he'll be fine."

I hugged him. "Thank you for caring about me."

He held me for a few moments. "Now go serve those drinks before you ruin our tips."

I laughed for the first time today. Then I added paper umbrellas to both drinks. "There," I said, "now you'll get a good tip."

I dropped the beers off first and then took the Peach Bum Fizzes over to Kellye and her friend.

"How are things going with Perry's spirit?" I asked, making sure to keep my expression nonjudgmental and my voice kind. Who was I to judge someone else's beliefs?

"I think he's letting go of this world," Kellye said, her voice sad.

"That's a good thing, though, right?" I asked.

"It is. He'll be at peace even with his violent death."

"You don't know anyone from the trapeze school who had a problem with Perry, do you?" I asked.

Kellye drew back in surprise. "Why would you ask that?"

I wanted to be tactful here. "Maybe someone followed all three of you down here. Was someone jealous of your relationship with Perry?"

"You're blaming me for Perry's death?"

"No. Not at all." This wasn't going as planned. "You didn't kill him." Or did you? I watched her reaction carefully, but Kellye gave nothing away. Rats.

"Joshua was upset when you started dating Perry," Kellye's friend said.

"Who is Joshua? Have you seen him down here, or anyone else from Chicago?" I asked.

"Someone I dated and no, I haven't seen him," Kellye said. "Can you just leave us alone so we can enjoy the beach and our drinks?" Kellye turned to her friend. "Let's go sit on the deck."

There went any chance of a tip and I didn't find out anything.

"You go on," Kellye's friend said. "I'm going to use the restroom."

Kellye flipped her hair and sashayed out to the deck. Her friend turned to me.

"She lied to you or at the very least left something out. Kellye told me she saw someone she knew down here from Chicago the day Perry was murdered."

"Who?" I asked.

"I don't know. A woman. Someone who knew Perry."

"Thanks," I said. Who could she be talking about?

* * *

At six we closed the bar and pushed tables together for dinner. I'd tacked up signs on the front and back doors saying we were closed for a private event. Wade was bringing food over. At six twenty there was a knock on the back door; everyone else was here so it had to be my brothers. "I'll get it," I dashed back to the door before anyone else could respond. I flung it open, and instead of inviting my brothers in, I stepped outside with them. I quickly filled them in on the whole feud thing and my relationship with Rip. Although Dale knew I was seeing someone, so Vivi must have been the one who told him. Still, it would be better not to mention him.

"Well, that explains a lot," Kenny said.

"What's that mean?" I demanded.

"It explains why you're so into the guy," Randy said. "You always did love sneaking around with some guy you didn't think we'd approve of."

"Oh, for heaven's sake. That's when I was in middle school." I blew a puff of air up in frustration. "Why wouldn't I like Rip? He's smart and handsome and—"

"Apparently rich," Kenny added.

"That's not what I was going to say. I was going to say funny." Or built, but I probably wouldn't say that to my brothers even though they had to have noticed.

"Ha, gotcha," Randy said. "Again."

I shook my head. "Get inside and behave yourselves." I followed them back inside and made more introductions.

The table was laden with Wade's famous savory cheese and rosemary biscuits that were still steaming, grilled grouper, fried shrimp, French fries, coleslaw, and greens with bits of ham in them. Soon everyone was busy passing food around.

"When did you get to town?" Vivi asked.

"Yesterday," Kenny said.

"It's nice of you to come visit," Joaquín said. He'd looked amused ever since my brothers arrived, like he was waiting for something to happen. I wanted to kick him but managed not to.

"We wanted to make sure our baby sister was okay," Randy said.

"They think I need a bodyguard," I said.

"Maybe they aren't so wrong. This is a bad business with your ex, and it doesn't seem like the sheriff has made any progress. I saw an update on the noon news with that 'we're making progress' BS." Wade helped himself to another biscuit. "I for one am glad you're here for Chloe."

Everyone nodded. Yeesh, so much for being viewed as a strong, independent woman.

"It makes us feel better knowing she has friends like all of you who are watching out for her," Randy said.

"It's almost a full-time job," Joaquín said. "She has a nose for trouble."

"And a loving heart," Michael added.

"Thank you, Michael." At least someone was sticking up for me.

Vivi called me Thursday morning while I was out for my run. I'd survived the dinner almost intact with some shreds of dignity left. She'd insisted I take the day off to spend with my brothers. Although they had left early to take out Boone's boat fishing, begging me not to tell their wives they were shirking their protection duties. They were comfortable leaving me home alone as long as it was daylight and the security system was on. I shooed them off because I needed some time alone and hadn't mentioned I planned to go for a run.

"I know I said you could have the day off, but can you meet me tonight? There's a gin distributor that's doing a tasting. There will be food. It would be a good time for you to meet more of the local people who are in the business."

"I guess that would work."

"It's at seven thirty. Cocktail attire. I'll text you the address."

I panted out an "okay."

After my run I sat on my bed doing an internet search on my phone. At least not working today meant I had more time to investigate Perry's murder. Lori's husband, Noah Clemens, was something of an enigma. From what I'd found on social media he was a real estate agent with a well-known firm in the area. His agent photo showed a genial-looking man. His carrot-colored hair styled. His flat, pale gray eyes didn't sparkle and his chin was soft and round. Even in the photo his smile looked strained, as if he had to work at looking genial. The pictures I'd seen of him at Lori's house made him look more human.

He didn't have a big presence on social media other than the real estate agent stuff. Either he didn't have accounts or they were so well hidden with an unusual user name and high privacy settings that I couldn't find them. I checked Lori's social media accounts, but none of them listed him as a friend. However, on Lori's accounts there was a picture of him holding Olivia and looking down at her adoringly. That made me feel better.

I went back to the real estate site to poke around. His profile was the standard stuff—native, this certification and that, organizations he belonged to. There weren't any top real estate agent badges or other things to make it look like he was really successful. I backed out of his personal page on the site and looked over the whole thing. Vacation homes. They rent vacation homes. I hadn't noticed when I looked up the house Kellye was renting what rental company the owner had listed the house with, but it was Noah's firm. Did that mean Noah would have access to the pass codes to the house? It probably did.

I pictured a scenario where Perry and Noah met at the house. They took a walk and Noah killed Perry and pushed him into the lake. The risk of doing that and getting caught made that scenario unlikely. It was more likely that they were inside, things went bad, and Noah killed Perry. It would be easy—relatively speaking—for Noah to then carry Perry's body out and dump him in the lake. It was only a few yards behind the house. Neither Henry's house nor the Rivers' backed to the lake like the rental did. They were angled slightly away. How Perry had ended up on the other side of the lake was something I didn't want to think about because it involved alligators. I shuddered. Or maybe it was the wind. It had been strong the day he died. But why would Perry have my photo in his hand if Noah killed him? To throw the sheriff's department off?

But all this was just speculation and didn't provide me with any answers. I needed to talk to Noah, but first I was going to see if the vacation owner had answered my request for more information. I checked my email and found a cheery message in response to me, telling me they would be happy to answer any questions. I'm not sure that was true, but I'd give it a whirl.

My message was simple: Can you tell me who rented the house last Saturday? Then I made up a story about finding a pair of glasses and a book on a table behind the house that I'd seen the renter reading when I'd been out for a walk the day before. *Not bad, Chloe.* I added we'd talked for a few minutes about the book but hadn't exchanged information and I'd like to return both to them. I hit Send and went back to cyberstalking Noah while I waited.

How could I talk to him without putting myself in jeopardy?

CHAPTER 32

An idea came to me. I could pretend to be looking for a house, but I certainly didn't want to go alone. I went and looked at the listings Noah had. There were three—a two-million-dollar house on the bay in Destin, a modest town house not far off Highway 98 in the oldest part of Destin, and a home in a small neighborhood not too far from the big shopping center, Destin Commons.

That house looked perfect. One level, three beds, two baths. A story formed in my head. I'd be looking for a house for my parents, who wanted to escape the Chicago winters. Now who to ask to go with me? I couldn't ask Rip. He was already in hot water and I didn't want to get him in more trouble. I went ahead and booked an appointment using the website's online booking system. That way I wouldn't have to talk to Noah in advance and give him the chance to figure out who I was. I set it up for an hour from now, hoping my brothers would be home and one of them would go with me. Kenny had always been the more adventurous of the two of them and more likely to do something a tad riskier than Randy would be.

I got a message back from the vacation rental owner saying they couldn't provide me with the name of the person who'd rented their house, but that they be happy to forward the items if I sent them along to them. Darn.

My brothers walked in just then.

"How was fishing?" I asked. They were empty handed.

"There wasn't any catching," Randy said.

"That's not true. You had an epic battle and caught that piece of driftwood," Kenny said. "He almost went in the water trying to haul that thing in. Randy was sure he had a shark on the line."

I laughed while Randy pouted.

"It was fun," Kenny said. "I could get used to this lifestyle."

Oh boy, that was all I needed, having family move down here. "What do you want for breakfast?"

Everyone pitched in and we made omelets, toast, and hashbrowns.

"I need to go get some groceries," I announced after we ate breakfast.

"It seems like we have plenty of food," Randy said.

"Female stuff," I said. Darn, I was good.

Randy and Kenny exchanged a look. I crossed my fingers behind my back.

"I'll go with her," Kenny said.

It sounded like they planned to tag team my every move. I could just picture one going somewhere with me, then the other. I liked being alone. Thinking about having one of my brothers around all the time gave me even more motivation to find Perry's killer. I knew my brothers would have to go back to work sometime soon, and if they had to leave before the murderer was found, my parents would show up.

My dad had always said he could take anyone even though as far as I knew he'd never been in a fight in his entire life. He was a talker and could talk himself out of almost any situation. Probably came from dealing with cranky customers who always wanted their plumbing problem fixed immediately but didn't always want to pay. And it wasn't that I didn't love my parents, but that would mean they'd have to meet Rip. It was hard enough introducing him to my brothers. I definitely wasn't ready to have him meet the parents. We just weren't there yet.

"Great," I said. "Let me grab my purse and go to the bathroom."

I closed the door to my room. After I went to the bathroom I grabbed my makeup bag and a spray bottle filled with water, putting both in my purse. At the last minute I added some hair gel. I changed into a low, V-necked, red tunic sweater to go over my leggings. I tossed a pair of heels in my purse too. It was getting a little bulky, but I didn't think my brothers would notice. Then I threw my ratty old Chicago Bears sweatshirt on to cover the sweater.

I walked back out into the living room. "Ready to go?"

Kenny pushed himself up from the couch and followed me to my car—an innocent lamb who hopefully wasn't being led to a slaughter.

After I tossed my purse in the back seat I took off and headed to Destin.

"Isn't going to Russo's Grocery Store good enough?

Isn't that where you got the cannolis?" Kenny asked. "You said it was a great local market. I'd like to see it."

"We have an errand to run before we pick up the groceries," I said.

Kenny turned in his seat. I kept my eyes focused on the road, all casual like.

"What kind of errand?"

"We're going to tour a house."

"A house? What for?"

"We're going to say we're looking for a house for our parents from Chicago. They're tired of the winters."

"And why are we going to do that?"

"I need to talk to the real estate agent without him knowing who I am."

Kenny was shaking his head. "Nope. Not going to happen."

I glanced at him before refocusing on the road. "You can go with me or I'll figure out another way to talk to this man. It's safer to have someone with me, but whatever. I can drop you off somewhere, or I'll just rebook for another time. Me in a deserted house with a strange man. No worries."

Kenny rubbed a hand over his face. "You're impossible."

"Thanks." I pulled into the parking lot of a restaurant that had closed a few weeks ago for a winter break. I drove around back. No one was there.

"What are you doing?"

I turned in my seat and hauled my purse onto my lap. I took my makeup bag out of my purse, turned the rearview so I could see myself, and started applying makeup. A lot of it. "I'm changing my appearance. There's a chance Noah's seen me around town or on TV. I don't want to

risk it." I applied a bright, purple-red lipstick, dark char-
coal eye shadow, and so much mascara that my eyelashes
were a quarter inch longer than they were when I started.

"How do I look?" I asked when I finished with the
blush.

"I went to a show with drag queens once. They wore
less makeup than you have on."

I slapped Kenny's arm. "Smart aleck." I thought I
looked pretty good. I took out the water bottle and hair
gel from my purse. I spritzed my hair with the water.
Then I slicked it back, squirted some gel on my hands,
and ran them through my hair. It gave me a whole different look from my usual tousled look. I'd done this once
before and it had taken a moment for both Rip and
Joaquín to recognize me.

Satisfied with phase one of my transformation, I went
into phase two. I pulled off my sweatshirt and tossed it
over the back seat. Kenny's eyes about bugged out of his
head.

"You are not wearing that out in public."

The sweater did cling in all the right places and was
really low in the front. I'd never worn it without something like a cami underneath it before.

Kenny twisted in his seat, grabbed my sweatshirt, and
lobbed it at me. "Put this back on."

I batted it away. "Didn't you ever watch *True Lies* with
Dad? Jamie Lee Curtis changes her outfit in the hall of a
hotel? Slicks back her hair with water and rips her dress
to show some cleavage?"

"If you're Jamie Lee Curtis, I guess that makes me
Arnold Schwarzenegger."

"Ugh. No. They were married. You're Tom Arnold.
Close your eyes."

"What? Why?"

"I have to wiggle out of my leggings."

Kenny shook his head but did what I asked.

"Okay. I'm almost all set." I dug my high-heeled shoes from my purse. They were black peep toes.

Kenny started shaking his head again. "Nope. My wife has a pair of those. She hauls them out every time she wants to have another baby."

"They complete the look," I said.

"They're too over-the-top. Any man with half a brain will realize something's off. Just wear the black flats."

I decided it wouldn't hurt to acquiesce on this one small thing. "Okay." I stuffed them back in my purse. "We're all set."

"What, I don't get a disguise? No fake beard? No glasses? I don't get to change clothes?"

"He wouldn't recognize you. Plus, trust me, you'll be the last person on his mind." I waved a hand to indicate my appearance.

"I can't believe I let you talk me into this," Kenny said as I restarted the car and pulled back onto highway 98.

Ten minutes later we pulled up in front of the house. A sign with Noah's face on it stood in the yard. It was a pleasant neighborhood of mostly one-story houses. Yards were mown, cars were washed, and hedges were trimmed. On the way over here Kenny had alternately sighed and muttered, "I can't believe I'm doing this." But once I pulled to the curb, he put on his game face and got into character.

"I hope we can help our poor, elderly parents find their dream home," he said to me.

I snickered at the thought of how mad our parents would be if we ever called them elderly. We'd decided to call each other by our rarely used middle names. We always knew we were in trouble if we heard our mom say Chloe Beth Jackson or Kenny Samson Jackson. We stood at the curb for a moment, taking in the house and neighborhood. A tan sedan was parked in the driveway.

I rang the doorbell. Noah popped open the door, a friendly expression on his face. His eyes swept over my outfit, but then he kept them up on my face. He introduced himself.

"Come on in, folks. You're looking at your new home."

CHAPTER 33

I hoped Kenny didn't throw up. "We're brother and sister," I said. "Our parents are moving here from Detroit and it's up to us to find them the perfect home."

"Great," Noah said. His hand was in his pants pocket and he jangled his keys.

I barely listened as he droned on about the house having a new roof put on a year ago, the heating and air conditioning being upgraded six months ago. The house was just two short blocks from the beach so it had all the advantages with none of the hassles of living on the beach.

"No traffic noise from old 98," Noah added. "And look at this open concept. Let's go to the kitchen. All the appliances have been recently updated." He continued to jangle his keys, which was getting on my nerves.

It was a nice house. Kenny and I oohed and ahhed, argued about the size of the closets—he said they were big enough, I was concerned they weren't. We hit just the right balance of enthusiasm and concerns. We settled at the round dining room table. That ended the key jangling, but then he started tapping the table. Maybe he was just a fidgety guy, but it was odd.

"Noah, I appreciate all you've told us today, but we'd like to hear more about you. Our parents are big on knowing who they're dealing with when they're doing business with someone." I paused and looked into his eyes. "You can imagine how difficult a move this will be, leaving all their friends behind."

"Their friends will love coming down here to visit," Noah said.

"If they can," Kenny said. "They are quite elderly."

"Yes, of course," Noah said.

"About you, then?" I asked, smiling.

Noah tilted his head to the side for a moment. "You look familiar to me. Have we met?"

Rats. He might have seen me the day Garth and I had coffee together. "I just have one of those faces. Everyone says that. And then they usually realize I look like the actress Rachal Bilson."

"That must be it."

Was he ever going to talk about himself? I wasn't getting any kind of an I'm-a-murderer vibe from him, but hey, what did I know about murderers? A third prompt would seem aggressive so I just looked at him politely.

"I'm a native of the Panhandle," he started. "I know this market like the back of my hand. This house won't last."

The house had been on the market for fifty-nine days according to the website, so not exactly flying off the real estate shelf.

"I'm married and have a six-month-old daughter," he said and got a little choked up.

"That is amazing," I said. "Pictures?"

Noah opened his phone and we spent the next few minutes going through pictures. I wanted to grab his phone and go through it myself, but he kept a tight hold on it.

"Your family is lovely," I said.

"I'm very lucky." His voice was flat.

He didn't sound like he felt lucky. Had he killed Perry and hauled his body to the lake? "My dad loves to go to the firing range to practice shooting. Is there one around here?" I asked.

"Yes. The closest one is only about ten miles from here, up toward Crestview. I could take him sometime. It's one of my favorite things to do."

So he was good with guns. That was scary, and I was glad Kenny was here with me.

"I have other houses I could show you," Noah said.

"This one seems like a good option. We love the one-story, split-bedroom layout," I said.

"We do," Kenny chirped.

I would elbow him to take it down a notch if Noah hadn't been there. "My parents are coming down soon and would love to stay in a vacation home instead of a hotel."

"I can help you with that," Noah said. "Our company has a number of beach homes and condos available."

"They were both geologists," I said.

Kenny's eyebrows popped up, but he managed to nod quickly.

"And they're fascinated by the coastal lakes. Do you have a house by any of them?" I watched Noah's face closely.

"There's one. It's rustic," he said.

"I'm sure that wouldn't bother them," Kenny said. "They traveled the world when they were working and are used to roughing it. A house is an upgrade from the tents and shacks they've lived in."

Oh, good one, Kenny. "Is there any chance we could see it?"

"Unfortunately it's occupied right now, but I could show you some photos of it." Noah opened his phone, typed in some commands, and then passed the phone over to me.

Kenny and I huddled over it. I quickly swiped open Noah's messaging app and Kenny tensed beside me.

"It is rustic," I said. I opened his contacts and swiped through them. Perry wasn't listed.

"I don't think it looks bad," Kenny said. "You're going soft. Say, Noah, we didn't look at the garage. Would you mind showing it to me while my sister decides if the rental is good enough?"

Noah stood. "No problem."

I could have hugged Kenny. As soon as they walked off, I typed Perry's phone number into the contacts. Boom. There was a series of calls dating back three weeks ago and ending the day of Perry's murder. I took out my phone and snapped a picture of all the calls. They weren't short. However, I was disappointed that there weren't any voice mails or text messages between the two of them. And I noted that some of the calls Noah had placed were in the evening, after Perry had been murdered. But maybe Noah had placed them to throw everyone off.

Even more striking was the realization that Lori had lied to me. She told me no one knew but her and Noah. If that was true, why would Noah be in touch with Perry? I closed his contacts and messaging app just as they walked back in. I stood. "The cabin looks just about perfect for them." I was amazed I managed to keep my voice even as my thoughts zinged around, puzzling over the calls.

We all walked to the door. Noah was jangling the keys in his pocket again.

"We'll be in touch about the house and the cabin."

Noah shook our hands and handed us business cards. "Thank you."

We got back in the car, waved one more time, and took off.

"Thank you," I said. "Especially for looking in the garage so I could snoop."

"Did you find anything out?" Kenny asked.

"Noah and Perry called each other, starting about three weeks before Perry showed up in town and ending the day of the murder. However, the calls continued after the estimated time of death."

"That could be covering his tracks."

"I agree, or it could mean he didn't do it."

"Not exactly a smoking gun."

"Not at all." I pulled in behind the restaurant again.

"What are we doing back here?" Kenny asked.

I searched my purse and pulled out a packet of makeup wipes. "I'm de-Jamie Lee Curtising myself."

Kenny looked puzzled.

"Erasing the evidence. If I go home looking like this, Randy is going to have questions."

"Are we still going to the store?"

"You bet. I need to pick up more food."

"Perfect."

After Kenny and I got home I decided to call Perry's

sister, Gina. We'd always gotten along well and I really did want to express my sympathies to her. It certainly hadn't worked calling Perry's mom, but I understood. As self-centered as she was, this had to be terrible for her. I went in my bedroom, settled on the bed, and called.

"Hello, Chloe," Gina said.

I guess she hadn't deleted my number when I broke off the engagement with Perry. We hadn't been in touch except briefly after it happened. I'd sent Gina a text saying how much I enjoyed knowing her, and that I hoped I hadn't caused the family too much pain. She'd written back saying not to worry, that her family was too screwed up to know what actual pain was like.

I'd always wondered what she meant by that, but with everything I'd found out about Perry since, I was looking at things differently than I had in the past.

"I'm so sorry about Perry. I can't imagine what you all are going through."

"No, you can't," she said. But she didn't say it in a mean way. "My family is so freaking nutty that each person is acting out in some horrible way."

That didn't surprise me under the circumstances. They'd been an unusual group of people.

"My mom is now in the how-could-Perry-get-himself-murdered phase of life. She thinks it reflects badly on the family and is damaging our reputation."

I didn't know what to say to that.

"And she's blaming you. She roams the house muttering your name under her breath like some crazed queen you'd read about in a Shakespeare play."

That made me a little uncomfortable. "Is someone coming down?" I asked. Maybe they could just make arrangements to have his body returned over the phone. But if it was me, I'd be down here hounding the sheriff's department for answers.

"Oh, right now there's a lot of arguing about that. Dad wants to go, but really I'm not sure he's up for it."

"What about Terry?" Terry and Perry were only twelve months apart. Irish twins. They even looked a lot like each other.

"He's been holed up in his room drinking since we got the news."

"He's living back with your parents?"

"Yes, and it's not healthy. The other two knuckleheads are avoiding going home, which is driving Mom even crazier."

"How are you coping with all of it?"

"Thank heavens for weed."

I'd laugh, but I knew she was serious. She smoked before work, after work, before bed, before going to a movie. If there was an occasion, she felt she should be high before it.

"And don't blame yourself. I should have warned you about him, but for a while there, it seemed like he got better when he was with you."

"Better?" I asked.

"Yeah. Like he was trying to be this regular guy. It's hard to be a regular person in a family like ours. A narcissistic mother. A father who traveled all the time to avoid said mother. We're all screwed up. It's why I'm high half the time."

This would have been good information to have early in our relationship. But I couldn't fault Gina. My relationship with Perry wasn't her responsibility. "Did he

really think the two of us were going to get back together? To get engaged again?"

"With every part of his shriveled soul. I'm sorry I
haven't been in touch. I should have told you what was
going on. But really, he kept me in the dark until I found
out he was heading down there. Even then I wasn't exactly sure about what he was up to. I know he'd talked
about trying to find a way to work things out with you. In
his own warped way, he loved you as much as he was capable of loving anyone."

How had I not seen any of this? Although what had
Joaquín said? Something about maybe I sensed something was off and that's why I ended the engagement.
Going with that theory made me feel slightly better. I'd
always thought Perry's family was different and we didn't
spend a lot of time with them. Now that I thought about
it, I didn't think Perry wanted me to be around them. To
find out who they really were. Yikes. Was I doing the
same thing with my brothers and my friends here? If so, I
needed to stop.

It made me think about Rip and his family. I didn't
know all that much about them, other than what I'd heard
from Vivi and some of the heritage business owners. I
didn't know if Rip's grandmother was just a cranky older
woman or if she had some terrible character flaw.

Rip's mother was sweet and polite when we saw her,
which wasn't often because she lived in Tampa. We
weren't at that place in our relationship yet to go visit her.
His father had died when Rip was sixteen and he'd had a
reputation as a playboy. Unstable. Unable to hold any job
but that of the tennis pro at the country club. Although
again, most of this information had come through Vivi,

and I wasn't sure how much I could trust her to be fair about it.

"Chloe? Are you still there?"

Gina's voice jerked me out of my reverie. "Sorry. I have the engagement ring Perry was planning on giving me. Are you still at the same address?"

"I am. Chloe, I gotta tell you something, but I'll deny it if you ever tell anyone."

"What?"

"Mom was down there the day Perry was killed."

I gaped at the phone for a moment while I tried to absorb that. "Why?"

"She found out that Perry was going to propose again and she said she'd stop him, whatever it took."

CHAPTER 34

A couple of moments ticked by before I could speak. "You have to tell the authorities."

"Not going to happen."

"She might have seen something that would help."

"She didn't. Trust me, we've all questioned her."

So the whole family knew and hadn't said anything? "She might have seen something she doesn't know was significant. Or someone." My thoughts sped ahead. "How long was she down here for?"

"Just the day."

"So she flew down here. That means there will be a record."

"She has a friend who's a private pilot and has her own plane. They came down in that. There's no record."

"You have to tell someone," I insisted again. "Or do you think she killed Perry?"

"Look, my mom is a lot of things. But she would never hurt one of us."

She'd hurt all of them in many ways. Was it too big of a leap to picture a narcissist murdering their own child in a rage?

"Mom's calling. I've got to run. Take care."

"*Gina*," I said, but Gina was already gone.

I thought back to my conversation with Kellye's friend. Maybe Perry's mother was the woman from Chicago Kellye had seen. Or maybe I shouldn't be taking what her friend said at face value. Maybe her friend was jealous of Kellye's relationship with Perry. I had more questions than answers. Not knowing what else to do with all this information, I called Deputy Biffle and told him what Gina had said about her mother. He hung up on me before I had a chance to tell him about talking with Noah. I'd have to get hold of him later.

With my brothers in tow, I mailed the ring to Gina. I didn't want it, even though my head was spinning with her news.

"I have to go to the airport in Destin," I told my brothers. I'd already filled them in on my call to Gina. "You don't have to go with me."

"Maybe we can help with your sleuthing. We're charming," Randy said.

"Yeah, as charming as an eel," I said.

"We'll slip in there, zap with our electric personalities, ask some questions, and get some answers," Kenny said.

It might be easier than having them tower over me while I tried to ask questions. "Okay. Divide and conquer." I texted them both a picture of Irma.

Thirty minutes later we arrived at the Destin Executive Airport. I didn't have a lot of confidence this venture would yield us any information. There was another small airport up by Crestview, and who knew how many private fields. I didn't have the tail number or even the type of plane. This was a busy place. Chances were no one would remember two women going through the airport on Saturday.

Five minutes later we were back at my brother's van with no new information. We'd been tossed out fairly quickly by a female security guard.

"Isn't this the point in the book or movie where someone comes over to us with information?" I asked.

We all looked around hopefully. The only person who paid any attention to us was the female security guard who told us to leave. She stood by the entrance, arms folded across her chest.

We piled in the van and left.

"Where to?" Randy asked.

"Bob Sikes Airport in Crestview." Maybe we'd have better luck there. An hour later we were headed back to Emerald Cove with no answers. At least in Crestview we managed to ask questions before security escorted us out. I hoped that Deputy Biffle would have better luck than we did. He'd probably have access to security camera footage that we'd never get our hands on.

"I'm hungry," Kenny complained.

"Let's go to The Diner," I said. I hadn't had time to talk to Delores about the day of the fight between Perry and Rip. It was three o'clock and it would be four by the time we got there. Maybe things would be slow and Delores would have time to talk if she was there.

*   *   *

The Diner wasn't crowded. Delores greeted us when we walked in. "Look at the three of you. I heard your brothers were in town."

Of course she did.

"You're like two giraffes and a—"

"Don't say warthog," I said.

"I would never say that about you, Chloe," Delores said. She sounded hurt. "I was going to say two giraffes and a gazelle on account of all your running."

I'd love to think of myself as a graceful gazelle. In fact, I would try to picture myself that way from now on.

Delores left us with menus and said she'd be back with glasses of water. She came back with the water and three chocolate shakes, which had become her habit when I came in because she thought I was too thin. I loved her for that. My brothers both ordered blackened catfish sandwiches with sides of hush puppies, onion rings, French fries, and Delores's famous Cajun coleslaw. I ordered a side salad, which made me think of Garth's mom, Savannah—only I planned to eat mine instead of pushing it around my plate. Vivi had said there would be food at tonight's event and I didn't want to be all bloated when I arrived. Heck, the chocolate shake was almost a meal on its own.

"Delores, do you have time to sit with us? I wanted to ask you about the day Perry and Rip fought in the town circle."

We both turned and looked out at the bench where it happened. It was about thirty yards from here.

"Sure. I'll put these orders in and be right back."

When Delores returned she had a cup of coffee with her. "It'll be good to sit for a spell."

I scooted over so she could sit next to me. By this point my brothers had given up trying to use their straws on their shakes and were spooning in the icy goodness. I'd warned them, but they were more the type to find things out on their own than take advice.

"How are you doing?" she asked. "I'm glad your brothers are here. We all need some family now and then."

"I'm okay. I wondered if you noticed anything out of the ordinary the day Perry and Rip argued in the park."

"You and Deputy Biffle. I've known Dan all his life and it still sets me on edge when he's in uniform and wants to talk to me." Delores sipped her coffee. "I'll tell you the same thing I told him. It was over by the time I looked out. I didn't see the fight, Rip, or the young man who got murdered. There was quite a crowd out there. I did see Savannah Havers hurrying off, but it might not mean a thing. That woman always seems to be in a hurry."

Then again, it might mean something. Lori had lied to me once. Maybe she'd lied about her mom knowing too. Thinking that made me wonder if Suni had put it together too. A waitress brought our food. After she left I reached over to snag an onion ring from Randy's plate.

"I knew it," he complained. "Don't be the woman who orders a salad and then eats everyone else's food."

Kenny dropped a couple of his onion rings on top of my salad. "Here you go, sis. I don't mind sharing." He grinned at me.

"I always did love you best," I told him while Randy gave an exaggerated sigh like he was being put-upon.

"Would you mind looking at some photos and seeing if you recognize any of the people in them?" I asked Delores. On the drive back from Crestview I'd pulled together ten photos of people I knew from Chicago. One of them was Irma Franklin.

"Sure. Am I looking for a killer?"

"I hope not." I passed Delores my phone.

She studied it while I ate my salad of tomatoes, romaine lettuce, corn, cheese, and grilled chicken with Delores's house vinaigrette. I was hungrier than I had realized. I looked longingly at Randy's quickly diminishing plate of food and he passed me over some French fries.

Delores took her time, but then shook her head. "I'm sorry, honey. I don't recognize any of them."

That was disappointing. "Thanks for looking."

"Why don't you send them to me and I'll see if Ralph recognizes any of them."

I hit Send, we finished eating, and left.

We spent the rest of the afternoon on the beach, throwing a Frisbee and looking for shells. Delores sent me a text saying Ralph hadn't recognized anyone in the photos either. While we played, I went over who had the most reason to kill Perry. The most obvious people were Olivia's family. They all had a solid reason for not wanting people to know about Olivia's real father. However, why kill Perry? Although I could picture Savannah killing someone. There was something off about her even with her attempt to be friendly.

Did Perry really want to help raise a child, or did he think that would help win me back? I picked up a piece of broken sand dollar. Something was very broken in whoever killed Perry and in Perry himself. Who had he hurt? Kellye and Suni. He used them or so it seemed to me. I was fortunate to have gotten away from him relatively unscathed. I shuddered to think of what life would have been like if I'd married him.

When it was dark we sat out on the screened porch, relaxing.

"Hey, Chloe, come on. We're hungry," Kenny said.

"Again?" It really shouldn't be a surprise anymore. I followed them back up to the house.

After we went back inside my brothers fixed sandwiches for their dinner. I quickly rinsed off in the shower, reapplied makeup, and searched for a dress to wear to the gin tasting. Vivi had said cocktail attire. I held up two dresses. One was black and one was purple. The black one was knee-length but had a split halfway up my thigh and a bare back. The purple was more modest-looking, but I knew it hugged me in all the right places. I went with the purple because I'd been wearing a lot of black lately and my brothers would hate it.

We argued about whether they were going too or not. We'd finally settled on them driving, dropping me off, and then going to the bar at the restaurant next door until I was done. Having them here was exhausting and caving was easier than arguing. I knew they'd follow me if I said no and why take two cars?

The address Vivi sent me was in Destin, at a restaurant on the harbor that had closed and now rented the space for private events. Fortunately, traffic wasn't bad. There were only a couple of main roads on the barrier island and if there was an accident or a lot of people out the drive could take fifty minutes or more. Fortunately, I made it to the place by seven forty. The parking lot was already full.

"Thanks for the ride," I said.

"Text us when you're ready to leave," Randy said.

"I will." I grabbed my purse and headed in.

I wasn't an introvert by any means, but sometimes, like tonight, I was reluctant to walk into a place where I might only know one or two people. It could be intimidating. I slapped on a smile and opened the door. The room was dim, the conversation muted. It looked like the last time the restaurant had been updated was back in the sixties. Long enough ago that the furnishings now gave the place a cool retro vibe instead of just looking old.

I stopped at the entrance to the room, stepped to the side, and looked around for Vivi. A man about my age came over to me.

"Hi, I'm Edward DeLouise," he said.

He wore an expensive-looking suit with a purple shirt that was almost the same color as my dress. It was open at the neck with no tie. He reeked of money and had a slight drawl that said, *I'm local*. Edward had wavy dark hair that was gelled so that it wouldn't dare go out of place.

DeLouise sounded familiar, and I realized he was part of the family hosting the event. DeLouise Gin was famous in the South, along with their line of cocktail and mocktail mixes.

"Chloe Jackson. I work at the Sea Glass."

"From what I understand you're part owner."

"Chloe, you made it." Vivi came up beside me. "And you've met Edward."

"Yes."

"I've heard a lot about you, Chloe," Edward said.

That surprised me. I glanced at Vivi and she was looking wide-eyed at Edward and gave a little shake of her head. What was that about?

"Your name has been on the news a time or two since you moved here," Edward added smoothly.

"Look at you two," Vivi said, gesturing toward our clothes. "You match."

"We do," Edward said. "Maybe a match made in heaven." Edward winked at me to show he was kidding.

I laughed, but my brain was doing some heavy-duty calculating. That little shake of Vivi's head when Edward said he'd heard about me. Vivi introducing me to Garth, Dale, Clay, and now Edward. All single men. I kept my face neutral but looked over at Vivi. The jig was up. *You're trying to fix me up with someone even though you know I'm dating Rip.* But how would she know to bring Dale to the bar? I wasn't supposed to be there that night. *Aha!* Any of us could check the security cameras from our phones. I rarely did, but that didn't mean Vivi didn't.

"Can I get you ladies a sample of our latest gin?" Edward asked.

"You go ahead with Chloe." She waved to someone across the room. "I have someone I need to speak to." She scuttled off like she was on a mission. And that mission was to leave me alone with Edward.

CHAPTER 35

That sealed the deal. I stared after her.

"Gin?" Edward asked. He moved his arm out for me to take.

I took it to be polite. "Sure."

"Do you have a favorite gin?" Edward asked as we worked our way around the edge of the crowd. Occasionally someone would stop Edward and congratulate him.

I racked my brain for gin brands. Something classy. "Hendrick's."

"Ah, well, if that's your favorite you're in for a treat," Edward said.

We came to a table that had spotlights shining down on it. Slim shot glasses sparkled and the bottles' metallic, steel-colored labels shined.

Edward gestured with a sweeping motion toward the display. "This is Titanium, our newest product."

I looked suitably impressed. "How did you choose the name?"

"It's strong and light, just like titanium. It's infused with our proprietary blend of citrus and herbs and aged in cabernet sauvignon barrels." Edward snagged two shot glasses and stuck them in his back pocket. He grabbed a bottle of Titanium and then my hand. "Let's find somewhere quiet so you can experience this fully."

And suddenly I was in the middle of the movie *Sabrina*. In the scene where the younger brother whisks Sabrina off and the older brother comes along to save her. The poor younger brother has champagne flutes in his back pocket, forgets, and sits on them.

"Do you have an older brother?" I asked as I followed Edward out onto a back deck that overlooked Destin Harbor.

Edward paused. "I do. Why?"

"No reason. Just making conversation."

"He runs a lot of the business end of things and is a ginnoisseur."

"A connoisseur of gin?" I asked.

"Yes. Everyone in my family is."

"That makes sense."

It was cool out here. Edward took off his suit jacket and insisted I put it on. After one weak protest I took it. The jacket smelled of juniper, citrus, and herbs. Maybe they made not only gin but aftershaves too.

Edward took the shot glasses from his pocket with a flourish, opened the bottle, and poured two shots. He handed me one. "A great gin is like a beautiful woman. Strong, mysterious, and intriguing."

I managed not to roll my eyes. I wondered how many

times he'd used that line before. It was smoother than this gin would be. Where was that older brother who was supposed to come save me? Sigh. This wasn't a movie and I'd have to save myself.

He raised his shot glass. "To you, Chloe."

I touched his shot glass lightly and braced myself to drink it—straight alcohol wasn't my favorite thing to drink. I guess holding my nose wouldn't be best. I tossed the shot back and it burned down my throat to my stomach. A warm glow expanded from there. I closed my eyes so they wouldn't water and gave myself a little shake. Whoo. Maybe I should have eaten when my brothers did.

I reopened my eyes. Edward was looking down at me with a slight grin on his face. His shot glass was still full.

"You didn't drink yours," I said when I could speak without wheezing. I never did like taking shots. When my friends did I always sipped mine.

"Gin is meant to be sipped, Chloe."

Well, I felt stupid. "Then why's it in a shot glass?"

"So we don't have to give as much away."

I laughed. "Excellent business strategy."

He grinned. "How did it taste?"

I decided to be honest. "I just felt it burn down my throat and hit my stomach. It had a nice afterglow, but not much flavor." I hoped their new brand wasn't a bust after all this hoopla. They had to shell out a lot for this party.

Edward took my shot glass from me and refilled it. "Try it again, but this time sip it."

Maybe shooting it would be preferable. But I did as told for once. Traces of citrus and herb lingered on my tongue. I liked it.

"What did you think?"

I took another sip. "It's like a handsome man. Delicious and gets bruised easily."

Edward looked shocked for a minute and then laughed. "You are a delight."

We looked out over the harbor and finished our gin.

"Vivi set you up with me, right?" A little bit of gin and I'd lost my filter. Maybe this was another reason I avoided hard liquor.

"You need no setting up." He was as smooth as the oil slicks boats left on the harbor's water. "Trust me, I've been set up before—beauties, overbites, smart women."

"You didn't answer my question."

"Vivi asked me to say hello. She said you were new in town and might be lonely."

I shook my head. "Consider yourself freed from any obligations."

"Oh, I'm a very willing participant."

A man stuck his head out the back door. "Edward, come on, it's time." He noticed me. "Always out in the dark with some pretty bimbo." He shook his head and went back in.

"They're almost never bimbos," Edward said. Edward poured two more shots.

I laughed. At least he didn't deny he was a player. "Here's your jacket back. Thanks for the gin tasting. It's a winner." I headed back to the party.

"Can I call you, Chloe?" Edward was right behind me when I turned.

"No. But thank you. I'm seeing someone." *And Vivi knows it.*

He pressed an engraved business card into my hand. "If you change your mind."

* * *

Once we were back inside Edward headed toward the front of the room and I headed toward the back. Those two shots of gin were swirling in my stomach like a whirling dervish. I wanted to find Vivi.

After looking around I spotted her on the far side of the room with a group of people I didn't know. I hung back a little because I couldn't confront her with all those people around. In the front of the room someone had a microphone and was effusing over Titanium. There were rounds of applause and then the talking points were over.

Waiters started circulating the room with shot glasses full of gin and trays of canapés. Thank heavens. I snagged a bacon-wrapped scallop, a mini egg roll, and a tiny cup of seafood chowder. Maybe confronting Vivi tonight wasn't a good idea. Even though I wasn't happy with her shenanigans, this wasn't the time or place to say anything.

After I finished eating I roamed around sipping my third shot of gin. That's when it hit me. I smiled. Revenge would be sweet.

CHAPTER 36

I found Edward. "I need your help with something."
He bowed with a flourish. "At your service, madame."

I explained what I wanted to do.

He grinned. "I'm going to be in trouble with Vivi."

I batted my eyelashes at him—shades of Suni batting hers at Joaquín—and walked my fingers up his chest. "But not with me."

"Don't toy with me, woman. You're in a relationship."

"You'll do it?"

"Yes."

I snagged another shot glass full of Titanium. I didn't exactly sip it, but I didn't down it either. It was more of a gulp. Then I practically skipped over to Vivi.

"Are you having a good evening?" Vivi asked.

"The best," I said with a happy sigh.

She smiled. "I'm glad."

Vivi introduced me to the people she was with—a wine wholesaler, a couple who owned a chain of local liquor stores, a vintner, and the woman we bought all our glassware from. I greeted each of them enthusiastically, saying things like "delighted" and "charmed." I pumped their hands and kissed their cheeks, all the while trying to maintain a giddy look on my face. The people all looked taken aback. I probably needed to tone it down. There was a fine line between giddy and wild.

Vivi was craning her neck. Perhaps looking for Edward.

"Vivi," I said in a low voice, "who are you looking for? You're starting to look like one of those people at a conference who is always looking for someone better to talk to."

"No one in particular. I was just looking for other people you should definitely meet."

I looked at the group. "Do you mind if I borrow Vivi for a moment?"

They all murmured a "no" and, frankly, I think they looked relieved to get away from me.

I took Vivi's arm and drew her a few steps away.

"Are you okay, Chloe?" Vivi asked. "Did something not agree with you? I know you don't drink spirits often."

"I'm fine. Wonderful. You know, I've never believed in love at first sight before. Oh, my parents always said that they knew the moment they set eyes on each other in eighth grade that they were meant to be together. I thought it was hogwash." My parents didn't meet until they went to the same community college after high school.

"Love?" Vivi said. She started shaking her head no. "I

have to agree with your first assessment, Chloe. Love takes time. Look at Wade and me."

Vivi had never admitted to being in love with Wade before. It shocked me so much I almost forgot what I was supposed to be doing.

"But Edward . . ." I sighed happily and looked off into the distance. "He's something." A player, but that was something.

Vivi drew her eyebrows together. "Chloe, Edward isn't marriage material. He has a reputation as a playboy."

Edward walked up just then. He slung his arm around my shoulders and pulled me to him. "That all ends tonight, doesn't it, babe?"

He laid a big old kiss on me. Scoundrel. It wasn't like I could pull away. It would blow my whole story. And he was one heck of a kisser.

"Could I take a few days off, Vivi? Starting tomorrow?"

"Well, I—I guess so."

"We're going to Vegas!" I said.

"Vegas?" Vivi sounded horrified. "To gamble? Biloxi is nice. It's closer."

"Life's a gamble, Vivi," Edward said. "And we're ready to take one." He squeezed me to him. "Tonight has been life changing. Earlier when I said we were a match made in heaven, it was just a cheesy line. Who knew it would come true?" We stood there beaming, first at each other and then at Vivi.

"Vivi, please wish us well." I grabbed her hands and squeezed them. "We have you to thank."

Vivi jerked her hands back and put them on her hips. She narrowed her eyes. "Okay. I get it."

I did wide eyes at her. "Whatever are you talking about, Vivi?" I said it with a fake Southern accent. If I got anymore Southern-sounding, I'd be clasping my hands to my chest and declaring things. "True love comes in all forms. Right, Edward?" Then I laughed. I couldn't help it. I couldn't keep up the pretense any longer.

"I get it. I was interfering in your life, Chloe," Vivi said.

I turned to Edward. "Thank you for helping me out."

"Anytime. Don't lose my business card." He looked at Vivi. "I'm a little hurt you don't think I'm marriage material."

Vivi gave him a light swat on the arm. "You know you're not. You will be someday, but not now."

Edward looked at me. "Marriage doesn't sound so bad." Then he winked and walked off. Seconds later he had his arm draped around a blonde in a sparkly, silver mini dress.

I shook my head. "He's something."

"And I deserved that."

"Yep," I said. "Let me live my life, Vivi." I knew she worried. Her daughter had had a terrible marriage and I'm not sure Vivi's was any better. Southern men were known for their charm, but in a lot of them it was a thin veneer hiding layers of ugly. "You're judging Rip not on who he is but on his family."

"And you haven't been here long enough to know what his family is like."

"I'm taking things slow, Vivi. Trust me, I'm the last person who wants to rush into something." The more I found out about Perry, the more I doubted myself.

"I'm sorry," Vivi said. "It was foolish. Please forgive me."

"Of course. I know you did it from a good place in your heart."

"And if you and Rip break up, I know a lot of eligible men." Vivi smiled at me and sashayed off.

I shook my head and laughed. You just had to love a strong, Southern woman.

At nine Vivi, Kenny, Randy, and I decided to swing by the Sea Glass to have a nightcap before we headed home. Joaquín, Michael, and Wade met us there. Wade had brought leftovers and everyone dug in. We'd been there about fifteen minutes when a knock on the back door sounded. I jumped up, eager to escape the ongoing conversation featuring me and my activities. "I'll get it."

I hustled back and opened the door. Deputy Biffle was standing there.

"Do you want to come in?" I asked. "We're having a drink. There's plenty." Duh. Of course there was plenty. This was a bar. Deputy Biffle made me nervous.

"No. I'd like you to step out."

I was mystified but did as he asked. I made sure the door was unlocked, stepped out, and closed it behind me. The sky was cloudless, the wind was cool, and I shivered. But I wasn't sure it was about the air temperature. More like I had a premonition I wasn't going to like what came next. I hoped Rip was okay.

"What do you need?" I asked.

"Lori Clemens is missing."

CHAPTER 37

I shook my head, as if I could clear the ringing that started in my ears. Lori missing? "I'm sorry to hear that, but what does it have to do with me?"

"We know you spent some time with her yesterday. Other than her husband, you were probably one of the last people to see her. A neighbor saw you enter Lori's house at approximately nine thirty and exit about fifteen minutes later. Does that sound about right?"

My thoughts were zooming ahead. "Is Olivia all right?" I couldn't imagine Lori abandoning her baby.

"Yes, the baby's fine. Lori's husband came home for dinner around six. The baby was asleep in her crib, but Lori was nowhere to be seen."

"That's scary. I can't imagine Lori abandoning Olivia."

"You didn't answer my question about when you entered and left Olivia's house yesterday."

"Yes. That timing is accurate. Have you checked out

where Noah's been? He's on my list of suspects." Noah, who had been so nervous this afternoon.

"You have a list of suspects?" He shook his head.

Put that way it sounded ridiculous. "I've been thinking about it. I know it wasn't Rip." Deputy Biffle was going to like this next bit even less. "I saw Noah this afternoon."

I saw a slight tightening of Biffle's mouth.

"Where?"

"He showed my brother and me a house in Destin. Why would he be working if his wife is missing?" Something wasn't adding up here. Shouldn't he have been out looking for Lori or watching Olivia?

"Your brother is moving here?"

Why prolong the pain? I might as well get this over with. If I didn't tell him Noah probably would. "No." Then I explained what we'd been up to. If Deputy Biffle's jaw got any tighter he was going to crack a tooth. "Noah was very on edge the whole time." Of course if my loved one was missing I'd be on edge too. But I'd be out looking for them, not trying to sell a house. "I looked through his phone while we were there and there were calls between Perry and Noah for the three weeks prior to Perry's arrival here."

"Did you have permission to go through his phone?"

"Sort of?" I explained how I happened to have Noah's phone.

Deputy Biffle shook his head.

"But you can get a search warrant to go through it, right?" I asked.

"Can you think of anywhere Lori might have gone?"

I guessed he wasn't going to answer my question.

"Since Noah came to us we've checked with her friends and family. Garth took us to their cabin in case she went out there to get away, but there was no sign of her. Savannah hasn't seen her for a couple of days either."

I hoped my conversation with Lori hadn't created some kind of mental crisis for her. But frankly, this wasn't looking good for Noah. I'm so glad I took Kenny with me when I went to see the house. "Why are you just asking me all of this now instead of yesterday?"

"We only found out a few hours ago that Lori was missing."

"Really?" That seemed odd.

"According to Noah, Lori would go for walks around the neighborhood sometimes if Olivia was asleep. Her smart watch would notify her if Olivia woke up and she could be back home in minutes."

Okay, I could get doing that.

"He assumed she was out for a walk at first. Then he got a text saying she was having a girl's night with a friend and would probably spend the night. So he didn't realize for hours that Lori was missing."

"In other words, he had hours to get rid of Lori and cover his tracks," I said.

The back door of the Sea Glass opened just then and Randy stuck out his head. "Everything okay, Chloe?" He spotted Deputy Biffle, took in the uniform, and stepped out.

Biffle put out a hand. "I need you to go back inside, sir."

Randy didn't move. "That's not going to happen."

Biffle's mouth barely twitched, but I could tell what was coming next wasn't going to be good.

"It's okay, Randy. I'm fine." I hoped I was. "Deputy Biffle's a friend and just wants to run something by me."

Biffle's eyes moved a fraction to the right at the friend comment, which for him was a huge eye roll.

Randy looked back and forth between us before nodding. "Okay. You holler if you need anything."

"I will."

Deputy Biffle didn't say anything until Randy closed the door with a firm click. "Is Vivi in there?"

"She is," I said.

"Let's go sit in my car because as soon as Vivi finds out I'm out here, she's going to show up threatening to call the sheriff and the governor."

"Front seat or back?"

"What?"

"I want to know where I'll be sitting, because if it's the back, I'm calling a lawyer right now."

Deputy Biffle sighed. "Front. Now come on."

Deputy Biffle turned and walked to his patrol car. I trotted after him, still leery, but he opened the front passenger door for me and I climbed in.

The fake leather upholstery was cold. The car smelled of sweat and oil. Some kind of rifle was between the seats, as was a lot of computer equipment. Once Deputy Biffle was in I turned to him. "Lori was fine when I left." At least she was fine physically. I knew our conversation had upset her.

He gave a slight nod as his answer. "Have you seen her since?"

"No. Did she go to the park this morning? She usually meets up with a group of parents around nine."

"No. We've checked with that group already."

"I've had someone with me all day and can account for every minute." Did he believe me? Did he think I'd conked her on the head and then dragged her out the back door? "Was her house okay? Were there signs of a struggle?" I asked.

Deputy Biffle opened his mouth and closed it again. It was like I could see his thoughts pinging around in his brain. I could picture him saying, *I'm the one that will do the question asking around here.*

"There weren't any signs of a struggle or forced entry."

It surprised me that he answered my question.

"Did she seem upset about anything?" Deputy Biffle asked.

Absolutely. Did I want to tell him that, though? I remained silent for a couple of moments. Lori was missing. If there was anything I could do to help find her, I had to, no matter how torn I was. I poured out my conversation with her—that Perry was Olivia's father.

His eyes widened. I think I'd finally shocked him.

"Why didn't you call me about this sooner?"

"I didn't know what the right thing to do was in this situation."

"The right thing to do is to always pass information on to law enforcement like you've been doing." Deputy Biffle's normally calm voice had a hard edge to it.

"Have you checked into Irma Franklin's whereabouts?" Maybe Irma did something to Lori to get her hands on Olivia. But why not take Olivia too?

"She's home. We confirmed it. Mrs. Franklin explained what happened the day she came down here. She did talk to Perry, but only for an hour or so. And before you ask, we have security camera footage of her coming and going from the airport. Mrs. Franklin couldn't have killed Perry so you can cross her off your suspect list." He used air quotes when he said "suspect."

Ouch. That hurt, but it was good information to have.

A knock on the window made me jump. It was Vivi.

"Dan, roll down your window," she said. "Chloe, get out and don't say anything else."

He ignored her. "You can go, but let me know if you find out anything else."

Not many people were brave or foolish enough to ignore Vivi Slidell.

"And Chloe, this is confidential for now."

"Got it." I opened my door and slipped out, looking at Vivi over the top of the car. She looked worried.

Vivi wasn't happy when we sat back down at the table. I'd been vague about my conversation with Deputy Biffle. I didn't want to lie to her, but I also didn't want to break Deputy Biffle's confidence and have it get back to him. At least now, unlike last summer, I knew Vivi's anger was concern for me. I'd told her I wasn't in any trouble. It was the best I could do.

The rest of the evening had been subdued. My brothers tried to bring the mood back around with a few of our silly childhood stories. People laughed, but mostly they shot worried glances at me. My brothers and I were back home by ten thirty. On the drive home I formulated what I would do next. I kept thinking about who would take Lori and why. I yawned a few times as we walked to the front door and went inside.

"I'm exhausted," I said as I locked the front door. I didn't set the alarm, but fortunately they were so worked up they didn't notice.

"It's been a day," Randy said.

I yawned. "It's been a *long* day." That was absolutely true. "I'm going to go to bed." That was a big fat lie. I stood on my tippy-toes and kissed them both on the cheek.

"I'll see you in the morning." Wow, this was like a game of two truths and a lie. But they bought the whole routine. At least I hoped they did. I had things I needed to do that I couldn't with my brothers tagging along.

I went in my room. After I heard the TV go on I quietly locked the door. If they heard the lock click, they'd be suspicious. My family had never been one of door lockers inside the house except for the bathroom of course. I changed into black leggings and a black sweater. I wanted to look nice enough to be in a bar. I added chunky boots. I looked longingly at the sliding glass door. It would be so much easier to get out of the house that way. But my brothers might hear the slider open or see me cross the porch to go out the door.

Instead, I opened my bedroom window. This was an old house so it was higher than most windows now. Fortunately it didn't stick. I pushed out the screen and managed to get it inside without making too much noise. I dragged over a chair from the corner of my room and stood on it. I swung one leg over the sill so I was straddling it. I ducked my head and then I awkwardly shifted around—sometimes being short did have its advantages—and managed to drop to the ground, landing on my feet.

A jolt went from the soles of my feet to the top of my head, but I hadn't done any serious damage. Thankfully, instead of the hard-packed frozen ground I would have faced this time of year in Chicago, I'd landed in soft white sand. I grinned. I hadn't climbed out a window since my junior year of high school when I was sneaking out for a night of partying with my boyfriend.

The beauty of driving the old Volkswagen was that I could pop it out of gear and roll it down the drive until I was far enough from the house that it was safe to start it without it being heard.

CHAPTER 38

I wanted to check up on Kellye and Suni. While I still had my suspicions about both of them when it came to who killed Perry, it didn't seem like they'd be involved with Lori's disappearance. And I was certain whoever killed Perry also had Lori. Maybe if I showed them pictures of Noah, Savannah, and Garth, it might help find Lori.

Those three had the biggest stake in Perry being Olivia's father. Although I still couldn't understand why someone would kill him. As far as I knew, Garth didn't know that Perry was Olivia's father. But what if he did know? How far would he be willing to go to keep that story quiet? Or Noah, for that matter.

Kellye might have run into them or Suni might have seen them in the town circle the day she followed Perry there. It came to me after I'd left Deputy Biffle. I'd been vacillating ever since whether I should tell him or keep my mouth shut until I talked to Suni and Kellye. Then I'd go right to him.

As far as I could figure, it would be more likely that Suni had seen pictures of Perry as a baby than Kellye because they dated in high school and she would have spent more time with him. Heck, she probably knew his whole family and had been to their house. However, if either Suni or Kellye had run into Lori and Olivia somewhere, they might have figured out, just as I had, that Perry was the father of Lori's baby. Could one of them have gone into a jealous rage, killed Perry, and then waited for the right moment to hurt Lori? My answer to that wasn't a no.

But why wait until five days after they killed Perry? I went over what I knew about Lori. The day I'd met Garth at Grounds For, he had said Lori had a very busy schedule. He'd complained he almost had to make an appointment to spend time with her. Finding Lori alone might not have been easy. Combine that with the fact that the convention ended tomorrow, which meant Suni would be leaving town, and Kellye could leave for Venice at any time, and I had to go tonight.

I was a little nervous about approaching them both on my own, but it would be worse if one of my brothers was tagging along. For that matter, I didn't know if they'd talk to me at all.

I drove to the house where Kellye was staying. It only took a few minutes to get there. The lights were off and there wasn't a car parked outside. "It doesn't look like anyone's home. Maybe they've already taken off for Venice already." Great, I was talking to myself now. I needed a sidekick. Even Winnie-the-Pooh had Piglet.

I got out and trotted up to the door. There wasn't a doorbell, so I knocked. Waited. Knocked again. I put my ear to the door but didn't hear anything. I waited a couple of seconds longer. I moved to the large picture window and cupped my hands against it. As far as I could tell, the house was empty.

I flipped on the flashlight on my cell phone and went around to the side of the house. It was dark and the ground was covered with pine needles. Their aroma shot up with every step I took. The windows on the side of the house were curtained and I couldn't see in.

There was a back door with a large glass window on the top half. I peered in. It was the kitchen. No one was in it, and everything looked neat and put away. That could mean that they'd left or that they were neat freaks. Or could it mean something more sinister? That they had Lori for some reason? I shook my head. Now I was really grasping at straws.

I trotted back to the car and headed to the Sandpiper in Destin. I drove north to highway 98 and headed west. Lots of cars were out and I hit almost every single red light. I wondered when the news that Lori was missing would go public.

I listened to the whump of the tires and the sounds of traffic as I entered Destin. The road was lined with strip malls, a huge outlet mall, restaurants, mom-and-pop shops, and antique stores. If you wanted ice cream or you wanted to work out, highway 98 in Destin had it all.

I pulled into the parking lot of the Sandpiper and found a space near a light. When at night, park by a light:

the advice my mother had given me when I first learned to drive. Unfortunately, it was one of those flickering lights that got on my already short and shredded nerves.

I got out of the car and stood by the trunk. I dialed Suni, identified myself, and asked her to come out here. It sounded like she was in the bar again with all the background noise of voices. I couldn't talk to her in her room or in the bar. I didn't want to see her husband and I couldn't very well have a quiet conversation with her in the bar. Especially a conversation that might make her angry. Besides, cars and people were coming and going out here so it was perfectly safe. Suni resisted at first, but finally agreed to meet me out here. I paced back and forth behind the car while I waited. *Breathe*, I told myself. *Look at the stars. All will be right in the world.*

Finally I heard the lobby doors swoosh open and saw Suni come out. I waved and she headed over to me. She was in a sparkly red cocktail dress. A halter with a plunging V-neck. Her killer heels were silver stilettos, tall and spiky. She strutted over. I'd break an ankle in those things.

"Thanks for coming out," I said.

"What is so effing important that I have to miss the last night at the bar? It's always the most fun." Her eyes swept over me. "We could have some fun if you came back in with me."

I repressed a shudder. I didn't want to dwell on what her idea of fun might be. "Listen, I need you to look at some pictures from the day Perry got in the fight with Rip. To see if you recognize any of the people from the park that day."

I started to hand her my phone, but Suni looked over my shoulder.

"I know you," she said. "You were in the park recording the fight the day Perry punched Rip."

I heard a zing and Suni slumped over. I wheeled around. Garth stood there with a taser in his hand. Now I was the one with the wide eyes. I watched as he pulled out another stun gun and pointed it at me. I turned to run as he pressed the trigger.

CHAPTER 39

When I opened my eyes I realized I was in the back seat of a moving car. My hands were duct-taped. My muscles felt like cranberry sauce and I tried to remember how I ended up here. Garth. I kept still, trying to figure out what to do. Never go to a secondary location: another thing my mom had always said when I was a teenager. Sorry, Mom. I didn't have a choice.

"What the hell, Garth?" It wasn't what I'd meant to do, but I blurted it out as I struggled to sit up. "Where's Suni?" I hoped she was still alive.

"In the trunk. Be grateful you aren't."

"Oh, I'm so grateful." Probably this wasn't the time to be sassy, but my brain and mouth weren't cooperating. We were on a small, dark, paved road. No houses, some fields, and patches of trees. I tried to make sense of what had happened.

Suni recognized Garth from the park. But why take me

too? Possibly I'd become a loose end because I saw him tase Suni. Wait. The other day when I'd walked off with Lori. Had he seen me with her?

"You saw me with Lori yesterday."

"I did."

"Then you scheduled some 'uncle time' with Olivia and kidnapped your own sister."

"No. I put her somewhere safe."

"Were you afraid someone was going to hurt her?" If so, why tase me?

"People are after my family. Of course I'm going to protect them."

"Did she go with you willingly?" There's no way she'd leave Olivia alone.

"More or less."

"You stunned her too."

Garth didn't answer. Garth must have killed Perry and now he was trying to clean up whoever might know. It was a fine time to be right. Why didn't I realize it when I was with Deputy Biffle sitting in the patrol car? I lunged for the door when we got to the next patch of trees, planning to roll out and try to hide until I could free myself of the duct tape and run. The door wouldn't open.

"Child locks," Garth said. "They're on the windows too."

Garth had made the mistake of duct-taping my hands in front of me. All I had to do was loop my arms around his throat and choke him. I pushed myself up into a sitting position.

"Don't get any wild ideas that you can hurt me. The stun gun is right here next to me and if you don't cooperate, no one will ever find Lori."

Lori. She must be so scared and frantic about Olivia.

And Suni—was she still passed out in the back or was it worse than that? I'd led Garth right to her.

"Why Lori?" I could make some sense of going after me or Suni. Then a bigger thought entered my muddled brain. "Why Perry?"

"He wanted to claim Olivia as his own. Thought you two were going to help raise her. As if."

That would never have happened. Perry must have seen pictures of Olivia somewhere. He'd have known he was her father right away too. "I had no idea he was thinking anything along those lines."

"I figured that out during our conversations at Vivi's party."

"A well-loved baby wouldn't be the worst thing in the world. Would it?"

"Lori brought shame to our family. I can't imagine anything worse than a public custody battle over Olivia. Either would kill my mother."

Screw his mother. What about Perry's mother? "Is Savannah in on this? She was at the park the day Perry and Rip fought."

"No. She was at Grounds For picking up coffee and pastries for some committee meeting she had. It almost ruined my whole plan."

"Why take me? Or Suni for that matter?"

"I saw the look you gave Olivia in Grounds For. You knew something was up and you just kept digging. Seeing you with Lori made me take action. It's why I followed you tonight."

Deranged. Out-of-his-mind. When had he started following me? There were no headlights behind me when I left my driveway, or Kellye's for that matter. Had I led him right to her? Would he somehow perceive her as a threat too? I had to figure out a way to calm him down. Garth turned onto a tree-lined, rutted dirt road. I gripped the bar above the door and held on so I didn't skitter across the seat or slam my head into something.

"You might as well tell me what happened with Rip and Perry in the park. How you set that up." If he told me, I'd know he didn't plan for me to ever say anything to anyone again.

"I told Perry that Rip was going to ruin his plan for the two of you to get back together."

"How did you even know about Rip and me?"

He looked in the rearview mirror for a moment. "It's a small town, Chloe. It was easy to find out."

"You knew about me; knew I was seeing Rip before we ever met at Vivi's party?" Even though I asked the question I already knew the answer. He'd played me and I'd bought the whole thing.

"Yes."

"And you just happened to be in the park to film the whole confrontation?"

He snorted. "Of course not. I also let Perry know where he could find Rip. People are creatures of habit. They follow the same routine. Lori goes to the park every morning. Then she takes Olivia home for a nap. Rip goes and gets a coffee and sits in the park on his break most mornings. What I didn't plan on was for that piece of filth in the trunk following Perry out there. She saw me filming. I thought I played it off as if I was a tourist filming lots of things. That was a mistake."

It burned me that he'd called Suni a piece of filth. "Were you the one who tried to break into my house?"

"Yes."

His answering these questions didn't bode well for me. "Why?"

"I was worried you were going to be a problem, and I was right."

Banging started in the trunk. Suni was still alive and had come to.

Seconds later I heard a clunk. I looked over my shoulder and saw the trunk was up. Garth slammed on the brakes and swore. Newer cars like this one had releases in the trunk and Garth hadn't disabled it. He slammed out of the car cursing up a storm. As soon as he was out of sight, I lunged over the seats into the front. Part of me wanted to drive off, part of me wanted to help Suni. The car had a button to call for help in an emergency. I pushed it, hoping it was connected, then worried some voice would come booming out.

I scooped up the taser and slipped out the driver's side door. Instead of heading to the back of the car, I scuttled bent-kneed to the front. Sounds of tussling and Garth's continued swearing covered my movement.

I scurried to the trees and slipped behind one. Thank heavens I'd worn black. I pictured myself as a ninja or Navy SEAL instead of the literal shaking-in-my-boots woman I was. I used a move I'd seen in a video, putting my hands behind my head and then snapping them forward. It broke the duct tape around my wrists. I couldn't believe it worked.

I peered around the tree. Suni was on the ground. She must have somehow managed to launch herself out of the trunk when she got it open. Garth was trying to drag her back to the car. She was twisting and turning. Fighting every inch of the way.

Garth's back was to the open trunk. One of her stilettos jammed into Garth's knee and he howled. I rushed out, pushed the button on the taser, and managed to hit him. He crumpled half in, half out of the trunk. I shoved him the rest of the way in and slammed the trunk closed. It wouldn't keep him for long because he probably knew where the trunk release was, but hopefully for long enough.

I rushed back to Suni and undid her duct tape. She lay there for a few seconds, but I pulled her up. "Get in," I shouted, pushing her toward the car.

She snapped to and dived in, slamming the door. I shoved the car into Drive and headed forward. Lori had to be out here somewhere. A calm voice was saying they'd located the car and help was on the way. It then asked, "What's your emergency?"

"We were freaking kidnapped," Suni yelled.

"Are you safe?" the voice asked.

"For the moment. I'm Chloe Jackson, but someone else who's been kidnapped is out here someplace. Her name is Lori Clemens. We're trying to find her," I said. "We were taken by a man named Garth Havers."

Suni looked at me. "Are you nuts? That man could pop out of the trunk at any moment."

"Probably, but we can't leave her out here. There's no telling what kind of shape she's in or what Garth would do to her."

"Ma'am, you need to get to safety," the voice said, taking Suni's side.

"You need to get us some help," I snapped back. I gunned the car forward. The rutted road tossed us around, I couldn't imagine what it was doing to Garth, but I hoped it was painful. "Can you tell me what's ahead?" I asked the voice.

"It looks like the road dead-ends a half mile ahead of you."

I jerked the wheel, missing a deep pothole. Blowing a tire out here could be deadly, not because of a potential accident but because of Garth. "How long before help arrives?"

"There's a sheriff's car about twenty minutes out and a state trooper not far behind him. There are multiple vehicles descending on your location."

The rutted road would slow them down. "Make sure there's an ambulance."

"Are you injured?"

"No, but someone might be."

Suni looked over at me.

"We don't know how Lori is or what will happen with Garth if he gets out."

"We'll just blast him again with the taser."

"Its low battery light is on, we might be out of luck. Look to see if there's any kind of charger for it." Did Tasers have chargers like cell phones? If not, our only weapon was this car. My driver's ed teacher used to tell us that cars were three-thousand-pound weapons. The idea of running someone over scared the bejesus out of me, but if it came to that, I'd run Garth over in a heartbeat.

Suni yanked open the glove box and started tossing stuff out and into the back seat. "No charger, but there's this." She held up a matte black gun.

I knew how to shoot. Perry had had a gun in his apartment and insisted I know how to use it. But I'd never shot anything other than a target at the gun range. When my hand was steady I wasn't a bad shot, but my hands were anything but steady. I noticed Suni's hands were shaking too.

"Put it down," I said. That's all we needed was for her to accidently shoot one of us. "Do you know how to use it?"

She lay the gun on the seat between us. "I know the basics."

"Hopefully they won't come into play. When we get there you cover the trunk and I'll search for Lori."

"Who is Lori? And that guy back there?" Suni asked.

"There's no time to explain."

"I saw him in the park filming the day I followed Perry. But there were a lot of people recording the fight. If only I'd mentioned him to someone sooner." Her voice cracked. "If I'd stayed with Perry, he might be alive."

Or you might be dead too. It was the second time she'd said this, and while she might not be my favorite person, I didn't want her to carry that kind of guilt around for the rest of her life. "You didn't do anything wrong. Garth did."

The road ended. There was an open space where the trees had been chopped away. A beautiful log cabin sat thirty feet in front of us. No lights were on. No cars were around. Lori must be in there.

CHAPTER 40

I left the headlights on as we tumbled out of the car. Suni grabbed the gun and headed to the back as I ran toward the house.

I heard Suni mutter something that sounded like "Make my day, punk," apparently channeling her inner Dirty Harry from the Clint Eastwood movies. How many times had my brothers said that to me? It was dark out here and very quiet. The better to hear you with, said the wolf. Only I wasn't Little Red Riding Hood. I was little pale scaredy hood. The cabin had a wide, deep porch. I tried the door. It was locked and solid, nothing I could kick through with a boot or shove open with a shoulder.

Why did someone even lock up out here? Half the residents of Emerald Cove left their doors unlocked. I went to the nearest window. Locked. So were the other two in the front of the house. I went around the side of the house. No luck. I edged my way around back. It was dark. The kind of darkness I was afraid of when I'd first moved here, so used to city lights. I'd come to like it, but not tonight.

Stars twinkled above, but not enough to light my way. I kept one hand on the side of the house, hoping my eyes would adjust to the dark. A gust of wind blew. Pine trees whispered, sounding like warnings. I ignored them or tried to. I tripped on something and pitched forward. Instead of falling to the ground, I landed on what I finally figured out was a short flight of stairs. I climbed them and ended up on a wide deck. I held the rail, following it until I hit the side of the house again.

I moved along the outside wall until I felt glass, not wood, underneath my fingers. I could see the glow of a light from a night-light and realized I was standing in front of sliding glass doors. I found the handle, tugged, and it moved a little. I jiggled it up and down, heard the pop of a release, and slid the door open.

Night-lights glowed here and there, along with power cords. It was enough to see that I was in a family room with a kitchen to the left and a hall to the right. Lori was most likely in a bedroom. Fortunately, because of the high-water tables in Florida, I didn't have to worry about her being locked in a creepy basement.

I ducked my head in doors. The first two were bedrooms. I didn't want to flip lights on in case Garth had overpowered Suni. Lights would give away my location.

"Lori?" Nothing. The next room was a bathroom. Then a closed door. I yanked it open. Linen closet. After that the last door. Another bedroom. I spotted a figure on the bed.

"Lori?" I called softly.

A whimper, some thrashing. Thanks heavens. I ran in, loosened the ties that bound her to the headboard, ripped duct tape from her mouth, and helped her sit up.

"Olivia." Lori grabbed my arms, sounding frantic.

"She's fine and with Noah."

Lori let out a small sob.

"Can you walk? We have to go." I was still worried about Garth.

"Yes." Lori's voice was hoarse.

We went out the back, started around the side of the house. A scream and a thunk sounded. It was Suni who had screamed. I grabbed Lori's hand and dragged her into the woods. I saw Garth cut across the headlights and head to the front door. He dug in his pocket, pulled out keys, and went inside. We worked our way toward the front of the house, staying in the woods.

"Stay put," I said. She sat down with her back to a boulder. "Help will be here soon."

I ran over to Suni. She was moaning and holding her head, but alive.

"He's got the gun," Suni said.

I checked the car's ignition. Garth had taken the keys. I helped her up, glancing at the house. Lights were flaring on inside. I put her arm over my shoulder and we staggered back into the woods.

I settled Suni with Lori and crept back to the edge of the tree line.

Garth was back out on the porch. "I know you're out there and I'm coming for you." He walked into the woods behind the house.

Why wasn't help here? They should have been by now. Did Garth somehow convince the emergency people that everything was okay? Maybe help wasn't coming and we were on our own. A twig snapped behind me. I started to turn, but a hand clamped over my mouth and jerked me back.

"It's me. Biffle." His voice low.

My knees sagged a little.

"Keep quiet. There's a team here. Is there more than one man out there?"

I shook my head no.

"Okay, I'm going to hand you off to someone. This will be over soon." He unclamped his hand from my mouth.

"Lori and Suni are back there. About twenty yards away, near a boulder. Garth went into the woods behind the house."

Deputy Biffle spoke quietly into a shoulder mic, relaying what I'd just told him. "We'll get them. Go with him."

A man stood a yard away. He came over and led me away from the cabin. I started shaking so hard, I kept stumbling along behind him. We cut back toward the road and a bunch of cop cars were there along with an ambulance. The man tucked me into the front of one of the cars. The heater was blasting.

I turned to him before he shut the door. "I'm worried about a woman named Kellye." I gave him the details of where she was staying and why I was concerned.

He gave me a brief nod and closed the door. Lori and Suni came out of the woods a few minutes later with another officer. She took them over to the ambulance.

I got out of the car and hurried over to them. We huddled together.

"Lori, Deputy Biffle told me Garth brought them out here and searched the cabin. Where were you?" I asked.

"He left me in an old shed on the property while they searched the house and then took me back to the cabin after they left."

That silenced all of us for a few minutes. We heard voices shouting and then word that they'd captured Garth. At last this night was over, except for the fact that I still had to face my brothers.

At three in the morning I was dropped off at my house. Lights were on, shadows moved beyond the windows. Great. I'd talked to Randy on the drive home, explaining that I'd gone out the window and gave him a general briefing of what else had transpired. Deputy Biffle told me that Kellye and her friend were safe and sound at the rental home. They planned on leaving in the morning.

As soon as I shut the door to the sheriff's car, my brothers were pounding down the front steps and yanking me into their arms. They waited until we got inside to start yelling at me.

"What were you thinking?" Randy sounded a lot like our father the one time he'd found me crawling back in a window.

Kenny was pacing back and forth. He alternated between throwing up his hands in the air and pinching his nose. "You could be dead or worse."

There wasn't much worse than dead, but I got what he was talking about. They went on like that for about ten minutes, until they wound down to "We love you," "You scared us," and "We're glad you're okay."

"Go get some sleep," Randy said.

"I put the screen back in your window and closed it," Kenny added.

I kissed them both on the cheek and thanked them. It was nice to have them here and I realized how much I'd miss them when they left.

* * *

I woke up Friday with my face pressed to the pillow, still dressed in what I'd worn the night before. At least I'd managed to get my boots off. During the night, or maybe it was this morning, I'd heard my brothers opening the door, checking on me, and softly closing it. It was a good thing I hadn't locked it because they probably would have broken it down just to make sure I was still here.

I sat up, and leaves fell out of my hair onto my pillow. I rolled over and grabbed my phone. It was one thirty in the afternoon. My phone was filled with text messages and voice mails, which I ignored. The one sock I still had on was halfway off. I ripped it off and tossed it on the floor, which was unusual for me because I was a throw-my-dirty-clothes-in-the-hamper kind of woman.

I crossed the room and opened the curtain that covered the sliding glass door. Light sparked off the soft waves of the Gulf. I leaned my head against the glass for a moment. The tides of my life had shifted once again. I could either fight them or relax into them.

After closing the curtain again I stripped off the rest of my clothes, leaving them on the floor too. Bending over to pick them up just seemed like too much work right now. My body hurt like I'd been in an Ironman competition. Voices murmured out in the living room. It sounded like more than just Randy and Kenny. I was hungry and wanted coffee but wasn't ready to face anyone yet. Maybe they'd go away if I took a long shower.

I stayed in until the water started to cool and my muscles started to relax. I brushed my teeth, finger combed my hair, and opened the door to my room wrapped in a towel. Rip sat on the edge of the bed, hands clasped.

CHAPTER 41

He looked up. Deep worry lines etched around his eyes, and I was sorry that I was probably the one who caused them.

He jumped up. "Is it all right that I'm in here?" He had on dark jeans and a long-sleeved, light blue T-shirt.

Thoughtful. "Yes." I adjusted the way I'd tucked in my towel around me.

He took two strides and gathered me to him. His T-shirt was soft, and I leaned on him. I liked leaning on him. It had been a long time since I'd leaned on anyone but myself. We just stood like that for a few moments. No recriminations. I finally pulled away. "It doesn't look like you've gotten much sleep."

"We had a big fire overnight. Then dispatch started to hear the calls about your situation. It was worrisome, but worse when I found out you were there."

"I'm okay."

"Thankfully."

"I'd better get dressed."

"Okay. I'll wait in the living room." He kissed the top of my head and left.

After I dressed I looked longingly at the window for a moment. Running away sounded like more fun than facing whoever was out there. I hoped it wasn't anyone official because I wasn't ready to answer more questions. But I would deal with it.

I yanked open the door and heads turned toward me. Vivi and Wade sat on the couch. Joaquín and Michael sat at the dining room table with Rip. Vivi and Rip coexisting in the same space without harsh words was a sight in itself. Randy and Kenny were in the kitchen cooking what smelled like sausages, bacon, eggs, and hash browns. A basket of Wade's cheesy biscuits was on the counter. The smell of coffee wafted across the room at me. I headed for it like it was a siren's song.

Kenny poured me a cup and pushed it across the counter. I took a big sip and closed my eyes. Heaven. I'd have liked to stay that way, but the sooner I dealt with everyone, the sooner they'd leave. I needed some time to process what had happened last night. What had happened to Perry. I took my cup over to the couch and everyone gathered round. Randy and Kenny sat on either side of me. Joaquín, Michael, and Rip were across from us.

"I never should have introduced you to Garth," Vivi said. "I'm sorry."

"It's not your fault. Perry told him about me." I took everyone through what had happened last night. Faces got paler, sterner, angrier as I talked. "But it came out okay. Garth's in custody. Lori's home with her baby." Who knew, maybe Suni would reevaluate her life and either make it work with her husband or get a divorce. "Have you heard how Garth got Perry down to the lake?"

"I spoke with Deputy Biffle," Vivi said. "Garth convinced Perry to meet him at a vacation rental, supposedly to pay Perry off and get him out of their lives."

"Why there?" I asked.

"Because Noah managed the place and if things didn't go well, Garth was going to try to set someone else up. First by egging Perry on with Rip and then by using the house. Garth knew Noah had been in contact with Perry because Garth overheard him calling him once."

"When Perry didn't cooperate Garth killed him," I said. So many people killed for greed or because they were evil, but Garth killed because he was exasperated— with his family and with trying to keep a secret. One that wasn't even that important in the larger scheme of life.

"Garth shot him and placed him in the lake. He put your picture in his hand to throw suspicion on you if blaming Rip or Noah didn't work out," Vivi said.

"That's awful," I said. So many people had been hurt unnecessarily. Perry, with all his faults, could have been part of Olivia's life. It was unlikely he'd even see her that much, with the path his life was on. People didn't have to die.

Everyone nodded. My stomach rumbled and Randy leaped up.

"Let's get you some food," he said.

"Hurry," Kenny said. "It will only get worse."

Everyone laughed and soon we all had plates filled with food. The mood had relaxed and after people had their fill, they hugged me and left. My brothers looked at me.

"Want us to go somewhere so you can be alone?" Kenny asked.

"And by alone he means we'll go sit on the porch or in the guest room," Randy said.

I smiled. I looked out at the Gulf and back at them. "First one in the Gulf wins." I leaped up and ran to my room, changing swiftly. By the time I was pounding down the walkway, they were running after me. I was in the water first. But I think for once maybe they let me win.

We spent the rest of the day having paddleboard races and lounging on the sand. After dinner at The Diner we drank wine on the porch, lolling with our full stomachs.

"We're leaving in the morning," Randy said.

"I can stay and fly back if you need me to," Kenny added.

It had been great having them here, but they needed to go take care of their own families instead of me.

"I've loved having you here." I really had too. "You can leave on one condition."

Randy and Kenny exchanged an oh-boy look.

"You have to promise to come back over spring break or the summer."

"That we can do."

Saturday morning after they'd packed the car I waved until they were out of sight and then I grabbed a paddleboard and headed out on the Gulf. My arms felt heavy, but I really think the heaviness was in my heart. Being surrounded by so many people this week had been good but had also worn me down. Not to mention being kidnapped by Garth Thursday night. I was completely out of the routine I'd established since I'd moved down here.

Stroke, glide, stroke, glide, the familiar activity gave

me plenty of time to think. I paddled down to the coastal lake and walked across the white sand to where I'd last seen Perry. The quartz sand squeaked under my feet. I dropped the board and paddle. The memorial was gone. Probably because it had all been scooped up as evidence the day I found the shell casing.

"You weren't who I thought you were," I said. "I thought you were just a dull, nice man. And I'm a little scared about my judgment of people now." Something I'd always prided myself on. Pride goeth . . . "But you didn't deserve this."

"He didn't."

I jumped. Suni stood a few feet off.

"Do you always talk to yourself?" she asked.

She had on a simple pink sweater and leggings that looked like they were leather. Spike-heeled shoes dangled from her hand. This was dressed down for her.

I smiled. Suni seemed to be no worse for wear, thankfully. "Not always."

"You're right, though. He wasn't who I thought he was either."

I felt better knowing I wasn't the only one who'd been fooled by him. "The memorial is gone," I said, gesturing to the spot where it had been. "Did you leave the things that were here?"

"Most of it. I wanted reminders of the things he loved around."

Suni had a good side to her.

"I'm sticking around for a few more days."

I raised an eyebrow. "Oh."

"My husband's heading back this afternoon." She glanced down. "At least some good has come from all this."

"How's that?" Did I really want to know? No. But it

seemed like Suni needed to talk and I guessed it wouldn't hurt to listen.

"I've made a mess of my life." She shook her head. "I've become someone who a few years ago I would have said was a slut. I don't like me anymore." Tears filled her eyes.

"At least you recognized it."

"Wow. Have you ever thought about becoming a therapist?" She laughed to lighten the words.

I laughed too. "Not in this lifetime."

I stared out at the Gulf. It changed all the time, from calm to angry to furious and back again. People changed too. Suni may not like who she'd become, but I bet she could work on being someone she liked again.

"Take care, Chloe."

"You too," I said as she walked away. After she was a tiny blip on the beach, I turned back to the coastal lake. Perry had made me doubt myself, but it wasn't just me he'd fooled. I needed to let go of my worries, just like I'd let go of him. Time to trust myself again. "Bye, Perry."

I paddled back toward my house. A little restless. Wanting to be alone and not wanting to all at once. Vivi and Joaquín had forbidden me from coming in today. But maybe I'd go anyway after a nap. People walked the shore, fishermen fished, boats, from sailboats to speedboats, were out on the water.

As I walked my paddleboard back up to the house, I spotted Rip sitting on the steps of my walkway. I felt shy all of a sudden. He stood when he saw me and walked down to meet me.

My heart accelerated. "Hey," I said. Wow, I was becoming a local. In Chicago it was all "hi" or "hello."

"Hey," he said. "Want me to carry that?" He pointed to my paddleboard.

"No, thanks."

"That's one of the things I like about you, Chloe Jackson. You're independent."

Was it hot out here or was it just me? We walked up the walkway together.

"One of the things?" I asked. I stored the paddleboard and paddle under the porch. "There's more?"

Rip pulled me to him. "How much time do you have?"

"All day," I said. I didn't add *and all night* because he knew. Rip and I understood each other.

ACKNOWLEDGMENTS

Thanks to everyone who takes the time to read my books and a huge thank you to reviewers.

Gary Goldstein, my editor at Kensington, always keeps me laughing. Thank you for buying my first book and continuing to support me with book number twelve!

John Talbot, my agent, thanks for taking a chance on me.

The team at Kensington is amazing and I have to give a special shout out to Larissa Ackerman. I'm so lucky to work with her.

Thanks so much to The Wickeds—Jessie Crockett, Julie Hennrikus, Edith Maxwell, Liz Mugavero, and Barbara Ross. I've missed you all so much during the pandemic. Zoom just doesn't replace sitting around with a glass of wine gabbing until the wee hours.

Barb Goffman, independent editor, always reads an early draft of my books. Your encouragement and support mean the world to me. If there are mistakes, it's on me, not Barb.

Jason Allen-Forrest, thank you for your wisdom and for being my sensitivity reader. Your insights are invaluable.

Christy Nichols, thanks for reading for me and finding errors. You and your family bring so much joy into our lives.

Mary Titone, thank you for always dropping everything and reading for me. This book is so much better because of your contributions. I'm so lucky to have you as a friend.

Also, thanks to Jen, you are so much more than a virtual assistant.

Mark Bergin, a retired police lieutenant and author of the book *Apprehension* (buy it!) and Michelle Clark, medicolegal death investigator, kept me from making a stupid mistake when Perry's body was found. Thank you both for answering my questions!

Thanks to my mom for reading to my sister and me when we were little and for filling our house with books. You passed on your love of mysteries.

Thanks to my family, who tease me, support me, and avoid me when it's near a deadline. You celebrate all of life with me and I love you.

KEEP READING FOR A SPECIAL EXCERPT!

A TIME TO SWILL
A Chloe Jackson Sea Glass Saloon Mystery

Best-selling author Sherry Harris gives us the second in a new cozy mystery series featuring a bartender sleuth in the tiny town of Emerald Cove, Florida.

Chloe loves her new life pouring beers and mixing cocktails at the Sea Glass Saloon in the Florida Panhandle town of Emerald Cove. But on the job, the only exercise she gets is walking from one end of the bar to the other, so in the mornings she loves to run on the beach. On this morning's foggy run, she spots a sailboat washed up on a sandbar. Hearing a cry, she climbs aboard the beached vessel to investigate and finds not only a mewling kitten—but a human skeleton in the cabin.

The skeleton is tied back to Chloe's friend Ralph, whose wife disappeared on a sailboat with three other people twelve years before. Believing his wife was lost at sea, Ralph remarried. Now he finds himself a murder suspect. Chloe is determined to find out who's been up to some skullduggery, but her sleuthing will lead her into some rough waters and some bone-chilling revelations . . .

Look for **A TIME TO SWILL**, *on sale now!*

CHAPTER 1

My shoes slapped the wet sand as I tried to make out what was up ahead of me through the swirling fog. I'd just arrived back in Emerald Cove, Florida, late last night. I'd driven through a dense fog the last thirty miles. When the advisory popped up on my phone, I'd thought, *how bad could it be?* Very bad was the answer. I'd crept along. Driving through gumbo would have been preferable. My hands still ached this morning from gripping the steering wheel of my vintage red Volkswagen Beetle.

I'd planned to sleep in. To unpack my worldly goods, which filled my car. Emptying my old life in Chicago into my new life in the Florida panhandle. But loud, angry waves pounding outside my two-bedroom beach house had other plans, so I'd gotten up, pulled on my running gear, and set out just before dawn. I squinted my eyes, but the fog danced and shifted like flowing Arabian head scarves, changing the view. There. There it was again, thirty yards ahead.

It looked like the mast of a sailboat angled oddly. Way too low for a boat to be upright. I tried to speed up, but the sand pulled at my shoes like wet hands trying to drag me under. Usually I found hard sand to run on, but this morning I hadn't found any. A groan and a creak floated across the air. The sound wasn't one I normally heard on the runs I'd taken to over the summer months. No one else seemed to be out. But the early hour and fog explained that.

The fog opened up just long enough for me to see a massive sailboat, listing to its side bobbing on the water.

"Hello?" I called as I got closer. I ran my hand through my short, brown hair. It curled wildly in this humidity. The boat was between the two sand bars that ran along this stretch of beach. The groan and creak seemed to be coming from the boat. A muffled cry sounded from inside the boat. A baby's cry. I whipped out my cell phone and dialed 911.

I thought of Julia Spencer-Fleming's opening line in *In the Bleak Midwinter*. "It was one hell of a night to throw away a baby." A terrible morning here.

"Where's your emergency?"

"Delores." Thank heavens it was someone I knew. "This is Chloe Jackson."

"What's wrong, honey? I didn't know you were back." Delores's voice was sweeter than the Mile High Pecan Pie she served at her diner when she wasn't working as a dispatcher.

"There's a sailboat that seems abandoned. It's stuck between the two sandbars. I heard a baby cry."

"Where are you?"

"The fog's so thick I'm not sure. I left my cottage about seven minutes ago and ran west toward Vivi's house. But I can't tell if I'm to her house yet or not."

"Okay, well, stay put while I get someone from the Walton County Sheriff's Department out there."

"Will do." I hung up and shouted again, "Anyone here?" I peered at the boat. The cry sounded again and tugged at my heart. I noticed a rope ladder dangling off the back end. It was like fate was telling me not to let the baby wait alone. I took off my shoes and dropped my key ring with its Chicago key chain in the toe of one of them. It looked like high tide, but I wasn't certain. I ran up the beach a few yards and left my shoes so they wouldn't get wet. There were marks in the sand like the boat had been farther up onshore.

I splashed through the water until it was waist deep and swam the last bit. I tried to keep my phone out of the water doing an awkward, one-armed stroke and kicking hard with my legs. The boat was farther out than I'd originally thought. It tilted up a bit, but I managed to catch the rope ladder and scramble up. As I boarded, a wave smacked the boat. It knocked me off my feet and I landed on my rear end, jolting every bone in my body. My phone flew out of my hand. I grabbed at it in midair but missed. A plop sounded in the water.

"No, no, no." The boat righted itself and I slid across the deck. My shoulder slammed into the side of the boat. *Ouch!* I gritted my teeth together. Another bounce, and it tipped precariously away from the sandbar. I clutched the side, managed to stay on the deck, and clung. The crying got louder, but now it didn't sound as much like a baby as it had from the shore. An animal perhaps? The boat began to move away from the shore and out to sea. What had I done?

CHAPTER 2

"Help," I yelled toward the shore. But the fog wrapped around my words and muffled them. No one yelled back. The boat moved quickly, probably caught up in a rip current. I eyed what bit of water I could see through the fog. Jumping in and trying to swim out of the current didn't seem smart, even though I was an excellent swimmer. I could become disoriented in the fog. The boat lurched in the waves. If I jumped, I couldn't be sure the boat wouldn't change direction and run me down.

The only thing worse than jumping in would be being tossed overboard. The boat tipped and tilted like the carnival rides I loved as a kid. Then there was the cry to think of. I couldn't abandon a baby if there was one. Moving would be perilous, but not moving wasn't an option.

A door that must lead to the cabin below banged open and closed with the motion of the waves. I eyed the distance. Standing would be foolish, but maybe I could slide over on my stomach. A wave pitched, I let loose. For a second I thought I was going in, but the boat rocked the other way. I took advantage and slid and scooted to the door. It banged shut behind me as I rolled down five steps, landing on the floor of the interior.

It took a minute for my eyes to adjust to the dim light that came through narrow, rectangular windows. I was in a living room, dining room, kitchen combo. The boat was a mess, with trash and clothing on the floor. The cry came from a room to my left. I stood and careened toward a door, staggering worse than any drunk I'd ever seen. I pushed on the partially opened door. A gray cat with long, white socks leaped off a bed and into my arms.

Not a baby, then. A cat. The boat pitched and we landed on the bed. I rubbed my cheek against the cat's head. "So, you're the one who caused me all this trouble." If not for the cry, I'd still be onshore. And my phone wouldn't be dead in the water. Literally. The cat purred and settled into my arms. The prudent thing seemed to try to wait out the waves down here now.

My stomach started to feel a little woozy even though I'd never been seasick before. I closed my eyes and tried to calm my breathing and heart rate. Both were banging along in double time.

"How did you end up on this boat?" Maybe the poor thing had climbed aboard when the boat was onshore. The door could have slammed shut when the boat was being flung around as it went back into the Gulf. The cat continued purring.

"Anyone else here?" No response. This room was a mess too, as if someone had tossed it or the boat had been whipped around by the Gulf for a long time. Clothes, bedding, and shoes were strewn everywhere. I hoped we'd be out of the riptide soon. Most riptides only went out about twenty feet. I prayed that's all this was.

Besides, Delores would have people looking for me. I hoped the waves wouldn't obscure where the boat had disturbed the sand. Maybe my phone would wash up onshore and someone would spot it, or my shoes. I wouldn't think about a scenario where none of those things happened and everyone assumed I'd gone home or continued my run. In that case, it would take hours for someone to realize I was missing.

I talked to the cat until I ran out of things to say trying to keep my mind off the dire situation we were in. We continued to be bounced and pitched at the whims of the Gulf. Down here the boat creaked and groaned like banshees had taken possession. My fear level was high as I wondered if the boat would hold together. I said some prayers and stroked the cat. I'd read in books that people said time had no meaning and finally understood what they were talking about. Then, at last, the waters finally calmed. Now what?

I was chilled because of my damp clothes, even though the air and water temperatures averaged in the eighties during October in this part of Florida. I grabbed a floral shirt off the floor and put it on. It was mildewed and the smell made my nose itch. I picked up a straw hat, with a tall, stiff crown and crammed it on my head.

"Let's go see where we are," I said to the cat and it followed me up onto the deck.

I gazed about trying to figure out where I was, disheartened to see that I was way farther away from the shore than I'd hoped. In three directions I saw endless views of the Gulf of Mexico. At any other time I'd admire the sparkling water and enjoy the warmth of the sun. Ominous clouds hung in what must be the southwest. Maybe that was what had passed over and tossed the boat around. *Please, don't let them be headed this way.* The fourth direction—north, I assumed—I could see fog still obscured the shoreline. It looked like I would have to save myself.

I stayed still for a couple of moments to get used to the gentle rocking. I wasn't sure I could sail a boat this size even though I'd been on plenty of sailboats on Lake Michigan. These sails looked ragged anyway. But if the boat had a working engine or a radio of some sort, maybe I could get help. I pictured myself sailing back to shore like a modern-day, older Pippi Longstocking. Hailed as a hero.

I went to the helm and put my hands on the wheel at two and ten. *This isn't driver's ed, Chloe.* The wheel spun a full circle, so it must have been disconnected from the rudder. That was no help. Even if I found a working engine, I couldn't steer the boat back to shore.

"Is there a radio around?" I asked the cat. It didn't answer but followed me as I went back below.

I opened doors off the main cabin. One of the doors opened to a bathroom, or the head, as my uncle always called it. I tried to open a second door, but something behind it wouldn't let me open it fully. I peered through the one-inch crack. This was another cabin with a bed. It too was in terrible condition, with things all over the place. Wood paneling that probably once gleamed was now dulled by sea air. What had happened to this boat and how had it ended up here?

The cat sat in front of a door at the far end of the main cabin. I threw it open. A skeleton sat at the head of a bed. I shrieked. It wore a hat and a dress. Its bony hand stretched out toward me. I stood as if someone had glued me to the floor. The skeleton's jaw had dropped down in what looked like a creepy grin. I slammed the door closed.

How could someone have died on this boat long enough ago for their bones to remain, yet this cat still be alive, meowing away? Never mind that now. I needed to find the radio. I scanned the room. There. There it was.

The radio was built in to a wall. If the battery that ran it had any juice, it wouldn't have much. I needed to try to figure out how to work it before I switched it on. A mic was attached by a curly cord to one side. I found the On/Off switch and a volume knob, which I turned up. It looked pretty basic. I hoped it was tuned to the right channel. But what to say? Something short and sweet. I took a deep breath, grabbed the mic, hit the On switch. Nothing happened, but I went on anyway, just in case. "Mayday. Mayday. Adrift off the shore of Emerald Cove. Mayday, Mayday—"

I hoped you were supposed to say "Mayday," and that wasn't just something you read in books or saw on films like *Jaws*. Ugh, why did I have to think about *Jaws* at a time like this? I released the button and listened. No staticky crackle. No calm voice assuring me they'd heard the message and help was on the way. Nothing but the sound of the ocean and the creaks of the boat. The cat meowed.

It was clawing on something wedged under the counter. It glinted in the dim light. I leaned over and saw a ring. It looked expensive. I pried it out and tucked it into the little pocket in my sports bra. I looked at a stain on the floor. Maybe it was only some dinner spilled, but I scooped up the cat. Where would help come from? A helicopter? A boat that heard my message? A plane? The Coast Guard?

How could I make myself more noticeable? A mirror or something shiny to reflect off the bright, bright sun? I searched the bedroom. It had a mirror securely attached to the wall. I crossed to the bathroom. It had an old mirrored medicine cabinet. I tugged on the door, trying to pull it off, but the rusted hinges fought back.

A crowbar would work, or a screwdriver. Tools? Where would they be? My uncle's boat had a storage space below the main cabin so I went back out. I scanned the floor, kicking stuff out of the way until I found a hatch. I pulled it up and looked down into the dark space below. It was small. Probably where the engine was. I lay on my stomach and dropped my head down. It was hard to see anything in the dim light. But as my eyes adjusted, I saw the outline of a toolbox sitting on a metal table and tools latched to a pegboard.

I eased myself down, dropping the last bit. The waves felt rougher down here, and I staggered a bit as I grasped the toolbox. I carried it back to the opening, lifted it over my head, and managed to get it out onto the floor. I went back and studied the tools. I picked out a hacksaw and a crowbar. I shoved them through the opening as another wave jolted the ship. The hatch cover creaked.

"No, no, no." If it slammed closed, I'd be stuck down here in the dark and could soon become the next dead body on this boat. I leaped for the edge, pulled myself up, and rolled away as it crashed back down. I lay on the floor for a minute until the cat licked my face in a time's-a-wasting message.

I opened the toolbox and found a couple of flares and the gun that shot them. They looked old, and I knew from my uncle that old flares could be dangerous. I picked up some tools, and the cat followed me to the bathroom, where I pried the mirror from the cabinet.

I took the mirror up to the deck along with the toolbox, which I set down. I almost blinded myself when the sun hit the reflective surface. Okay, so this might work. As long as I didn't look at it. I scanned the horizon again. The fog seemed farther away. I hoped that meant it was receding and not that I was farther from shore. I spotted a tanker on the horizon, but it was so far away that I doubted it would be able to see the tiny speck I must be in the vast Gulf.

Usually when I ran on the beach I saw fishing boats dotting the horizon. None were out today. Maybe the fog had kept them in their harbors—the small one at Emerald Cove and the much larger one in Destin. Joaquín, the head bartender at the Sea Glass Saloon, where I worked, fished every morning before coming to work. Was he out here someplace? Did he know I was missing? News traveled faster than a radio message in a small town like Emerald Cove.

My shoulders slumped as I realized no one was racing to my rescue. The cat meowed something that sounded like *don't give up*. Or maybe it was just a plain meow and I was losing it.

I held up the mirror and turned in a circle, hoping as I wiggled it around it would catch someone's attention. My arms ached, but I kept at it. I saw two fighter jets scream by overhead. Probably from Eglin Air Force Base. They'd be too high to see me. But it was a good sign that the fog was dissipating. Otherwise they wouldn't be flying.

The bad news was, I couldn't see fog or shore. I'd drifted farther out to sea.